Our Gentle Sins

Noreen Lace

ReadLips Press

Editors: Jack Odman, Rebecca Brooke

Cover Artist: Naae Studio

Interior design: Rebecca Brooke

Los Angeles

ISBN: 978-1-7331813-9-6

ACKNOWLEDGMENTS

In the spring of 2017, I was filled with fire for so many reasons. These characters began speaking to me when I was asked to teach The History of African American Literature. The students were expecting another teacher; when I walked into the room, I sensed doubt, concern, but we forged ahead and that semester, that class, became one of the brightest lights in my teaching career. I became inspired by the open communication and authentic emotions expressed. It felt like that is what the world needed.

Our Gentle Sins made it through the first round of beta readers with minor suggestions; everyone thought it was ready. However, something else bubbled up. At its earliest inception, the story was about Valerie. A woman realizing her husband is not all he seems when she meets Jack, an open, authentic, yet imperfect young man who inspires change. Yet Jack had not finished speaking. He'd only just begun. I found myself writing first person notes to myself about what Jack would say or think or do. His voice came through so clearly, it needed space. Therefore, *Our Gentle Sins*, was rewritten.

Love and gratitude are given to Jo Rousseau who has continued to inspire, support, read, reread, and reread all my drafts, catch my errors, and guide my writing path for these last some years. And for Ron Terranova, fellow writer and ardent supporter of the novel. I'm truly blessed to have such a talented and tender souls as my dearest friends.

.

PROLOGUE

"I'm stretched thin on a three-inch mattress set upon a steel frame that's bolted to the floor and surrounded by reinforced iron bars. Club Fed. Federal prison. How does the son of an LAPD detective end up in federal prison?

It feels like my whole life has been a fight. I'm alone, metaphorically speaking, Dad gave up on me years ago. He had every right, but I still feel betrayed. Mom's dead. I'm probably the one responsible for her death, although no one's actually said that out loud. And my sister. Claire. Claire. Claire. She's probably given up on me as well. She should have, long ago.

When they brought me in, I was so freaking high I could barely walk, so they practically carried me, dumped me into a cold metal chair and handcuffed me.

I half remember them asking, 'who do you want to call?' Some fog lifted, and I could see the officer's face. Brown, thick, serious. For a moment, his skin paled, his eyes lightened, and his face morphed into my father's. I didn't have anyone to call. I didn't speak though. My tongue didn't work, mouth couldn't move, I just shook my head slowly and dropped my gaze.

'You're batting a hundred, aren't ya?' My father's words from the officer's mouth.

Another officer comes in; she's petite, indifferent, but her military posture tells me she doesn't take jack, literally or figuratively. She dumps the contents of my torn and dirty backpack on the table between us. The first officer picks up what I have jokingly referred to with my friends as my survival kit: clean needles, a glass bong, a meth pipe.

'These yours?'

The shameful and guilty part of my body wants to just admit it and say, throw me the fuck away, put me out of my and everyone else's misery. The plan is always to just keep my mouth shut. But my brain, all wrapped up in whatever the hell I took last, is the one that responds, even beyond any control I have, and I shake my head no.

He searches further, sifts through my jeans, t-shirts, nothing else incriminating. I only planned to go to Tijuana overnight. But my friends had other plans."

1

Morning should shuffle in softly, the Golden streaks crawling slowly across the floor until they caress the sleeper's cheek. That is the way Valerie used to wake up every morning. Now, the buzz like a bus horn barrels through her.

Alexander waits a moment longer, watching her body react, before he turns off his alarm. "Wakey wakey, sleepy head," he whispers. When she doesn't turn to him, he drops his open hand to her naked thigh.

"Oow," she murmurs and fights to open her eyes.

He squeezes the same spot, watches her face. "Was it that hard? I didn't mean to hurt you."

"I'm up. I'm up," she says with more breath than voice.
When she hears the bathroom door close, she pulls the blanket over herself and clicks the remote on the automatic blinds. The morning sunshine spills in and warms the cool, shadowy room. She stretches sleepily allowing the morning sun to gently nudge her from the shores of nod.

"Aw, hon." Alexander reaches for the remote, the blinds hiss to a close.

He is tanned and toweled at the waist standing next to her. The whole first year of marriage, he'd wake her like this. They'd made love every morning before work; a better way to start the day than his alarm bleating through her dreamy sleep. Things had changed in the last six months; they use to make love two and three times a day, but lately it's been once or twice a week. Alexander assures her this is the way marriages grow; the passion of newlyweds gives in to a comfortable married life.

Reaching for his towel, her morning blush fades as she smiles.

He backs away. "You'll make us late."

"I can be late." She throws off the blanket, revealing gentle curves under a silken gown.

Alexander's eyes move slowly up and down her silhouette. He raises one side of his mouth in a suggestive half smile as his gaze lingers on her face. Then he glances away. "Why do you need so much attention?"

Her mouth gapes open as she watches the slight shake of his head back and forth before he walks away.

She's not initiated sex for some time, but she longs for him, to be in his arms, have him between her legs, his hot breath on her neck and face, her nails digging into his spine, but he's brushed her off more often with remarks such as this. Sex, she thinks, has always been on his terms. She'd just never realized it before.

They'd met when she was finishing her Master's Program. Alexander's confidence and decisiveness were attractive as she and her peers struggled with their own place in the world. His gentlemanly behavior the first few months gave way to suggestive words, passionate kissing, and him reaching for her. She'd only had a few boyfriends, but they'd always waited for her. Valerie felt ready for the big love of her life, so when Alexander said, "you might as well be with someone you love," she believed he meant, "I love you." Later, she realized he'd intimated, "you love me." It seemed to matter little in the fresh bloom of their relationship. He fawned over her, impressing her with fancy dinners and glittering gifts.

However, she'd come to understand, marriage is not fairy tales and moonbeams. "Marriage is two people working toward a common goal. Sometimes the work is hard. It takes two people to make a happy coupling and only one to cause a rough patch. No one loves you like your father, and even your parents' marriage may have not been what you thought." It made sense. Everything Alexander said was logical, well thought out, researched, and asserted in a tone of affable but unquestionable authority.

Showered and dressed, Valerie canters down the stairs. The door to the guest room stands open and shadows seep into the hall stopping her at the bottom stair. She peeks in the dark and daunting room. Their guest room vowed to be for family, far away friends, and someday a child. She'd pictured long weekends with Nan, visits from friends, one day a crib. But the room remains real estate white; the bed, still wrapped in plastic, leans against one wall. The window shuttered by boxes. An old shelf is at odd ends, sideways shouldering, daring someone to enter. The room is a little crippled piece of their promised life together. It unsettles her. She reaches in and pulls the door to a close before slinking by.

"Vaaalll..."

She appears around the corner as Alexander begins to call.

"Ah, there you are. Toast." Alexander motions to the empty toaster with the spatula. Alexander does the cooking while she butters toast, pours the coffee. He prepares their dinners for the week on Sundays while she's visiting Nan. The color coordinated instructions are in chronological order on the refrigerator just behind his head; most nights, when she returns from the school, she places the covered dish in the oven or on the stove as per his instructions.

"The door to the guest room was open." She wants to open the conversation to that room; she wants to explain how the darkness trips her up, how it spills into the hall and makes it difficult for her to pass.

He doesn't glance up from scrambling eggs, adding cheese, salt, pepper.

"Did you…a..?"

He plates the steaming eggs, tops one with a single slice of bacon. His gift to himself; the workouts, the healthy lunches; this is his morning cheat. "Looking for something."

"I was hoping," she starts slowly, quietly, "maybe Nan could come for a visit. We could clean..."

Alexander sighs audibly and leaves the room with the plates.

She grabs the matching Roscher plates, follows him with the toast. As a child, her family ate toast straight from the toaster. Her mother received a new set of Corelle one Christmas, and for a full month they ate from plates that matched their bowls and cups. Then one broke, then another, and they were back to mismatching and making do with whatever was close. In college, fast food on paper plates was the norm. This is grown up life, she thinks, matching and purposeful plates.

"We've talked about this." Alexander is nearly twelve years older than Valerie. A few gray hairs grow near his temples, barely perceptible to anyone but him and the woman who shares his bed. When she first noticed them, she laid next to him as he slept, excitement shooting through her as she thought, this is my husband, this is my life. She believes it makes him look distinguished, except when he acts like this. She sees the hardboiled attorney, frustrated with a corporate deal. "Young couples shouldn't have permanent guests and that room is a mess right now. You want your grandmother to stay in a room like that?"

She'd never seen this side of him before they married. "Not as a permanent guest, but I thought we might clean it and paint it. She's getting older..."

"And shouldn't be living with people who can't take care of her. If she needs help, she should be among experts in a home."

"No, she doesn't need..." Valerie struggles to keep up with his changing tactics.

Alexander sets down his fork. "Okay, honey, you win. We'll talk about this another time."

Valerie half smiles: she hasn't won anything, but at least he's open to the conversation. The first and last time Nan visited, he sat silently in the dining room reading briefs, making them both feel like invaders in his time and space.

After breakfast, Valerie loads the dishwasher. Alexander kisses her on the cheek. She reaches her arms up for a hug, which he leans into and out of quickly, checking his phone with the door closing behind him even before she drops her arms.

Above the sink is a picture window so wide it affords a view of the entirety of their patio and yard. The wood deck has a full set of furniture: to one side, a table with four chairs; to the other, two recliners. The whole of the yard shaded by two live oak trees. Birds alight to a new circular feeder filled with seed in the center of the yard placed it at Alexander's prompting. The yard is green and lush and beautiful, the patio is welcoming if not pristine, but they have yet to use it. If she leans forward and looks left or right, she catches a glimpse of the neighbors' nearly similar expanses of green over the wooden fences. She turns toward the kitchen, the center island where Alexander cooks, running her hand over the cool smooth surface of the marble countertops. As she walks toward the stairs, the view of the living room is picture perfect too. National Geographic's *Stunning Photographs* lay elegantly centered on the coffee table. The spine remains uncracked. She wonders if this is what grown up life is all about, pretty pictures and guestless guest rooms. Her childhood was messy, loud, chaotic. She wanted a different life, quiet, calm, orderly. Valerie takes a deep breath which catches and clogs her throat before she reminds herself to be happy.

2

Being a kindergarten teacher was not her first choice. Working at a small private school in a suburb far from her family was not her original plan. The degree in Educational Design was meant to serve the larger public school system of Los Angeles which struggles with student success. However, West Oaks Youth housed in a modern set of buildings with painted concrete pathways clearly marking the direction to the main office, the grade levels, and the green walkway that leads to the kindergarten yard boasts "Today's Children, Tomorrow's Leaders," is selective in who they accept into their fold.

Valerie enjoys the sense of community, and she's fallen in love with the twenty little five-year-olds. In her few years here, she's made friends and created scholarship opportunities for underprivileged children. By her design, they now sponsor a Halloween carnival for the community; all families have a safe and exciting night. And the Spring Gala where faculty, staff, and community members are welcomed for a night of food and entertainment funds the scholarship and other school activities.

"Good morning!" Jenny, the student teacher, is already waiting near the kindergarten door as Valerie appears.

"You're early." Valerie feels fortunate to have the positive and energetic student teacher.

The classrooms boast two and sometimes three people per twenty students, and the school buzzes with activity. When some students are sitting quietly, studying, or taking a test, the music room is in use with the door open to allow the sweet sounds of piano or violin to fill the courtyard while other children play soccer or volleyball in the exercise yard. The school is always in motion, the children chattering happily as they move around the buildings. A carefully crafted illusion to create confidence should a parent drive by or have a reason to stop in. "Parents pay good money," the director reminds the faculty, "make certain they feel their money is well-spent."

"Birdhouse day!" Jenny bubbles over with excitement. She's short and quick with a round face brightened by her permanent smile. The students love her, and Valerie knows she'll make an excellent teacher.

From the school approved lesson plans, the students learn about life cycles, beetles, butterflies, and birds. Birds, they learn, have homes before they have families. The building of the bird house, and the incubator with chicken eggs, which comes next month, are tweaks inspired by Valerie and her Kinder-partner, Lucy, to make the lessons fun.

The gluing and decorating of the bird house are done outside with Valerie, Jenny, and an office helper, Gabriel, running nonstop.

"Wet cloth!" Valerie calls out.

Jenny hands her a cloth from a bucket of sudsy water as another child hollers, "owww!" Gabriel helps a little girl with glue in her hair. Jenny struggles to keep the children's sleeves rolled up. It's February, but southern California's three hundred days of sunshine allows for many outside activities, which saves hours of classroom clean-up.

"My eye!" another child hollers.

Gabriel quickly hands a towel to Jenny.

"Mrs. V," he leans toward her. "Should we start cleaning up?"

Valerie glances at the young man. Office helpers are nieces or nephews of staff or faculty. Her Kinder-partner whispers they also report any deviations of schedule, lessons, or improprieties to Mr. Stewart. Valerie glances at the schoolyard clock and back to the young, freckled man.

"Oh my," Jenny bubbles. "Ten minutes."

"Thursday!" Valerie nods for the clean up to begin. The school bell rings at 1:10 on Thursdays instead of the usual 2:30. The early day means time with Lucy; sometimes they see the latest children's movies and plan themed assignments to make learning fun. Most days she has a few hours before Alexander gets home, so she prepares for the next day of class, runs errands, and makes certain the house is clean with dinner in the oven. Thursdays leave her with even more extra time, and today she and Lucy sit with their feet up and sip on a hot coffee before heading their separate ways.

"Okay, everyone. If we didn't finish the bird house today, we will finish them tomorrow. Let's stand in line and wash up. Then we'll go inside and sing our end of the day song."

The kids rush to the outside sinks and stand in makeshift lines as Valerie repeats herself with an encouraging tone. Gabriel starts the clean-up and Jenny helps with handwashing. This is a practiced dance of intuition and precision. People who work with children know the steps. The movements must be fast but gentle, helpful but not overbearing, encouraging without urging. One person absent, one person out of sync, and the dance loses its fine balance.

Jenny grabs her guitar and strums her thumb across the strings. The children race to the front of the classroom and sit quietly. This was Jenny's idea, and Valerie plans to continue it for future classes.

"Which one shall we do today?"

The children call out: "Old MacDonald." "Twinkle." "Mouse ran up the clock."

Twinkle, Twinkle, Little Star rings out as the children fall in sync with Jenny whose sweet voice leads the children in a makeshift harmony. Valerie pauses to watch joy brighten the children's faces.

She gets teary – all of life should be this happy.

Jenny walks the children out to meet the parents, and Valerie sits on a hard, wooden chair exhaling a slow relaxing breath, thinking longingly of that afternoon coffee with Lucy. They'll kick their feet out and push back into the hard steel patio chairs at Starbucks. She credits the indefatigable kids for keeping her in shape, even slimming her down since her pizza and taco college days.

Valerie is straightening up paperwork when Jenny returns to the classroom holding Tommy's hand. Tommy is a blonde haired, blued eyed forty-pound ball of energy.

"Want to wait on the carpet?" Valerie asks, but Tommy jumps up and down, hops from one foot to the other.

"Uncle Jack's coming today." He drops his lunch box; his uneaten apple slices and half eaten peanut butter sandwich spill onto the floor. Then he steps on them.

"Wait. Wait," Valerie tries to still him. Jenny hands over a few paper towels. Valerie wipes Tommy's sneakers and starts on the floor.

"Uncle Jack!" Tommy jumps, landing on Valerie's hand.

"Tommy, my man, you've smashed Ms. V." Tommy is lifted into the air by the tall, presumable Uncle who has short, backcombed hair and tattoos on both arms; his t-shirt reads "Saffarri's Automotive," the name of Tommy's father's business, but Valerie stands quickly. He is still a stranger with one of her charges in his arms.

The man takes her hand and turns it over. "You okay? No permanent damage?"

"I'm sorry, Ms. V." Tommy lowers his head in practiced regret.

"I'm Jack, Little Man's uncle." He still holds Valerie's hand, smiles warmly, and stares at her, waiting for a response.

"I'm.. a.." His smile is engaging. Something about him feels familiar.

"Okay, Toms, let's get you cleaned up." Jenny retrieves Tommy from Jack's arm and starts down the walkway toward the main office. This is protocol. If someone unfamiliar shows up for a child, an aide or teacher removes the child until permission is granted from the parent and the director, Mr. Stewart. This happens at least once a month because parents often send a sister or a babysitter, forgetting to notify the office.

"Uh-oh. We're in trouble now, Little Man." Jack watches them hurry away.

"Not at all" Valerie starts to step away, but he takes the paper towel from her free hand and wipes the peanut butter from her fingers.

"Love me some Goober Grape," he chuckles.

Valerie smiles and steps away. "They'll be right back. You're welcome to have a seat." The friendly and familiar stranger has given her goosebumps. She's a little embarrassed and, as if she's forgotten all social etiquette, she doesn't introduce herself or show him around the class, which is the usual routine when unannounced family members show up for a child. She busies herself at the gold-star-good-behavior-poster and the whose-lost-a-tooth-chart in the front of the classroom.

"I came to the wrong gate," he chuckles. "They wouldn't let me in, made me go all the way around."

Valerie nods, "Yes, those are the rules. No strangers on the campus."

"Then I waited at that gate, but it seemed he wasn't coming back out."

"Protocol." Valerie offers. "Children must be returned to the classroom if a parent or guardian is late."

"Got a lot of rules around here."

Valerie smiles and nods before turning back to her day-end paperwork.

Jack meanders around the chairs, desks. "Is this the little man's desk?" He sits in the tiny chair, legs sprawling between the rows of desks, and smiles as he reads Tommy's bird poem written this morning.

Lucy marches in, the usual hasty gait of energy and purpose;

she stands next to Valerie before anyone realizes she's there. "Hey, guess who's in charge of planning the Gala this year?!" she hands a folder to Valerie.

"Nooo," Valerie mumbles low and silly; a tone she'd only use with Lucy.

"Yep. We're on it together. It'll be fun." Lucy is half Japanese and a good half a foot shorter than Valerie, darker hair, with enviable skin.

"Can't do coffee today."

"You're full of good news, aren't you?" Valerie craves a long rest with a cup of hot black coffee in front of her. Birdhouse day is exhausting, and Lucy is her only friend outside of her husband's business associates.

"Hubby's home sick. Biggest baby of all."

"Ain't we though?" Jack's voice surprises them.

"Sorry," Lucy leans into Valerie, "didn't see him." Faculty are not to hold personal conversations in front of families. They could receive a verbal reprimand if any of the runners or parents reported it.

Valerie has more free time than Lucy and they both have come to treasure their Thursday afternoons together. Lucy struggles with family ideals of traditional gender roles while trying to maintain some semblance of independence. Valerie has her independence, but more and more misses family regardless of the struggles they brought.

Jack catches Valerie's eye. "I feel like I'm the one stepping on toes here."

"Please don't worry," Valerie moves toward him. "The school has a lot of rules." She realizes that too could get her a verbal reprimand.

Jack pushes himself up from the tiny seat and moves toward Valerie when Tommy races in with Jenny close behind him.

"Tommy's ready to go! Okay to head out, Ms. V? I have a class."

Valerie nods. "Have a good afternoon."

"Got your backpack, Little Man? Ready to go? Hey, Teach, got a little star for this guy?" Valerie peels off a sticker and starts to place one on Tommy's forehead when Jack captures her hand and guides it to his forehead. "Not that little man. This one. I was a good boy waitin'." He smiles down at the blonde little boy.

Valerie notices the family resemblance as she places stars on both of their foreheads.

"Thanks, Teach."

"Her name is Miss V."

"Your Uncle Jack knows that, Little Man. Don't he, Miss V?"

"Can we get a happy meal?" Tommy says.

"Yes, sir. You're going to get some french fries and Uncle Jack is going to have a big coffee." Jack widens the space between his hands, "Big, supersize."

Valerie's stomach growls. French fries sound good; she rarely eats them these days. The coffee sounds better, and she considers a pickup order on the way home. Thinking of being alone in that big empty house for hours, she bites her lip. Alexander works late on Thursdays, which is why she has even more time than usual. It feels different if she has plans and then heads home. She runs though the laundry list of errands she might do, but it makes her feel alone and isolated.

"Can Miss V come too?"

Valerie laughs.

"Definitely. Come," Jack says.

She shakes her head, still smiling. "No."

"Come on, I know your coffee date canceled." Jack winks.

Valerie hesitates. She'd love to go but feels it may be inappropriate.

"Let me guess," Jack leans in, "That's against the rules too. Don't you get tired of rules?"

Valerie nods absentmindedly.

"Toms and I won't tell."

"Are you coming for reals, Miss V?"

She hesitates, still resolute on saying no when Tommy jumps

up and yells, "yessss!"

She tells herself she agrees because of Tommy. She tells herself she would have gone for the coffee anyway before returning to clean the classroom. She reminds herself that one of the rules is to be congenial to their families and thinks of how she might argue it if she's ever asked. Don't other faculty members sometimes dine at family homes? And as they walk toward McDonalds a block away, she considers how refreshing it is to be out in the sunshine, about to eat fries, and watch children play while not having to instruct their movements.

Although Valerie only orders a coffee, Jack keeps pushing fries across the table to her, "eat, eat," while Tommy races through the colorful tubes and jumps into the ball pit. "That little guy has a lot of energy." Jack widens his eyes and then smiles. "How do you do it?" He turns his attention to Valerie. "I mean twenty little Tommies running around. How do you do it and look this relaxed at the end of the day?"

Valerie chuckles. "Relaxed? I think the word you're looking for is exhausted. But it helps when they're in a herd."

"I think you're just bein' nice, Teach." Jack sprawls his legs out from under the table and leans himself over the fries. He's tall and seems oddly comfortable in the hard fiberglass seats. Jack is near her age, she guesses, but seems younger. He percolates as he talks, thought and motion all bubbling up with a frenetic energy. It reminds her of college, everyone filled with vitality and passion.

"Are you Claire's or Danny's brother?" Tommy's parents are good people, thoughtful about their son's education.

"Claire's. Twins, in fact," he offers. "I know, don't look like it. She's all petite and cute as a button and I'm..." he laughs and waves his hand toward himself, "a raggedy bean pole."

"No, you're not," she giggles at his self-deprecating humor.

"I am, I know I am. Claire though, she's an angel. Saved my life. And that man of hers. Danny's a good man. I was a mess. Dropped out of art school, got in trouble..." Jack's expressive face keeps up with his words, softening when talking about his sister and curving into practiced angles when the subject turns to himself. "I mean... trouble. But I'm good now. Danny offered me a job." He sits up and gazes across the table at her. "Do you know what we do over there?" he asks.

"Automotive," she points to his shirt, which he bashfully forgot he was wearing.

"Ah, yeah. Danny's great with the studio execs, what they need and want. And I deal with the drivers, stuntmen, and what they need the car to do. I do the artwork, too. The studios want two identical cars; one they can use throughout, and one for scenes where the car might get botched. I brought Dan a whole other side, street racers. The street racers want fast cars, and they want hot cars. So, I thought why not. Street racing might be illegal but working on their cars is not."

"Do you race?" Valerie asks.

He nods and winks as he says, "No. Street racing is illegal."

Tommy pops his head up. "Boo! Did I scare you?" he giggles.

"Little Man, you 'bout gave me a heart attack. You can't do that to an old man." Jack puts his arm around Tommy as the boy climbs up next to him.

"You ain't old." Tommy takes a bite out of his half-eaten burger. There's a resemblance between uncle and nephew, but Jack's face is thinner, his hair darker blonde. Tommy has white blonde hair, like his mother, with his father's round face.

"Did Uncle Jack tell you he talked to me before I was born?"

"No." Valerie wonders if the little boy is confusing fantasy and reality. At five, it's easy for a child to do.

"When I was in my Mommy's tummy, Uncle Jack read me stories and told me to be a good boy when I grow up. That's why I'm a good boy."

"Is that right?"

"That's right, Little Guy." Jack hugs him. "Imprinting."

"Then he was gone for a while." Tommy takes another bite.

"Hey, I'm here now, right?"

"Yep." Tommy sees another boy jump in the ball pit and runs

off to join him.

"It's supposed to help the baby bond with family members to hear their voices talking to them."

He meets her gaze, and she realizes she's staring, watching his face light up before twisting into humor, then warm with affection as he talks to Tommy. Her face flushes and she drops her eyes to her hands.

"Is this the hand Tommy stepped on?" He picks up her hand. "No permanent damage I hope." He chuckles as if making a joke, but then adds softly, "You have the most beautiful hands I've ever seen." He strokes his finger gently over the soft skin.

Valerie's enjoying herself much more than she has in a long time. "It's fine, really." She is completely comfortable, feeling among friends. Her jaw nearly aches from smiling and laughing. These were her family days, her college days. Fun, easy going.

"You are beautiful," he whispers. There's a long pause before the bubble of children's happy calls comes between them and he leans back.

She pulls her hand back and sit back, a pink blush working up her neck to her cheeks.

"Ah and look at me. T-shirt, unshaven." He runs his hands over his scruff. "I like it this way though. It's soft. I use a special shampoo, Detroit, has tea tree oil." He leans forward and grasps her hand, rubs the back of her hand over his facial hair; the surprise on her face causes him to let it go quickly, chuckling. "I am so sorry. I feel like I've known you for a hundred years. Claire is going to kill me for making a fool of myself."

Valerie laughs out loud and shakes her head. "I won't say anything."

There's a shared moment of comfortable amusement, exploring each other's smiling faces before Tommy races over, climbs up and rests his head on Jack's shoulder. The moment fills Valerie with a warm awe.

"I'm bored," Tommy whines.

Realizing she's lost track of time, Valerie lifts her empty cup as she stands, "I should be getting back."

They walk back in the afternoon sun. The grass is green, the trees are in bloom, and early spring jasmine fills the air. The breeze lifts Valerie's rose and vanilla scent in Jack's direction. He moves closer to catch another hint. Tommy runs ahead to chase a butterfly, doubles back, only to take off again.

"I sincerely hope I didn't make you uncomfortable," Jack offers.

Valerie sways her head from side to side. "It was fun, refreshing." A cool breeze sweeps up behind them and she pulls her sweater closer.

"Do I get to know your name or should I just continue to call you Ms. V."

"Valerina Graham, but everyone calls me Valerie" she says. "There's another teacher with the same last name, so the kids call me Ms. V."

"Well, Valerie Graham, my real and full name is John Fitzgerald Rose Jr., but everyone calls me Jack. I guess daddy was hoping I'd become president or something," he pauses and his voice drops, "He's just a little disappointed." They stop at the gate to the kindergarten yard.

"Thank you for the coffee, John..."

He waves his hand fanatically, "Jack."

She giggles, "Jack."

"Thursdays I'm on Tommy duty. Next week, Krispy Kreme?" Jack holds Tommy's hand and leads him away before Valerie can refuse.

"Yeah, Krispy Kreme! Let's go now," Tommy calls out excitedly.

"Next week," he shoots a smile over his shoulder, "Miss V will come."

Valerie shakes her head no while smiling. Of course, she will not go to Krispy Kreme with them, but likes Jack's humor. She spends the next few hours cleaning up the classroom, prepping for the next day when the children will finish their bird houses, paint them in an array of hearts and flowers, and take them as Valentine gifts to their parents. But as she cleans up, she's humming, feeling lighter than she has in some time. Her routine, she thinks, has been weighing on her. She thinks of Tommy's smiling face racing through the playland. It's good to spend time with children outside of school. One day, she wants to be a parent. She wants to see children happily playing, looks forward to the day her little boy or girl climbs up on her lap, hugs her like Tommy hugged Jack.

Then she thinks of Jack. There is something wonderfully familiar, as if they were old college friends who picked up where they left off. Valerie sits in one of the children's chairs and looks around her. College friends promised to stay in touch, get together. Her mind wends around the last of her college years. The sweet freedom of dorm life and school friends faded away, the parties ended with finals, and everyone pushed forward for their degrees and their new lives. Her mother had passed, and her Nan moved to a new condo; life changed so quickly. Then Alexander appeared.

She touches her hands, remembers the feel of Jack's soft whiskers against her fingers. Alexander is always clean shaven. Sometimes, if he has a late meeting, he returns home and shaves his five-o-clock shadow before going out again. It was Alexander's mature and logical manner that attracted Valerie to him. He was an adult; a suit-wearing, nine-to-five attorney, while her friends and herself seemed to be playing at life. With Alexander, everything was black or white; there was no indecision. So different from her family and friends, pitching around ideas until the point became moot.

Valerie arrives home later than usual and finds the table set, the wine uncorked; when Alexander sees her, he smiles and begins to pour the St. Estephe. She pulls out the chair, sits down, dropping her bag on the floor next to her.

He fills his glass and stops short of a swallow in hers. Her face is soft, a smile at play on her lips, and her thoughts are elsewhere. "You've forgotten dinner."

She glances up, her eyes widen in realization, "I... Yes... I..."

Valerie is without an answer.

"Honey," he says gently, "I only ask you to be responsible for dinner one night a week."

"I can cook something," she offers. The single slight raise to his left eyebrow signals to Valerie a coming question. She straightens her spine in response and says, "I received a new project today," she wonders if she's changing the subject or creating excuses; she doesn't want to tell him she lost track of time, doesn't want to see that other eyebrow raise into suspicion or drop into anger. She can already hear his lecture: "Faculty shouldn't fraternize... your contract..." He must be horrifying, she thinks, in a board room or courtroom. "Lucy and I are to plan the spring gala." She fumbles to reach in her bag and pull out the folder.

He leans forward, brings the glass of wine to his lips, never removing his eyes from Valerie. She was so young, so very sweet when they'd first met. The creamy skin, those creole eyes: Beautiful. And Naïve. Malleable. Everything he wanted in a wife. He smiles thinking of her in front of her little kindergarteners. Some of his colleagues' wives were designers, writers - too much to reign in. He didn't want a battle ground at home, that was for the office. They'd given up real careers for their families and their husbands; giving up a kindergarten class wouldn't be hard. And working with children was good practice for her.

"I'll talk to Stewart, ask him to find someone else."

"Oh, no," she says too quickly, returns his smile as she pauses to slow her thoughts. "I want to do it." She has no idea why that pops out of her mouth; she doesn't care one way or another. She wants something of her own, even if it is just the power to make the decision. If she decides it's too much, she can talk to Mr. Stewart. She lifts the glass, notices the small swirl of wine in the bottom as she brings it to her lips.

That night in bed, Valerie is restless. Sleep flits around the room, teasing her. Then Alexander pulls her tight to him. She's slept comfortably many nights in the curve of his arm, feeling safe and loved. Tonight, though, it feels constraining. She desires to toss and turn, to wander the hall in the cool night air in search of sleep, but she lies there long into the night until sleep finally comes to her.

3

"All that poison I pumped into my body leaches out in giant drips of agony. I spend the next few weeks in a hospital, chained to the bed with a sheriff's deputy making regular rounds. I'm sick from detoxing, can't eat, can't sleep, intravenous fluids flow into my veins so I don't dehydrate and turn into a rubbery piece of skin on their clean white sheets. And it hurts. My whole body is one open throbbing wound. I've been in rehabs where they give you meds to make the come down easy. Not here, no way. They want you to feel it. They're not doing you any favors here.

I can't blame anyone. It's my own freaking fault. I sincerely wish I could die. The body is pretty amazing though. Survival instinct is born into every cell. Maybe that's been my fight: wanting to die and at the same time wanting to survive.

When I do get to Club Fed, the five a.m. bell rings for us to get up. Shower: Mandatory. Breakfast: Presence is mandatory. Then, our choice, back to the cell or to a meeting.

I don't know what day it is. I don't care. This is the end of the line for me. I'm here for the next ten years minimum. With any luck, I'll die long before then.

After breakfast, the guard calls out my name: 'Rose.' I step out of line and wait. He comes and gets me, walks me down the line. I don't know where he's taking me, and I don't ask. You learn fast here. Follow the rules, keep your head down, don't ask questions. These cops will mess you up.

I'm sat in a metal room handcuffed to a clip on the wooden table. A suit shows up, briefcase in hand. Public defender, I assume. I don't say anything. Barely look at him.

'I'm Mr. Gonzales, I'll be defending you.' He goes on to list the charges and ask me questions, which I don't answer. I'm not really listening. 'Mr. Rose, you'll only be helping yourself to talk to me.'

'I got nothing beyond this.'

'Are you admitting guilt?' he asks. 'You put the drugs in the gas tank and knew they were there?'

I didn't know what my friends were up to, but I don't respond. Even high, I would have never agreed to that. I'm not a dealer, not a thief, just an addict looking for my next high.

'Mr. Rose, if you turn state's evidence, you could walk out of here before you're thirty.' He doesn't even pretend to give a shit what happens to me.

I glare at him, eyebrows lowered; if we were on the street, I'd smash him hard. If I snitch, there'd be no street to walk out on. I'd be dead before I hit the sidewalk. I'm dead anyway.

The following day, I appear in the brown and black courtroom in bright prison orange. I stand out like that storm on Jupiter, three times the size of earth, a mar on an otherwise beautiful swirl of gasses and clouds. They'd thrown out everything, my clothes, backpack, ID. Right now, I don't exist.

I keep my head down, gaze at my feet. There are public defenders lined up behind the tables, prisoners lined up next to me, people in the galley, and the judge taking his seat at the pulpit. Can't say I've ever been in court before. Definitely not in this position. I imagine this will be my only view from now on.

'Jack,' a woman's voice whispers. I try to remember who else was in the car with us. But no girl. I'm hallucinating.

"Unca," I hear this tiny little voice call out. I'm imagining things. The after-effects of addiction. Then I hear the whine. My head rises.

My attorney's standing at the table. Behind him, a hand waves. I don't recognize them at first, but then my eyes clear and Claire's face comes into focus. She holds little Tommy on her hip with Danny's arm around her. I suck back the glob that forms in my throat and bite down hard on the inside of my jaw, flex it to keep from sobbing.

'Mr. Rose, how do you plead?'

Tommy's a chubby little guy, and he's giving his mom hell, reaching his pudgy little arms toward me, struggling to get down. I can't do nothing but look away or burst out in tears. Wish they'd never seen me like this, especially him. The last time he'll see his Uncle Jack is looking like a skinny broken wishbone soaked in orange glow.

My attorney says, 'My client wishes to plead guilty.'

'No!' Claire calls out. Danny takes little Toms, who starts to cry, and leaves the courtroom.

The judge glances up. I expect he's going to give Claire a verbal lashing. But he looks pretty sympathetic. 'Mr. Gonzales?'

'Sir,' Claire says. 'We haven't had a chance to talk to my brother. Can we please talk to him before he pleads?'

The judge is unlike any I've heard of. He glances from her to me, then back again. 'Bailiff, take the defendant to the visitor's room. Mr. Gonzales, show your client's family where he'll be. I'll expect you back here in one hour.'

Claire sits down across from me. I can sense it's her, her small frame, her light step, even the chair barely makes a sound in this echo chamber of a room when she sits, pulls it in. My head hangs low. I couldn't pick it up if I tried, and I'm biting the inside of my mouth just to stop from crying. One word from her soft, sweet voice, I'm going to vomit sobs. Sobs of apologies for being such a freaking disappointment and problem. She deserved a much better brother than me.

I can't look up at her lovely face. Her expression will dim with concern or warm with love. She won't shade me with blame, not now. But I don't want her or anyone to see me like this. I know I look like shit, paper thin, malnourished, probably half dead, all in a neon traffic cone that accentuates every mark, bruise, enlarged pour. They didn't choose this color by accident. This is humiliation by the billionth power.

She reaches across the cold metal table for my hands. She puts her hands in between mine, and I grasp on like I'm holding on for dear life. I'm not going to cry, I say to myself, not going to cry to my sister, the one who I'm supposed to protect.

'Jack,' she says softly as if the room will hear her and eat us up. 'You can't do this. Plead not guilty, and let's see what we can do for you.'

I shake my head, still don't raise it to meet her eyes. 'Can't do it anymore.' I whisper into the metal table. 'Just let me go.' I cannot hurt my family any more than I have already. Just let me disappear into the system that welcomes people like me, that keeps us from the society that doesn't want us, the family that rejected us because of too much pain, from the people who don't deserve for us to be put on them.

'Jack,' her voice is stronger. 'You can't do this to your family. They'll put you away for like ten years.'

I get angry, just to keep from bawling. 'Really, Claire. I can't do this to my family? After all the shit I have done, all the pain I've caused, you want more? They should put me away if only for your sakes. Forget about me, forget you ever had a brother.'

'That's not going to happen, Jack.'

'Is this the kind of brother you want?'

She's quiet. I can't always read Claire, which is amazing considering she's my twin. Fraternal, but we still shared that space, that bond. But I do know Claire, and she's like our mother, always prepared with love and kindness for anyone who crosses her path.

'Yes. If this is what I'm offered. There's a reason and purpose for you being my brother, so, yes, I'll take it.'

I let go of her hands. Then she grabs my hands to make me look at her.

'I love you. You are a part of me. You're my baby brother, and I'd be lost without you.'

The 'baby brother' comment makes me smirk, even in my current state. Claire is one minute older than I am. When we were younger and she wanted to tease me, she'd call me her baby brother, as if she had to actually take care of me. I look at her, think about that. She is taking care of me just like she's always tried.

'Tommy can't lose his uncle.'

And now, I gulp back a sob and choke on it. My face tenses, my jaw flexes. My lips curl and eyes water. I know Claire sees it. She leans over and kisses my hands. 'Fight, Jack. Please fight.' She runs out before she can start crying.

In a few moments, my attorney comes back. I've choked back the thick emotion; it's stuck in my throat.

'What did we decide?' He already knows the answer.

'Not guilty.'

'Alright, we can probably get some sort of deal for you, but I wouldn't count on it.' Public defender burnout maybe. What penance is he doing? I don't know. I don't care. What's clear is that he doesn't give a shit what happens to anyone on this side of the table.

'Your sister's gotta set of lungs on her.'

I dart my eyes at him, narrow them.

He adjusts his attitude. 'This is up to you, but she wants you to sign this form giving me permission to give her information about your case.'

He doesn't want me to, which is probably the only reason I do it. When I think about it later, there's so much I don't want her to know. But this public defender isn't going to try very hard, and Claire's on the outside, has access to more information than I do. I don't want to get my hopes up though. I may never see the light of day.

When we go back into court, Danny is there. I wonder if Tommy's being fussy, but Claire is probably bawling her eyes out. I hate myself. But if this is what she wants me to do.

'In the case of Federal Government vs John Fitzgerald Rose, Jr, how do you plead?'

My attorney answers for me. 'Not Guilty, Sir.'

The judge glances from him to me. He nods as if he approves of my plea. He continues the case, slams his oak hammer on the oak gavel. I'm led out, back to the prison bus and back to the federal lock-up.

That night, lying on my cot, listening to the sounds of men snoring, burping, farting, gasping, even sniffling in the darkness, and the guard walking by for the late-night check, I think of Tommy. That beautiful little blonde baby boy. His tiny hands pulled on my goatee as soon as he could control those fingers enough to hold on. That baby smell always reminded me of my own mother for some reason. I haven't seen that little man in almost year, he'll be nearly two now. I want to say I'm shocked he remembered me, but something inside me is glad he did. He was barely walking, taking his first steps when Mom died, when I lost it again, when I disappeared from their lives.

I start sniffling. I turn into my thin fabric pillow and bite my lips so hard I taste blood. My chin pulsates, body reflexes to sobs that I won't allow to escape. My eyes water, nose runs, but I keep my jaw clenched. If I get out of this, I'll make sure Tommy becomes a better man than I could ever be.

After breakfast, an intimidating shadow falls over me as I lie on my cot. One of my first days here, a big Jamaican guy gave me his bread. I didn't ask, but I was hungry. I haven't said another word to him besides thanks.

'There's a meetin',' he says in a thick accent, 'you want to go?''

Jack pauses for the first time, taking a deep breath. "And that is how I come to be among you fine folks. Thanks for having me."

"Thank you, brother." A guy in the front row nods his head.

"Thank you for your share," someone else offers. The rest join in, nodding and thanking him.

Jack feels at home here. Belonging is a fluid road with many stops along the way. Sometimes he felt he belonged nowhere at all but being with those who've traveled similar paths is comforting.

4

White waves of shoulder length hair frame the thin, tanned skin, brightening her sparkling blue eyes. Ruth was a Betty back in her day. Dark auburn hair, flaming spirit, and a strong woman who not only raised a daughter nearly on her own, but her granddaughter too. She'll be eighty soon, but her soul still feels twenty-five. No one ever warned her that aging happens so much faster on the outside than on the inside. She wakes up in the morning with a desire to run on the beach and dive into the waves, but then she moves and her body is slow to respond; her knee feels spongy, her hip aches, and she gives her shoulder a little rub before making any big moves.

"What's wrong with your shoulder?" Valerie asks when she sees Nan reach for it during lunch.

"Old football injury," Ruth snipes.

"You played football?"

"No, I didn't, you smart girl."

They share a giggle before the spry woman launches into an update of her frenemy, Charlotte, at whose birthday party they will "make an appearance" this afternoon.

"She suddenly wants everyone to call her Char, like she's the new Cher or something. She begins planning this talent show and suddenly, she's a superstar..."

Valerie chuckles watching Nan's expressions as she speaks. In her younger years, Nan became a welcomed staple on weekends, holidays, and special dinners. Her regular appearances were met with excitement. It wasn't until after her father's death when Valerie was a preteen that Nan became the most important stable figure in her life. Her mother's diabetes was under control, more medication and a diet low in sugar, fat, and salt. But, after the death of her father, her mother fell into a depression and spun out of control, neglecting her medication, gorging herself on bread and sweets. Valerie missed much of her first year of high school trying to care for her mother. Her grades suffered, and she became uncomfortably close to failing, not to mention losing her mind. Her mother's emotional highs and lows led to angry fits and pouting to get what she wanted. They'd nearly lost their little house; the landlord ready to boot them to the curb for nonpayment. When Nan moved in, Valerie regained some semblance of a normal life. Nan became the calm in the storm of loss and chaos. Even though her mother's ups and downs continued, Nan dealt with the brunt of the issues, allowing Valerie to finish high school then encouraging her to go away to college.

"Does that mean we're not going to the party?" Valerie asks facetiously.

"Of course, we're going. I may not be a fan of Char's, but I am a fan of cake!"

Valerie picks up the plates from lunch; she'd made Nan's favorite shrimp and spinach salad sandwiches, but Nan's left half of hers untouched. "Nan, you barely ate."

"Just wrap it up, honey. I'll have it for dinner. Tell me about your week, anything new and exciting?" Nan sips her tea and tucks a stray wave behind her ear.

Valerie pauses at the sink, "The school asked me to help with the spring gala," she says without enthusiasm.

"What's Alexander think of that?"

Valerie turns to Nan, "Not much."

Nan nods, "Figures. How're those kids treating you?"

"We made bird houses," Valerie returns to the table with the pitcher of tea refilling both of their glasses, sits down, and leans in. "Kids are just always so excited about every little thing. I could say, hey we're going to the box factory to build boxes, and they would scream with excitement. I love that."

"Maybe you should try that with your husband."

Valerie searches Nan's face. Without explanation, Nan intuits Valerie's feelings. "Think that would work?"

"Couldn't hurt to try."

"Was I that way when I was a child?" Valerie curls her hand to her cheek. "Was I happy and excited about life?"

Nan nods noncommittally. "I think more so before your father passed."

Valerie glances out the patio door, watches the hummingbirds sip from the feeders swaying in the breeze.

"But I was happy, right? Seems like so long ago."

"We had some great times. Don't allow the bad times to overshadow the good."

Valerie pictures her teenage years; she and Nan laughing over jokes, painting together, shopping for her prom dress. Then the shadows take over: Mom's crying fit as she'd nearly ripped the dress because she didn't want to lose her baby.

Nan pats her hand. "I want you to be happy, honey."

"I'm happy." Valerie sits up and straightens her spine. "I have so much to be thankful for."

Nan smiles thoughtfully, still patting Valerie's hand. "Good. Tell me the highlight of your week."

Valerie thinks for a moment and gleefully launches into the story of Tommy's peanut butter fiasco, how she'd eaten fries for the first time in years, and chatted with the boy's oddly familiar, funny uncle.

"Uncle, huh?" Nan winks.

"No, no, Nan. Don't make anything of that."

"I won't if you won't. But I saw how your eyes just lit up."

Valerie muses, "I definitely need to get out more, make some friends."

"If Alexander approves." Nan sips her tea and turns her head. "Oh, look at that sky."

Valerie chuckles mirthlessly. "He's not that bad. He just wants what's best for me, for us."

Nan hmpfs. When Valerie first met Alexander, Nan thought him too old for Valerie. But the girl seemed happy, and Nan knew he'd provide a good life. She'd not desired to pick up where Valerie's mother left off and tell Valerie what to do; children need to learn to make their own decisions. She wonders now if that was a mistake. Her gaze lingers on Valerie; she's still so young, but she'll find her way. Nan closes her eyes, asks the angels to watch over her granddaughter.

At the party, Nan hugs her frenemy Char; the two older women laugh and even, at one point, dance together. Valerie knows Nan tells the stories more for entertainment than out of any real annoyance. The women are clearly friends.

The retirement community is located on the sands of Huntington Beach. Each resident has their own condominium, and each building has a nurse-concierge at the front desk. Although the complex offers a community ride service, many of the residents are independent enough to have their own cars. Some of them have families who visit regularly, but others do not.

At one time, Valerie pictured returning to the home where she grew up with Nan waiting for her; she understands now, when she sees Nan with her friends, living among people who share circumstances is clearly a benefit. They help one another, plan outings together, and are generally joyful. There's rarely an outlier, no lonely wallflowers as they watch out for one another.

Walter, another resident shows off his dance skills and pulls any stragglers onto the floor. He begs a dance from Char then Nan but, when waved off, he shuffles over to Valerie to tug her into the group Bunny-Hop.

The day slips away. The sun setting over the ocean somehow seems sad, even in all its grandeur. It's a painting, wavy, moving north and south even as the gold, pink, and blue melt into the horizon. A chill washes in with the rising tide.

"Going to storm tomorrow," Nan says as she and Valerie walk arm in arm back to the condo. "Shouldn't you be scooting?"

"Trying to get rid of me, Nan? I saw that Walter makin' eyes at you."

"Oh, please, honey. That man is crazy."

Valerie knows that when they say goodnight, she'll have second thoughts about leaving. When she gets in her car to drive off, she'll think of turning back and worry until she reaches her own front door.

Halfway through her college career, her mother passed. Valerie came home for the summer and, even though the doctor didn't like the test results and warned them that her heart was close to failure, her mother seemed fine. It was a good summer. They cooked together, finished puzzles, and visited the beach. Her mother was back on her medication and eating healthier.

Valerie packed her old Toyota Corolla on Sunday evening to drive the two and a half hours north to the University. She'd only just arrived, dropped her first bag in the dorm room when her phone rang. They'd known it was coming. The diabetes had eaten through her body, nibbled at her organs, stressed her systems, but death is always a shock.

"You know, Nan. You can visit anytime." Valerie thinks of that room at the bottom of the stairs waiting to breathe in life.

"Hmmm. What will Alexander think of that?"

"That's one of the reasons we chose that house," Valerie defends. He must see reason, she thinks. What if it were one of his family members? She resolves to bring up the topic again, to ready that room for guests.

"Honey, I'm happy here. I have my friends. I have the beach."

Nan knows Valerie worries; the later she stays on Sundays, the harder it is for her to leave. "I have that extra room anytime you want to stay here." Nan tugs at her arm.

Valerie's lips turn up, the line in her brow decreases. She is comforted knowing she is welcome.

5

The morning light is hazy; thickening clouds gather, dampening the bright streaks crossing the beige carpet. The room appears gray, melancholy. Valerie sits on the edge of the bed, waiting for the sound of the shower to stop. She's worded and reworded what she wants to say.

The steam pours into the room as Alexander leaves the bathroom. He's clean shaven, still wet, the towel wrapped around his waist showing he is tan and fit. His Sunday softball games are complemented by regular workouts at the company gym. He smiles widely, pleasantly surprised to find Valerie awake. He doesn't have to pull her out of that sleep she seems to love too much. There are a few things he'd like to change and this is one. The penchant for sleeping-in denotes a laziness he hadn't detected prior to their marriage. A year and a half later and he hasn't successfully broken the undesirable habit.

He kisses her head, reaches for the remote, and the curtains shimmy to a close. "You know I hate it when you open those." He drops the remote next to her on the bed and walks away.

She decides the discussion can wait.

This morning, when she comes down the steps, he leans his head to one side. "Studies show women who wear their hair up are taken more seriously." He returns his gaze to the waffle iron. "Strawberries."

Valerie presses the start on the coffee maker and retrieves the chopped strawberries from the refrigerator. "They're kindergarteners."

He pauses midway through transferring the waffles to the plate, and shakes his head, amused. "The kids are not the only ones who see you throughout the day. There are parents, faculty…" he chuckles as they move in unison toward the dining room.

Alexander thumbs his iPhone screen as he eats.

"I thought this Saturday, we could start on that room." She uses a confident tone. It's not as singsong as she might use with the children, but upbeat and positive.

"Did you order some sort of incubator? I need to call the credit card company." He clicks, puts the phone to his ear.

"Yes. Yes. I did. It's for class."

He ends the call and sets the phone down. "An incubator, hon?"

"It's for the chicken eggs that will be coming soon."

"Chicken eggs?"

"I do it every spring. Don't you remember?" She smiles thinking of the kids' excitement. They will run in every morning enthusiastically checking the eggs for movement or cracks.

He nods. "I guess I do now. Why isn't the school paying for these things?"

Valerie laughs. "The school doesn't pay for these. They're considered extras, non-essential items. But we do get tissues and pencils, which is more than other schools offer."

Alexander chuckles as he reaches for her plate and places it on his own. He heads for the kitchen, pausing to kiss her head on the way. This is her signal to pick up any other plates and follow, but she waits for him to come back. He'll have another nip or two of coffee before he leaves for the day.

When he returns, she says again, "Saturday, then?"

He sips his coffee and contemplates as if trying to remember something. "Saturday." He pauses, "Oh, yes, honey. I've signed you up for cooking classes. Thanks for reminding me." He leans down and kisses her lips and her nose, leaves her sitting there as he grabs his phone and walks into the kitchen.

The cup clinks in the porcelain sink and his briefcase slides across the counter. She catches him before he walks out the door to the garage. "What?"

He backtracks toward her as she stands in the center of the room. She folds her arms, momentarily afraid of what he might say or do, but he half-hugs her, phone in one hand, briefcase in the other. "We discussed this. I can't do all the cooking forever, hon."

She searches her mind for the conversation. A year ago, maybe more, a light-hearted taunt, "you need training," after he'd tried her chicken and rice. She'd cooked a handful of meals on her own, all of which he found problematic. For a while, they prepared the meals together, but his gourmet ideals weren't practical to begin when he arrived home late.

"Do I get some choice in this?"

He laughs heartily. "Of course, my dear." He pulls her into his arms and hugs her. "I'll send you the information this afternoon. Choose whichever time suits you."

Valerie leans her body into him, her head on his chest, the guest room forgotten.

*

Last year's Gala's theme brought the 80's Madonna and Punk scene into mimicking life. Anyone who lived through the 80's would argue it's a stereotype. Not everyone dyed their hair blue or hung chained crosses to their waist, but that's the post MTV view for those too young to remember or too old to care. The year before was inappropriately black tie. A fail for teachers and parents, too formal for a June event.

This week her extra time is spent planning; she and Lucy brainstorm ideas in the few minutes before school and when passing each other. And it's with excitement she carries the ever-thickening folder of ideas for their Thursday meeting. Her mind is beaming with a masquerade ball of sorts when Jenny returns with Tommy and gives her a wave good-bye.

The little boy is waiting almost patiently, not jumping, but bouncing from foot to foot and counting the numbers learned in class today. Valerie feels the same excitement as she holds the folder in her arms. She's used the gala planning as a reason not to commit to the cooking class. She'd imagined a romantic evening cooking class for two or even a summer session for herself to learn to produce the rich sauces and the complicated dishes Alexander prefers. But cooking alone on a Saturday morning in the spring feels more like a punishment than a gift.

Lucy speed walks into the classroom, glances at Tommy. "Leftover?"

"I'm sure it'll only be a minute or two."

"Did you tell Stewart you didn't want to do the gala?"

Surprised, Valerie says, "Of course not. I've been planning all week." She excitedly opens the folder to show Lucy notes and photo print outs. "I'm having a blast running through ideas. I thought we might..."

Lucy shakes her head, interrupting Valerie. "Stewart reassigned this."

"What? Why?" Valerie reflexively closes the folder, laying it to her chest.

"I thought maybe you said something to him. I have to work with Wankle." She leans closer to Valerie and whispers, "Wankle." The older woman harbors the old school stereotype: strict, shuffling, a little bit loud and even more hard of hearing

Valerie offers a sympathetic smile as she, reluctantly, leans the folder toward Lucy. She wonders if Mr. Stewart doesn't trust her. Next August will be her third year. She's the one who brought the gala idea to the board, designed other programs, helped plan other, albeit smaller, events. As Valerie watches Lucy go, she realizes their regular Thursday coffee date is off for the foreseeable future.

"Excuse me," Lucy pauses at the door allowing Jack to enter before she disappears.

"I got the gates mixed up." Having heard part of the conversation and now noticing the sad eyes, the bitten lip, he feels guilty for eavesdropping.

"Uncle Jack!" Tommy races over to him and up into Jack's ready arms.

"You have a good day, Little Man? Were ya good to Miss V and Miss Jenny?"

Tommy nods hard. "Yes, let's go now. You said if I was good."

"Yep, yep. But let me ask Miss V. if Toms was a good little man."

The corners of her mouth turn up as she focuses on them. "Yes, Tommy was very good today. Thank you, Tommy, for your hard work."

"You're welcome," he says. "Come on, let's go. You promised."

Jack smiles and sets Tommy on the ground. "Go get your stuff, Little Man." He steps further into the classroom. "I didn't mean to interrupt, I'm sorry."

Valerie shakes her head and waves her hand.

"We did promise you some Krispy Kreme if you want to join us."

Valerie's eyes start to smile along with her face. She'd forgotten the kind gesture but sways her head from side to side. "Thank you, but no."

"You can come Miss. V. It's okay, I don't mind."

Jack and Valerie chuckle as Tommy heads toward the door.

"Hold on there, Toms." Jack steps closer to Valerie and lowers his voice. "You doin' okay, got some bad news?"

Valerie appreciates the sincerity. "Thank you for asking. I'm okay. You guys have fun at Krispy Kreme." She waves to Tommy who is becoming impatient in the doorway.

"They have chocolate, Miss V." Jack backs up to where

Tommy is starting to jump with both feet in and out of the doorway. "Chocolate makes everything better."

Valerie's smile widens. "Thank you," she says again. "But I really do have plenty to do here."

Jack adjusts Tommy's backpack and takes his lunch box from him, holds his hand and with one last look says, "You know where it is, right? Next to the movie theater." Jack winks. "The whole world looks better after a cup of coffee."

"I don't want to go to the movies. You said Krispy..."

She watches them go. Tommy holds Jack's hand and chatters while Jack gazes down occasionally adding a word or two. Before they turn out of sight, Jack glances back, catches her eye, and smiles.

Valerie's disappointment about the gala causes her to stand in the center of the class, scanning the room. Tomorrow's preparations are finished in anticipation of event planning with Lucy. The star chart, the tooth chart, the posters are all updated. She sincerely can't think of anything that needs to be done. She slowly spins toward her desk considering her work for next week, the emails she could check or... the cooking class. She wonders if there's one for Thursday afternoons; a short tense breath brings a sob into her throat, moisture to her eyes.

She grabs her purse and backs away from her desk. She'll go shopping. She'll order a large Mocha Frappuccino and sit at the duck pond. Jack was right, coffee and chocolate. As she turns her car toward the local coffee shop, she passes the entrance to the movie theater. She decides, without thinking too long, to turn around. It's only when the electronic doors of Krispy Kreme slide to an open that she pauses to think about what she's doing.

She barely knows Jack. It could be misinterpreted by others. He's not even expecting her. She spins to leave when Jack calls out, "Miss V, over here."

Blush rises to her cheeks.

"Miss V, you came!" Tommy climbs off his chair and runs to take her hand. Tommy leads her to the table and points. "My backpack is in this seat, so you have to sit next to Uncle Jack."

"Thank you, Tommy, but let me get..."

"I got it." Jack jumps up "Black or a mocha?" He smiles warmly.

Before she knows it, she's telling Jack about the gala. "I thought a masquerade ball, like you see in the movies, a live band."

"I feel ya. Yep. Why don't you go ask this Stewart guy to put you back on? Tell him your ideas."

"He already reassigned it. I feel like he doesn't trust me."

"You gotta show him, girl. March in there and give him a what for." Jack sits back, listening intently, offering his support.

When they get up to leave, Tommy sees an advertisement for a new movie that features talking animals. "Uncle Jack, look."

"A talking rabbit? Is this a scary movie?" Jack jokes. "Cuz bunnies scare me."

"Rabbits aren't scary, are they Miss V? They don't even eat people." He traces the poster with his finger.

"You've never seen Zombie Rabbits from the Black Lagoon." Jack quips as they pass the billboard showing fuzzy creatures in a garden.

"Miss V, you got time for a movie?"

Valerie loves children's movies. She and Lucy have designed assignments around some of the latest releases to get the kids interested in learning numbers and letters. If the movie falls under the educational realm, they can apply for a grant to take the children to a matinee. But with her planning buddy working with someone else, she feels a little cheated.

"I've imposed enough on your time. But thank you. I really do appreciate you listening."

"Nonsense. That's what friends do. They listen. And they go see movies together."

"We're going? Yay!" Tommy yanks on Jack's hand. "Come on. Come on Miss V, hurry."

Jack tips his head toward the theater, a playful light in his eyes, a smile on his lips. He had her the moment he said friends. She checks her watch. "Only if you're sure I won't be intruding." He grabs her hand and lets Tommy pull them both toward the theater.

When the movie ends, Valerie thanks both of them sincerely. She calls in an order to Olive Garden for pasta, pizza, and salad. It's not Alexander's favorite, but it is a full meal and she believes he'll appreciate the effort.

The early spring weather inspires her; she sets the table on the patio. She opens the wine to let it breathe. When Alexander gets in, he glances toward the dining room, and sighs heavily believing she's forgotten dinner again. Valerie sweeps in, "Hi, honey." She stands on her tippy toes and hugs him, kisses him.

"Did you forget?"

"I did not." She's feeling good as she takes his hands and leads him outside to the set table, the covered plates, the poured wine.

He glances around the back yard, then over to the neighbor's yards. "Okay." He loosens his tie and picks up his glass. "What brought on this mood?"

She shrugs, dips her head to the side. It reminds him of when he first met her. He likes the tilt of her head, finds the small shy smile seeking approval sexy, but somehow it's also immature.

"I felt pretty bad. Mr. Stewart gave the gala to someone else," she explains, "but then I went to the movies..."

"You went to the movies in the middle of the day? Alone?"

She smiles, reaches for his hand. She waited excitedly to share her day with him. The anticipation, the disappointment, the new friend. "No, with one of the families from school. The little boy, Tommy, he's..."

He pulls back, sets his hands flat on the patio table as if ready to rise. "Is that acceptable? Doesn't your contract stipulate no fraternization with the clients."

Her smile dims, she pauses, searching for the words. "Mr. Stewart wants us to remain friendly. Some people even go to dinner at family's homes. Mr. Stewart himself..."

"That doesn't mean a thing, honey." Alexander leans forward. "All that matters is the wording of the contract. The whole Mr.

Stewart did it will not hold up in court."

Valerie leans back. Her good mood interrupted.

Alexander reaches across the table and takes her hand. "I'm sorry, honey. I'm just trying to look out for you." He drops her hand, picks up his plate, and stands, "This is really sweet, hon. But the dining room table is more appropriate."

Slow to follow, she picks up her wine and her own plate and works her way in. She doesn't offer anything more but listens as he talks about his day. When they make love that night, she doesn't think about the way he feels in her arms. She thinks about the movie, about the donuts and, then for an instant, Jack's face, Jack's laugh, the feel of Jack's beard when he grabbed her hand; Valerie moans.

6

"I wake up before the prison bell sounds in the morning. It's easier for me to be awake instead of that horrendous bell yanking me from dreams. We dress. We're counted. Yes, counted. Five or six times a day; we stand in lines and they count the population. I can't see how anyone might escape, but I guess they're worried about us disappearing into the concrete walls.

My Jamaican friend, Kaio stops by after breakfast again. 'Meetin' bro?' His voice is deep, rhythmic. It's like a blues guitar, musical.

I hop up out of bed, but not because I really care about the meeting. It's just better than being in my cell with nothing but flowing thoughts.

Kaio tells a story of how he found God and how God guides him, says this God helps him to handle the hardest times of his life. I don't speak, I just listen. 'Most people,' his deep balanced voice sounds like a song, 'Think of God as a man who is pulling strings, making decisions, ruinin' der' plans, Mon'. But the truth of it is that the program is talking about power, about turnin' over your power to something else. See, Mon', you don't have the power. That's what you got to realize. The powerful one can be in that big blue sky, the oceans you swim, it can be in nature, or it can be that chair. You just got to realize there is a power greater than you. Those drugs told you that you were the powerful one. And, Mon', where are you? Are you powerful here? No. And this is where everyone ends up who thinks they have it all under control.'

He walks off and I stare at the chair he sat in. I shake my head, not believing a word he said.

'So you're the all powerful one, huh?' I say to the chair all mocking like. I get up, head back to my cell, and I trip over that very chair!

I stay real still on the floor and stare at the four-legged, wobbly, aluminum seat. I laugh. I laugh at that chair. I laugh at myself. I laugh at the irony. I laugh until everyone turns around and looks at me like I'm crazy. Kaio says, 'you alright, bro?'

I wave a hand.

It's blank inside here. You're not a person. No one comes to see you. You don't call people. You can't eat what you want or when you want. Everyone in here is in the same spot as I am; some of them are in more trouble and some ain't coming back after trial. Some are going away for a long time. It seems strange to me that they are looking for salvation. Later, I say to Kaio, 'isn't it a little too late to think about all this now?'

'How else you goin' to get through this death?'

I think he means to say life, but he's serious. And he's right. This is a different kind of death. It's a life in blankness. What does one do on the inside of a cell for fifteen or twenty years? There is nothing. But these people are serious about their salvation.

I get it. It's too late to turn their life around. All you got is your soul. So you turn that around.

Kaio tells me that many of them will get out and spend five minutes in the sun before they hit the nearest corner looking for drugs. 'They'll be back in here,' he assures me. But maybe that's where they want to be.

I ask, why?

Kaio takes my shoulders with his big hands and squeezes me a little, says, 'you don't worry about those other people. You ask yourself why? Those are where the answers are, Mon.'

Why do I do it? It's a way to fool around, have fun. It's a way to get away from the pain. But when I think about it, most of it's not fun, most of it is a void. Big empty moments. What pain am I trying to get away from? It's the pain I create.

All while this stuff is happening to my head, a guard comes to get me. I follow. Head down. Don't ask questions. Leads me to a visitor's room.

Danny comes in. Claire's husband. He's a little chubby, shorter than me. He's like a teddy bear, but he surprises me all the time.

'Is Claire out there with Tommy?' I ask.

He stares down at the table and traces some invisible line with his finger, 'No, she doesn't know I'm here. I took the day off to drive down here.' He pauses for a moment. I can see he's working some things out in his head.

'If...' he stops himself.

My heart sinks. I watch his face, but I don't meet his eyes when he shoots me a glance. I feel like he's here to tell me to stop fucking up, to stop hurting his wife, my sister.

'After...' he interrupts himself again.

I sit back a little. I don't want him to think I'm not listening or I'm shutting down; I've gotta face up to whatever he says. I'm already thinking of what I need to agree too, how I need to apologize again, the promises I shouldn't make again until it's all for real.

'I'm needing help at the shop, thought maybe when you're done here, we could get you started working there. I think you know a little about cars, but I can train you. It's not a lot of money or a big, fancy job, but we do work with the movie studios these days.'

I lean back all the way, slouch against my chair. Danny doesn't say if you can stay clean or after you get out of jail. He offers me a job like I'm any other upstanding citizen.

'Claire tells me you're a great artist, so maybe we can get you to design some art for these studio cars...' And Danny keeps going.

I feel like such a shit.

When he finally stops tripping over his words, he looks at me straight on. 'What do you think?'

I nod. Want to bawl my f'n eyes out. Not even about the job, but that Danny would trust me, give me a chance. Treat me so good when he barely even knows me.

'Cool, cool,' he says. 'So whenever you're a... finished here... you'll like come up there, we'll get ya all set up...'

Facing a shitty three to four hour drive back home in mid-day traffic, Danny shoots his hand across the table. 'Well, nice seeing you, Jack.' And he shakes my hand.

I can see now how Danny is with the studio execs, how he must be with everyone he meets.

The guard opens the gate and I get up, and damn it if I don't trip over that chair. Someone is definitely tryin' to tell me something!" Jack laughs.

His friends and his sponsor laugh with him.

7

Saturday morning is cool and chilly, Valerie wears a summer dress with a sweater. Her hair is clipped back, and her apron tied on as she stands alone behind a cutting board at the Studio Grille for the beginner's cooking class. Everyone else shows up in pairs. There are two women who are friends, a few young couples, an older couple, a gay couple, and Valerie who numbers nine and feels out of place.

Elsa, the instructor, leads them step by step through the process of making soup. Valerie has done this many times, except for the additions of salt, oil, and spices. Her mother was not allowed to have too much salt or oil, and Valerie never learned much beyond a pinch of dried oregano here and there. The class will be easy, if not boring.

The class pours out into the center of the farmer's market. The location allows the residents and visitors to gather and wander the stalls, support the local farmers, and buy fresh fruits and vegetables.

Valerie hangs her sweater over her arm as she browses the market, picking up vegetables in case Alexander expects her to repeat the soup recipe sometime this week. Remembering spices, she turns suddenly and nearly smacks into Jack carrying a yoga mat.

"I am so sorry..." he realizes it's Valerie and his face lights up.

"My fault. I'm sorry. Yoga?" Valerie chuckles.

Jack nods. "Yes, Ma'am. Gotta get all grounded and zen with the world around me. How about you, getting some fresh veggies for dinner?"

"I need spices."

They walk together. "What do you need? This place right over here has basil, but there's a place further down with a better selection."

Valerie shrugs. "I don't know. Whatever goes into soup."

Jack laughs. "What kind of soup?"

"Vegetable. Alexander signed me up for a cooking class."

He bumps her shoulder with his. "You can cook. You're teasing me."

"I cook! It's just that..." she pauses. "My mom was diabetic. I made healthy things, chicken breast, salads. I make great salads!" She picks up a cucumber to point at him.

"Okay, okay. Well that's good. So you can cook, you just need to get creative, huh?"

Valerie looks at the plants blankly.

"This is rosemary," Jack picks up a plastic bag of the herb.

"I think I need them all."

Jack chuckles. "You sure?"

Valerie shrugs, picks up the basil, oregano, mint, and lemon balm to add to the rosemary.

They fall into a quiet step with one another as they head to the parking lot. "Is the class that bad?" Jack asks.

Valerie shrugs again. "I feel out of place. Everyone has a partner. The teacher came to help me. It's like middle school Home-Ec all over again."

Jack laughs. "Next week, play hooky and come to yoga."

"I might!"

"Did you talk to that principle about the party?"

"Monday."

"Good. You march in there and you say, Look here, Mr. Bossman." Jack puts his hand on his hips and tosses his head as if he's tossing his hair.

Valerie chuckles.

"Joking aside, tho," Jack's voice gets drippy-smooth and serious. "You are smart and capable; you remind him why he hired you."

Valerie watches Jack's face. No one's told her that in a long time. It feels nice to be reminded that she has a brain and someone believes in her. When they approach her car, she pops the trunk with the beep of her remote and sets the food inside.

Jack steps ahead of her and opens the car door. "Hug?"

"Yes." She accepts his arms around her for the momentary, but warm and friendly hug, and returns the gesture. "Thanks for the help."

"Anytime. You have a great day," he calls as he walks away.

*

Valerie washes the vegetables in the sink as Alexander comes in. "How was class? Ready to whip up some Carbonara?"

Valerie chuckles. "I think I'm a long way from that. But the class, Alexander, is for couples."

He sniffs the spices, places them in the refrigerator. "Take a different class."

"They're for couples. Why don't you come with me?" Valerie dries the cucumber, red pepper, squash, and tomatoes, before handing them to him.

Alexander laughs loudly. "No." He places them, one by one, in the crisper.

"Honey."

Shutting the refrigerator, he mimics her, "Honey," then adds "Don't whine. It's unattractive." He leaves Valerie standing at the sink.

She follows him to the doorway, intent on defending herself but stops short. The argument's not worth it, she tells herself.

Instead, she stalks off in the other direction. She pushes open the door to the guest room, intent on cleaning it.

She begins with her own boxes of teaching materials. She doesn't need everything. some she can leave at school; some can be hauled to the garage. She'll pile Alexander's boxes in the corner and let him decide.

An hour passes before Alexander comes in search of her. "What are you doing?"

"Cleaning. I put your boxes," she points to the dim and dusty corner, "over there. You can decide what to do with those."

Alexander puffs out a mocking snicker. "I decided to put them here."

Valerie ignores his attitude. "Put them in the den upstairs."

"That's my office. My man cave, soccer games, bourbon."

Valerie's aware he has never watched a full game of anything, nor has he spent much time there unless he was preparing legal documents for work. "And now it can be for boxes."

He stares at Valerie. He does not like this. He does not like her cleaning out this room and he certainly finds it unacceptable for her to be telling him what to do. He lifts that one eyebrow. "What brought this on?"

"I want this to be a room. A real room for people, friends, guests. We have the bed." She points to the plastic covered mattress standing against the adjacent wall.

"For your grandmother?"

"If she wants to visit." Valerie doesn't turn to look at him.

Alexander stands there, waiting for her to turn to him. When she doesn't, he steps up to her and puts his hand heavily on her shoulder. "Honey, come here." He walks into her body and holds her close. "Let me hire someone, sweetheart. I'll hire a contractor. We'll get a little dresser in here, nightstand. But we should leave it to experts and not try to throw something together that might embarrass us." He feels Valerie's posture soften, knows he's got her. She'll agree.

"When?" she asks.

He pauses in the center of the room and takes a deep breath. "I'll try a contractor on Monday."

Valerie doesn't completely believe him.

Tugging on her hand playfully, he t ilts his head toward the door in a charmingly boyish way. He offers a half smile, a wink. "Let's go shower." He pulls her into him. "I'll soap your back, rub your shoulders."

Valerie follows him out, up the stairs, holding his hand as he leads her away.

8

"**D**ates in my head don't always work. Numbers don't stick. Don't ask me how many times I've been clean or how long or when it all started. I can't talk like that. Talk to me about places, faces, lives. That I can do.

I was seventeen when I saw my first junkie friend die of an overdose. That was before my first stint in some pay-for-play rehab bullshit. So many rehabs are there for the money, people running them think they know what's best, or they don't give a shit; they're there for the dinero. Not that the addicts care anyway. Never takes the first time, or the second time, because we don't think we're sick. We think we can handle it. Addicts think it takes willpower or just a change of scenery – hell I did that too. I blew off art school and went to New Orleans. A change of scenery. I told my dad and sis, just gotta get away from these people who are using me. Truth is addicts use one another. Addicts will use whoever they can. This is what I saw; no one had any sort of morals, ethics. There is no honor among thieves. No honor among people who need drugs more than they need friends, family, love, food, a bed to sleep in.

I blew my art school tuition and got a little place in NoLa. A little apartment I shared with two other people, just footsteps North of Bourbon Street. I told myself, right where a drug addict needs to be. I can at least control it here. No people trying to use me, buy me, sell me. I can get clean here. I'm not sure if we are born liars or that shit we put into our veins turns us into vapid, mindless machines serving bullshit.

Bourbon street is a freaking bust though. Tourists, drunks, robberies. A haven for the criminal element. I have to admit to lifting a few wallets myself. The guys I stayed with showed me how and, on Bourbon Street, where every one's drunk and bumping into one another anyway, it's easy. But I had my rules. Ronnie, the guy that taught me, would lie and steal anything from anyone. I'm pretty damn sure he stole my shit a few times too.

It's a hot Saturday night. All nights are hot in the sticky, steamy humidity of the French Quarter. There are no breezes comin' off the Mississippi. Vendors sometimes boast ac in their shops to get people in, but most just leave their door open and suffer the swell. Vendors in the French Quarter are locals, they live in the city somewhere; they lose a lot of merchandise to tourists stealing, but they don't tolerate the locals pilfering from them. And after a few weeks they know we're locals, so we're not welcomed in their shops at all.

Ronnie goes up to this woman; it's late, she's tipsy, giggling with her girlfriends. He makes like a drunk and bumps into her. Her bag is half open, didn't shut it all the way and slung it over her shoulder. He got the wallet the minute he bumped into her, but he turns around and apologizes, squinting his eyes like he's drunk and starts flirting with them. 'Oh, man, look at these beautiful ladies.'

They giggle.

'You beautiful ladies got to be from New Orleans. Are you college students?'

They're obviously over college age; he's flattering them and they're eating it up.

'Oh, yes,' one of them laughs, 'Just graduated, celebrating.'

'Graduates. Oh my god!' It might be kind of funny if I was

watching this on Tosh, if Ronnie was really drunk and half meant what he said and wasn't stealing from them.

'Oh, no, no, babies, we gotta party. Jack, Jack,' he drunkenly calls me over, but I do not want any part of it.

Figure I better act a little buzzed if I gotta do this, so I stumble over to them.

'Jack, we gotta buy these ladies a graduation drink.' I think Ronnie might be serious about buying them drinks with their own money.

'Ron, man. Our wives'll kill us. Remember last time you bought some pretty college students a drink?'

The ladies' smiles shrink.

Ronnie waves his hand at me. 'He's messin' with you.'

The ladies walk off.

'You ass,' he says when they've disappeared into the crowd. He takes the money from the wallet, drops it on the ground where we stand. I look around but no one cares, no one's watching us.

As we turn around, he bumps into a man accidently, 'so sorry, man,' and picks his pocket as well.

Bourbon street is thick with gettoweed. People find stuff in the garden trash, grind it up with some crap they've grown in their basement and sell it to tourists. The tourists are either too drunk or too ignorant to know the difference. It'll get you high – if you've never been high in your life.

Bourbon street, after the bars close, is putrid from piss. Bad city plumbing and drunks taking a leak anywhere they want. There's an old wives' tale circulating down here; if you fall in the bourbon juice that lines the gutters, you're a gonner. They say, if you lose a shoe, you lose your foot. May as well cut the damn thing off before you get gangrene or some shit from that swell.

I paid my rent six months in advance with my art school tuition. Told myself at that time it was smart, so I couldn't use the money for drugs. But it made me not have to work, and I still had enough money to drink, get high. I grew to hate Bourbon street, so I head north to Treme where there's a bunch of jazz clubs and the air is thick with G-13. The drinks are shit, watered down, but the pot is touted as top-secret government grown.

This, I have to admit, is where I meet the best addicts a man could know. Marlon plays the trombone harder than anyone I've ever heard. When he comes off stage between sets, the waitress hands him a drink. He sits at the nearest table to smoke, drink before he gets back up there. This isn't the safest neighborhood. There are low lives who will rob you, leave you dead in the street, but then there's the people who hang out here. Good people. The waitress helps a drunk up from the table, tells the bouncer to get him a cab; she takes his keys away from him and says, 'I'll get 'em to you in the mornin'.'

I don't leave until the bar's closing. I walk out at the same time Marlon Lasch does. There's a few girls, maybe fresh out of high school, going to college age, too young to be out here alone, waiting near the curb, sweaters pulled up around 'em.

'What're you girls doin out here?' Marlon's voice surprises even me.

'Waiting for our ride, Mister.' They look him up and down. Marlon's probably got a good fifteen years on them, so it's okay for them to wonder about him. But he's probably safer than some stupid kid my age.

'No cabs come 'round 'ere.' He's stumbling a little himself, but he keeps his distance so as to not scare 'em.

There's a gang of young punks on the corner looking for trouble. If any of us were heading that way, the smartest thing to do was to walk the other way, clear around the block if we had to. But the girls start walking down that way.

'Hey, no, no.' He waves his hand at 'em. 'We'll walk ya home.'
'Uhm. No.'

I know they're scared and they're acting tough, but they're out of their element.

'Ladies,' I say, 'Do you know who this is? This is Marlon Lasch. He's with the band in there. Did you hear that sweet, sweet music?'

I know they trust me because I'm closer to their age. They turn around to me. Their bodies relax; they release the iron grips on their sweaters.

'Which way you ladies going? Maybe we can help you find a cab.'

Marlon's watching me. Doesn't know me from any other stranger in the bar, doesn't know if I'm trying to trick them, but I think he knows I'm not.

'We're staying in the French Quarter,' one of them offers.

'Me, too. Marlon,' I tap his arm, 'You're right down there, too.' I point straight ahead. We'll have to cross the major intersection at night, but it's safer than crossing those corners where the lights are, where the gang of assholes is hanging.

'Yes, Sir,' he says, 'We're walking right down there toward Bourbon. We could walk behind ya'll, make sure no one bothers you.'

They seem to like that better than the alternative of standing there or walking the streets, not quite alone, but enough alone. Some of these side streets are dark, no streetlights, easy for someone to hide against one of the buildings, in one of the alleys.

The French Quarter is touted as a fun place to have a good time, but I learn fast it's also one of the most dangerous cities in America. Too many drunks meet too many criminals.

Marlon and I talk music as we keep pace behind the ladies who whisper, giggle, occasionally look back. When they see we seriously don't mean them any harm, they say a few words to us. By the time we get them to their hotel, they're giggling like the little girls they are.

'Hey, you guys wanna come in?'

I want to. I'm not ready for the night to be over. I assume they have some alcohol in their room, some ragweed.

Marlon grabs my arm. 'No. You ladies get on up to that room. You don't come up there to Treme,' he says like a father. 'That's a dangerous place for nice, young ladies to be.'

'We were just trying to have some fun,' one of them mouths

off defiantly.

'Those boys on that corner had some other plans for you,' he says. 'They leave your little bodies in the cemetery 'ver there for your mommas to find. You like that kinda fun?'

I'm shocked. But they march angrily into their hotel.

'You pissed them off,' I chuckle.

'They'll get over it.' He looks down at the bricks, 'you gonna walk me back now young man?'

'What's that?'

'Got some talking to do to you too.' He turns and starts walking away, not waiting for my answer.

I'm not sure what to expect, but right now I'm a little amazed with this man and want to know more.

'Why'd you do that?' I ask. 'Harp on those girls like that.'

'Seen too many of them end up in a ditch, side of the road, trash bin somewhere. Kids come here trying to have some fun and they run into the wrong kinda people. Lots of them here.' He looks up, watches the street, the meandering spectral bodies still lingering in the shadows of the French quarter. 'Lots of bad things in this life.'

I shrug, keep pace with him.

'I seen you got your own kinda trouble.' He doesn't look at me, but I know what he's talking about. 'I got my own too. But it's all how we handle 'em. How you gonna handle yours?' He asks, but he doesn't wait for an answer, so even as my mind is trying to catch up with his words, he keeps talking. 'You can handle your own trouble and not let it spill out onto other people. You hear what I'm sayin' young man. You got my meaning?'

I start to mumble a yeah, or sure, or whatever I think might be appropriate.

'We all make choices.' He stops and looks down at me. He's a big man, dark eyes, dark hair, darker splotches on his skin. He's seen some life, I think, a whole lot of life. 'Don't let your life choices hurt other people, ya feel me?'

I nod, a little dumbfounded. He ambles off back toward

Treme. I'm closer to my apartment, so I stand still, not sure whether I should follow. I feel he's said his peace.

'Maybe I'll see ya,' he says without looking back.

I become a regular at the club where he plays. Once in a while he talks to me, sometimes he doesn't. He's got a lot of fans and even more friends.

Almost every night I'm there, I see what he's talking about, young people not getting what they expected. I walk some home, sometimes, take his cue and never walk them in. I decide to be a gentleman, the way he is.

I don't rob tourists, like Ronnie. And, one day, Ronnie doesn't come back. The other guy doesn't worry, he shrugs. 'Probably got his due, ya know?' That's a drug addict for you. Your best friend one day, doesn't give a shit if you're lying in a ditch the next day.

We hear from others that he got pinched, picked up, going away. None of us go see him. None of us know if it's even the truth.

My place becomes a mess. Dishes in the sink. Pizza boxes on top of the trash. Drink containers lying around. Fridge empty, except for condiments. And more and more people in and out. I keep my door locked, not that I have anything in there except for a dresser with some clothes and a mattress on the floor. I carry my wallet on me at all times. If I have drugs, they're on me or hidden. There's always a spot to hide drugs, or you have to create one. Mine is a faked electrical socket. If you plug something into the top one, it works. That's where the lamp is plugged in. The bottom one is cracked, looks broken. It takes a screwdriver, kept in another room, to unlock it.

With Ronnie gone, we gotta come up with extra rent. I'm running low on cash and do a few jobs with people I know. I help someone paint a house. I drive for someone else. But I need something else. I start searching the place when the other roommate is out. He wants to move two other guys in here; I don't like these guys, don't trust them. I can tell they're trouble. They're always looking around like they're expecting a problem; they check cars that pass, see if someone is following them. They're either really gone on too much sesh or they're on the run.

I want to search Ronnie's room, see if he left any cash or hash behind. I doubt it. My six months' worth of rent is almost gone anyway. I'll find another place, but I gotta make some regular cash and I gotta figure out how.

I sit back and try to work out where the rest of my cash went. I took one semester's worth of funds: that's almost ten grand. Rent and utilities was like a third of that at most. Food couldn't have taken up another third. But if in any way it did, that leaves another third that I've blown on drugs, probably more if I'm honest with myself. That doesn't include what the other guys bought or the ready cash I'd spent from side jobs.

One day, when my roommate and his new friends are out, I go into Ronnie's old room. I know they've all been in here, doing what I'm doing. The better you know a person, the closer you get to understanding where they'd hide their stash.

Ronnie's room is full of shit. Things he'd stolen from tourists and locals. He used to drop wallets, but I guess he brought some home. His whole top drawer is full of men's and women's wallets, IDs, credit cards, pictures of kids, spouses, parents, etc. There's other random things, a tissue with a lipstick print, a note, maybe poem, written on the back of a business card. There's some cheap jewelry, plastic tourist crap bought on bourbon street. There's even a woman's scarf. I pick it up, unlike Ronnie to keep something pretty, but it looks like it might be worth some cash. I toss it aside. Not worth my time to try. I check his other drawers, look for false bottoms, fake backs, pull them out and check underneath each, search under the dresser itself, behind. He's got a cot like bed in here; I check it out too, but nothing. Ronnie's pretty damn smart, so I try thinking like him. Since he's big on grifting others, he'd be expecting where people would look. I check his closet. Besides a jacket that's clean, there's a t-shirt on the floor, a pair of old shoes that look like they've been kicked off and left, an old backpack. I pick it up, really not expecting to find anything. There's an old notebook, looks like it'd gotten wet, it's wrinkled, wilted, can't read a thing in it. I toss the thing back on the floor, turn and walk out into the room again. I'm kinda jonesing now. I need something. My stomach's starting to hurt, my head's feeling fuzzy, starting to get sick. I got maybe twenty bucks. It's enough for a quick hit, but not enough for food. I wonder how much I got left in the bank, maybe a hundred bucks. I sit on the floor, try to figure Ronnie out. It's here. Something is here. Everyone keeps a little something hidden.

I hear the front door. I think Kyle and his new friends are back. I'm getting angry now. I fucking hate them. I don't trust them a damn bit. Kyle doesn't realize what he's getting in to. He's some rich boy who gets a monthly check. He has his drugs delivered. He doesn't go out and get to know the people, know the streets, that makes him vulnerable to stupid shitheads like these guys. He can't smell trouble. He's a happy go lucky guy. So am I, for the most part, but you gotta know who you're dealing with at any given time. Ronnie was the worst of us three and Kyle didn't know half the shit he was in to.

I back into the closet, kick the backpack and shoes aside and sit down. I'm listening to them. They've settled the money of moving in with Kyle; they feign that they're going to get their belongings, clothes, pick up a bed, and offer him a couch for the living room. We used to have one, but it stunk like piss and alcohol from too many drunken parties. There's a table out there, no chairs, busted up from the same drunken parties. Who cares; it's not like we sit at the table and eat. We occasionally lay things on it, separate dope on it. Otherwise, we crash in our rooms. Kyle's got a tv out there. An old one. He had a new one when he first moved in, stolen in the first week. That was long before I moved in.

I'm sitting in the closet when I feel the floor is uneven. I think I'm sitting on one of the shoes or something, so I move over, but still kind of lumpy, uneven. I consider it's a bad carpeting job – but then it occurs to me. I forget those freaking people are even here when I push the stuff aside and start looking for a way to pull up the rug. I'm pretty damn sure I've just found Ronnie's stash.

I dig at one of the corners. He's good. I'm not sure how he had easy access or if he has a tool somewhere else in the room, probably in that drawer of junk, wallets, plastic beads. Explains a lot now.

I dig at the corner, rip it up with my bare hands. A carpet staple catches my finger and I start bleeding. There's plywood that I yank out, then there it is… neatly stacked…cash, some envelopes of coke, a few bags of pot. I take the pot, stick it in my pocket, open one of the envelopes and rub it over my mouth and nose. Then I pick up the packets of cash. It's hundreds, about three packets held together with rubber bands. Thrilled! Got a couple grand easy. Moving out cash.

I hear a voice that calls me out of my enjoyment of the find. It's a woman's voice. My brain knows who it is even if my mind doesn't yet. I only know it's familiar, soft, sweet, and I can't, at first, even make out what is being said. I don't even know how I heard it since the guy's voices faded into oblivion in the joy of my discovery, as if the whole world disappeared for a moment while I was living my bliss on the bottom of a closet floor.

I sit up, pull myself out of the closet, stuff the money in my waistband.

'Jack? He doesn't live here?'

'We didn't say that, pretty lady. Tell us what a fine beauty such as yourself is doing with a loser like that?'

'Is he here or not?' Claire's voice cuts through my drug haze and I jump up.

'Don't be like that, Baby.'

I throw open the door, let it slam on the wall behind me as they all turn to look at me. One of the guys has his hand on Claire's arm. I step right up to them and grab his hand, twist his fingers back, 'Get your stinking hand off my sister.'

'Bro,' his brother steps up, 'You ain't gotta be like that, bro.'

'Bro,' I mock him. 'This is my sister. You touch her, I will kill both of you.' I get in their faces, start pointing and spitting. You gotta act like a madman sometimes. And, no one touches Claire.

No one touches my sister! I will kill them, or I'll go at them until they kill me.

They back off, then I turn to Claire. I move her into another part of the room so I can talk to her and watch them. I don't turn my back on anyone, especially someone I just threatened.

'What are you doing here?' I speak quietly to Claire.

'Well, hello to you, brother. It's nice to see you too. How have you been?'

I calm down and smile. I give her a hug. She's a foot shorter than I, maybe more. She looks good. Her skin is clear and tanned. Her hair is shorter than I remember. 'How've you been?'

Now she smiles. 'I'm good. How about you?' She wipes something from my face, which I think is probably some of the cocaine dust that I just shoved into my nose. I'm quickly ashamed, but I try not to show it.

'Jackie, I want you to come home with me.'

The guys leave and Kyle goes into his room; it's just us now.

'What? Why?' I try to laugh off the concern I hear in her voice.

'So you can get your life back on track, clean up your act, go back to school.'

I force a smile, but I'm biting the inside of my jaw. 'Yeah, I will. You know I will. Just needed a little break.'

'Yeah, well, it's been a long break. What have you been doing here, painting?' She looks around the room, not for proof that I've been doing anything, but just to take in the lack that takes up the space. She knows what I've been doing here. She knows what a drug apartment looks like. I'm ashamed. I shift from foot to foot, hunch over a little.

'Well, time's up. Anyway, I want you to come home with me. I'm getting married.'

'Married?' I hug her hard, joy fills me. 'Married! When?' I'm expecting her to say a year, two years. I know she's got at least a year left of school.

'Next week,' she says.

I stop and look at her, don't want to believe her. My first

thought is she's trying to trick me to get me home, maybe an intervention on that end, but that's not it. She's serious. She doesn't lie to me. And I can even see there's something else there in her face, like she's scared or nervous or something.

'What? Why the rush, hon?'

'You'll like Danny, he's a nice man.' She doesn't meet my gaze.

'Yeah. Nice men wait.'

Now her eyes dig into me. 'I'm pregnant.'

I'm not sure how to react. I'm not sure what she needs from me. But I put my arm around her and hug her close, holding her next to me. I think about her at home with Dad, how he might have reacted, or I can guess she hasn't told him. But, if she's getting married so quickly, he's wondering why, pressuring her to not do it.

'I need you there.' Her voice shakes a little when she says this. So I know what I have to do.

'I'll come.' I hold her out at arm's length and look her in the face so she knows I'm serious.

'Now.'

'Now?'

She also knows I mean what I say right now in front of her but let me get a bit of hashish inside me, a little drink, some liquid discouragement via the pipe, any meaning or intention will be lost. I don't argue with her. I nod.

I go back into Ronnie's room and pick up that backpack. I check the pockets. If I'm getting on a plane, I don't want any illegal substances on me. I push the money into the bottom, shaking off any white powder that may have fallen on it.

Then I go into my room, grab the clothes that I can fit, anything else I think is necessary and meet her back in the living room. Those guys are just getting back as we are leaving; they call behind me, but I ignore them. I don't tell them I'm not coming back, nor explain anything. I want to believe this is what Ronnie did too. He went home. He found hope. He ran toward sobriety. I want to hope so, but I will never know what happened to Ronnie.

And that happens to drug addicts. Sometimes they just disappear, and no one ever finds them.

As Claire and I walk down the street, I put my arm around her. I know it wasn't difficult to find me because of the check I wrote to the building manager five months ago, but that would have been Claire's only clue as to how to find me. Had I rented the place in cash, had I moved more than once, been streeted for the lack of rent, had I left New Orleans for greener pastures, or had I ended up in a tomb over there in one of those graveyards, no one would ever know. This is what happens to drug addicts. Lost. I kiss Claire on the head as we hail a taxi from the corner.

I'm hurting by the time we get to the airport. I figure I'll grab a drink or two from one of the bars, but Claire won't let me go in. As we sit and wait for the flight, she pulls out a sleeping pill from her purse. The woman's got my number. I can't last a three to four-hour flight without something in my system. I'm ashamed and want to refuse, but there's not a cell in my body that lets me, so I take it and pop it in my mouth without water, swallow hard. I know what's waiting for me on the other end of that flight. An angry father, rehab, detoxing. I figure, I can handle it. I can get clean any time I want. I think drug addicts lie to themselves more than they lie to everyone else around them."

9

Valerie is frozen, her fist in the air, in front of Mr. Stewart's cream-colored door. She is running over scenarios in her head. She's wording what she wants to say. Does he not trust her? It sounds weak, she thinks. She'll start with, "I'm wondering why..." She shakes her head at that thought when the door opens suddenly and Mrs. Cruise, the administrative assistant, nearly runs into Valerie. "Excuse me," she says, glancing back at Mr. Stewart.

A blush rises to Valerie's cheeks. The option to turn and walk away is gone. She feels unprepared.

"Come on in," Mr. Stewart waves her in with one hand as he brushes the tan crumbs from his half-eaten coffee cake off his blue suit and lavender tie. "Shelly is so good to me. Would you like some?"

"Thank you, no." Valerie folds her hands in front of her as Alexander's words ring through her head, "that looks childish," and unfolds them. She straightens her spine and smiles confidently at Mr. Stewart. "You've reassigned the gala. I feel I had a good grasp on what was expected. Did you feel I didn't have enough experience?"

"Oh, heavens, that's not it, Mrs. V. Have a seat here." He stands as he offers the chair on the other side of his desk.

"No, thank you. I won't take much of your time." Sitting, she feels, will make her more nervous.

"Mrs. V, I understand you're a young wife making a home, taking cooking classes. You have enough on your plate. I trust you implicitly. I'll tell you what, if you want to help plan the Halloween carnival, we could always use the assistance with that."

Valerie nods, not quite certain what else to say.

Mr. Stewart moves closer to her, places his hand gently on her shoulder, turning toward the door. "You talk that over with your husband and let me know."

Valerie turns to him in the doorway, "husband?"

"And that reminds me, Mrs. V, we had to put the kibosh on the chickens. Some of the West Oaks families felt farm animals on campus might be a little dangerous to have around the children." Mr. Stewart leads her out the door and begins to push it to a close between them.

"Mr. Stewart, you've approved it for the last two years. It's just eggs in an incubator. After they hatch, we donate them to the local farm."

He nods his balding head and puts his hand on his pouchy stomach. "I know, I know," he smiles falsely, "but we do what makes the West Oaks families comfortable."

He closes the door gently, but completely. Valerie stands there for a moment longer before turning and walking slowly toward her class. Replaying the conversation in her head, something didn't feel right, didn't sound right, and just as Jenny pops up and says, "Hi, Ms. V," with her usual excitement, Valerie thinks "cooking classes." How did Mr. Stewart know about the cooking classes? An unfamiliar fire rises from her feet to her chest, heat growing upward, nipping at her throat.

"You okay?" Jenny pauses, touching Valerie's shoulder lightly.

Releasing a deep breath, Valerie smiles. The kids come first. "Yes, Jenny. Thank you." She returns Jenny's touch; they walk toward the kindergarten yard.

That evening, Valerie opens the refrigerator searching for the clear covered glass dish described in Alexander's instructions.

The list includes the day and exact time to place them in the oven. He has turned his dinner into a science. If he's due home at six, and the meal needs to warm for thirty minutes, she is to put it in at 5:15 and cooks it until 5:45, leaving it to rest on the counter for his prompt arrival.

She thinks, as she sets the dining room table, maybe she'd become a little complacent. She'd grown used to Alexander taking control of the meals. She didn't appreciate his dislike for her healthier versions to the point of insult. He'd grown up with a cook and a full-time mother who prepared on a daily basis what Valerie's family would have considered a special meal. Rich creams and sauces were on the no-no list for her mother; deep fried, oil laden, butter filled dishes were not on the list either. Alexander, she thinks, might benefit from a chicken breast lightly sprayed with lemon juice and seasoned with rosemary or some jasmine rice with spring vegetables. But he'd made his position clear.

Maybe she'd been unfair not learning to cook exactly what he wanted and the way he wanted, but she'd tried. An overcooked eggplant parmesan did not win his approval and he didn't want to rely on what he called her "experiments."

It didn't excuse his behavior of talking to Mr. Stewart behind her back, but perhaps she needs to take responsibility. After cooking for her own mother, helping her grandmother, and then opting for takeout through her college years, the idea of having someone cook for her felt rather good.

Oven on, timer set, the sweet scent of orange blossoms carries in with the breeze, the birds build nests in the trees, and their songs call Valerie. She picks up her wine and decides to enjoy the patio.

The first breath of March has arrived, a gentle evening breeze leans Valerie back into the chaise lounge. The appearance of a man wandering into the yard causes her to jolt upright. The gate is locked, she's certain. But she's not alarmed. He's familiar; caramel skin, bright eyes, with his hair curling around his ears. Young and healthier than she remembers him as he kicks a stick, pushes at leaves with his shoe. She smiles as he leans down before making his way toward Valerie. His old work shoes clomp up the two stairs and across the wooden deck, taking the seat next to her.

"Dad," she exalts happily, unquestioning.

A feather lay in his open palm. "White means an angel is watching over you."

She reaches for it when his watch starts beeping. "Your watch."

His kind face stares into hers, "Not mine."

The beeping grows louder.

"Honey." He moves the feather closer to her as the beeping grows more urgent.

Valerie shakes herself awake. The beep, beep, beep of the timer barks through the window. She runs into the house; pulling the glass dish onto the hot plate, she lifts the foil to see an overcooked Chicken Italiano.

The garage door rattles announcing Alexander's arrival. Returning to the patio, a small white feather lay next to her chair. She smiles, thinking of the dream, and pinches it between her fingers as she returns to welcome Alexander home.

Alexander halts his inspection of the crispy-around-the-edges dinner. Grabbing a napkin, he strides toward her, and snatches the feather from her hand. "How many times do I have to tell you not to touch those things? They're filthy. Now go wash your hands." After he tosses it in the bin and kicks the cabinet door to a close, he leans himself on the island staring at the ruined dinner.

Tears sting her eyes; a dry pain strikes her throat. "There is no need to speak to me that way." Her voice shakes, and she spins toward the stairs.

While Alexander occasionally comes home in a bad mood, he'd only ever spoken to her like that once before. Years before when they were walking through a park and she'd found a green parrot's feather. She picked it up, and he'd done nearly the same thing, took it from her hand and lectured her. She'd never picked one up in front of him again.

Feathers are a way to remember her father. She began collecting them years ago on walks with him. As in the dream, he explained what the colors meant. Green, she remembers, signaled health and prosperity. Yellow was joy, and white, he'd always said, were angels watching. The jar now, filled mostly with white, dotted with yellow, a lone owl's feather floating among them, sits in the corner of her classroom. The students occasionally bring one in to excitedly drop among the rest.

As she settles on the edge of the bed, the dressing mirror reflects a sadness so deep she can't bear to glance up at it. It's been a long time since she dreamt of her father, and those dreams took place at her childhood home or the park near her house, never here. While she wonders if there's meaning found in dreams, her father's image remains a calming essence.

Alexander appears at the door, pauses before joining her. "I'm sorry," he pulls her into him. "I should never speak to you like that."

She hesitates before resting her head on his shoulder.

After a few minutes, he offers, "I was out of line." He kisses her head. "Am I forgiven?"

Valerie nods, watching their reflection in the mirror. She used to think they looked so good together. She loved his presence, his arms around her, the feeling she could count on him for anything. Although the image remains, the reflection blurs and shifts as if wind is blowing through the frame. It's her, she thinks, that's moving, blurring the image. Whether she's not living up to the image or not living up to his expectations, something's wrong, something's changing.

"Should we go down for dinner?"

"I talked to Mr. Stewart today." She allows the space between them breathe before she finishes, "Did you speak to him about the gala?"

Alexander pushes a hair from her face. "I did. I thought you had too much on your plate."

"And the incubator?"

Alexander hesitates, "I feel…" he pauses, chooses his words carefully. "Honey, animals carry diseases. I know your heart is in the right place. The topic just came up and, in the end, it is his decision to make."

The sincerity in his face, the tone of his voice draws her in. Attorneys, she thinks, factual, powerful, convincing.

"I care about you."

Manipulating.

The silence grows between them until it alone seems to loosen his arms and stands him up.

"Dinner?" he strikes back at it.

Valerie sways her head from side to side slowly, her eyes on the beige carpeting. She hates it. All the beige: the walls, the curtains, the carpet. Beige doesn't say anything. It's mute and meaningless. "I'm not hungry," she says to the beige. "I'm going to take a bath."

The gap widens between them, the beige growing larger. Fear appears and rises.

"Alexander," she calls to him as he steps out of the room. "The cooking class is a good idea. I should do my share around here." She expects a smile, a raise of approval on his lip, or even the gentle arch of an eyebrow, but he's blank, beige, and offers no response.

10

Jack slipped right into that split of emptiness. Lucy busy with planning, Valerie felt alone. Even in those quiet moments when she questions the appropriateness, concerns about her contract, she argues with herself that the need for friendship was valid and, sometimes, overwhelming. Watching Tommy play so energetically, listening to him share his stories, funny jokes, and feeling the love between him and his uncle became the highlight of her week.

On Thursday, Jack appears in the doorway with Tommy beside him. "Free?"

Valerie's smile is instant and genuine. "How about the duck pond?"

"Great idea. I gotta get the little man something to eat, meet you there?"

Valerie smiles and watches them go before turning back to her desk to retrieve her purse.

"Hi, you." Lucy strides in, her familiar quick gait gliding across the classroom.

"Lucy! How are you?"

"Mrs. Wankle isn't too bad to work with. She's excited,

suggested a fifties' sock hop."

"That sounds fun."

Lucy nods, moves closer to Valerie, and lowers her voice. "Hey, I gotta tell you to be careful of that Dad you're seeing."

"Dad?"

"Yeah. People talk."

"He's not a dad, and we're just friends. I mentioned it to Mr. Stewart." A quick email because of Alexander's contract concern and the response offered a diplomatic, "all of our families at West Oaks should be treated as friends." Of course, she could surmise that "this would not hold up in court" if she bothered to bring it up again with Alexander.

Lucy meets her concerned gaze with surprise. "You did? Okay, good. Sometimes people around here, you know? You might want to tone it down. Don't want anyone to get the wrong idea." Lucy hugs her hard. "Lunch next week, okay? I want to catch up."

Valerie checks and rechecks, keys, purse, phone, and wanders toward the door, turning back to see if she forgot anything. The idea that people might be gossiping concerns her. She doesn't want to sneak around, make it seem and feel like something it's not. She has no desire to be underhanded or dishonest. "We're just friends," she whispers to the empty room. And then, "I deserve friends," as she starts her car.

The duck pond is a manmade installation for families and exercise enthusiasts, and part of the original community plan. Tracks for running surround it, while jungle gyms and covered picnic centers stand at one end. The pond itself was originally stocked with ducks and koi, other wildlife followed. Butterflies and dragonflies flit at the water's edge and families make themselves comfortable at benches or on the grass. Jack leans against the car while Tommy plays on the nearby jungle gym. As Valerie greets them, he offers her a cup of coffee and a paper wrapped Mrs. Field's chocolate chip cookie.

"You are going to make me fat." She smiles a thank you as she sips the coffee.

"What? These are 100% calorie free, all-natural eggs and butter. It's almost like having breakfast," he chuckles.

"Come on!" Tommy hops off the gym and grabs their hands, pulling them to a spot he likes near the pond. Jack unfolds a blanket as Tommy races around, tossing crumbs from his pocket to the ducks.

The tattoos on Jack's arms are full of color and movement, lines and graphs and meanings unknown to Valerie. They are a mystery and a maze. Jack sees her studying his tattoos and turns the inside of his arm toward her.

"This is a cross, a heartbeat, and a heart, means faith, hope, love. I got this one," he pulls up the sleeve on his other arm, which traces two heart beats separated by a semi colon, "after I got clean." He pauses a moment and watches her reaction. "I'm in recovery, have been for three and a half years." He waits again, gives her time for questions, concerns, as he watches her face to see if the statement has made her uncomfortable. There's a sugar skull on one forearm, a compass with a bow and arrow through it on the other.

"Do you have more?"

"Yes, Ma'am, I do. I have my mother's birth and death dates on my chest here," he pats his hand over his heart.

"I'm sorry. I hadn't realized."

"It's okay now. She died of cancer after Toms was born. At least she got to see her new baby grandson." Jack forces a smile. "But you lost your mom too, huh?"

"Yeah, I was in college. Type II Diabetes led to heart failure."

"Oh, man. And I'm feeding you all these sweets. Bad on me."

"It's okay. I hardly ever eat them."

"How about your Dad?"

"He passed when I was around twelve." Valerie watches Tommy play happily in the grass.

"Oh, man. You lost both your parents?" Jack leans in with his arm out, "Okay to hug you?"

Valerie smiles, "yeah." He gives her a big squeeze as Tommy

runs over to them. "Can I hug too?"

"That's right, Little Man, always ask."

Tommy throws himself into them and squeezes tight before he climbs off and runs to chase a nearby bird.

"Why do you tell him to always ask? It's a good thing, but I can't say I've heard it often."

"A lot of women in the program…" he pauses, considers his wording as he gazes at her. "Let's just say that not a lot of people ask."

Valerie nods in understanding.

A comfortable silence lays down between them, the sweet kind that draws in the space between two people, bringing them closer together, and they unconsciously lean into it.

"Ms. V! Ms. V!" Tommy runs toward them. "I found one. I found one. Look, it's blue. Ms V!" Tommy skids to a stop on his knees right in front of them. "Blue!"

"Thank you. It's very pretty."

Jack leans in. "Ah, nice."

"We keep feathers in a jar in the classroom." Her mind turns to Alexander and quickly away. "Blue, I think, means peace."

They get up, brush off the grass, and Jack folds up the blanket. "Forgot to ask, how'd it go with Mr. Stewart? Did you give 'em" he glances at Tommy, "a what for?"

"Yes, he said he thought I was too busy."

"What? Why did he give it to you in the first place then?"

"Alexander spoke with him." She drops her gaze. "I'm embarrassed. He says he has my best interest at heart, but…" She wonders if she should talk about it. But friends tell each other things, even uncomplimentary things, don't they?

"Relationships are about inspiring each other to soar, not clipping each other's wings. Did you talk to the hubby?"

"I did."

"How could…" Jack pauses and glances over at Valerie who won't make eye contact. "My bad, this is your business. I'm sorry."

"It's okay. I'm a little upset with him. These cooking classes. I am not that bad of a cook. He just wants something fancier, but instead of letting me experiment or take fun classes during the summer, I'm standing there alone feeling like a reject from charm school."

"Woo hoo! You go girl!"

Valerie chuckles. "I'm sorry. I didn't mean to dump this on you."

"No apologies, it sounds like that needed to come out. What are friends for?"

Valerie nods, feeling a weight lift from her. It's different than talking to Lucy. Lucy commiserates; they end up talking about their husbands, and then laughing together. But Jack makes her feel better in a different way, as if she has a right to be upset. And that maybe Alexander is a little bit of what she thinks sometimes - out of line, a little controlling.

As they reach the parking lot, Jack asks Valerie to wait. He straps Tommy into his car seat. Tommy waves, "Bye Ms. V."

"Bye Tommy. You have a nice rest of your day."

"Okay."

Jack hands her a rolled parchment paper tied with a pink ribbon. "A gift. Hope it cheers you."

Valerie releases the ribbon, unrolls the paper. It's a detailed sketch of a girl with long flowing hair surrounded by flowers.

"You drew this?" Valerie's mouth gapes open, which makes Jack smile.

"It's you as the spring solstice. I know we have another week or so, but you've brought an early spring to my life." Jack swallows hard, wondering if he's said too much.

Valerie reflexively launches into a hug, then backs off just as quickly, "I'm sorry, may I?"

Jack chuckles as he holds out his arms. "Anytime. An-nee-time." And pulls her in.

"It's beautiful, absolutely beautiful, thank you."

*

Valerie dances around the kitchen feeling lighter and happier.

She decided to try to repeat the soup from cooking class. Although she didn't remember how much of which spices, she believed she could do it.

On some of those long nights in college with dorm mates, she whipped up pizza from whatever scraps they could find between them. They'd all raved about the spinach, beet, parmesan midnight miracle on bagels. Her spaghetti surprise with chilis and enchilada sauce won her extra privileges from the RA, but then again they were twenty, some of them were high, and some were just plain too hungry or too tired to actually taste what they were woofing down. She giggles at the memory, cutting basil, oregano, and then what else had she'd picked up? A lemon scented something or other. She tosses them all in at the same time.

When Alexander walks in, the table is set, the bread in the warming basket, and the wine breathing; he seems to approve. "Soup?"

"This is what we made in class. I thought I'd give it a try."

As they take their seats across from one another at the dining room table, he smiles noting her happiness. "You're in a good mood."

"I was feeling inspired." Her heart warms for the sketch tucked safely in her purse.

He raises the spoon to his mouth, smells lemon. "Mmmm."

"We went to the park after class, it was so warm and beau…"

Alexander gags, dropping his spoon in his bowl, broth spewing out onto the white tablecloth. "Did you taste this?"

She opens her mouth to answer.

"What did you put in this?" Alexander laughs out loud. "It tastes like…" he sniffs, "Lemon Pledge?"

She raises the spoon to her mouth. Okay, so it did not taste exactly like the soup they made in the class.

"I'm sorry, honey." He shakes his head and grabs for a piece of bread, smothering butter on it and taking a big bite to replace the taste in his mouth. "But you tried."

Valerie bites her lip. Too much lemon balm? She tries again, sipping the broth from the spoon. The lemon flavor is a bit much.

Alexander takes the bowls. "It's okay honey, you don't have to eat this. I'll whip up a salad or something."

The sun disappears behind the neighbor's house; pointed shadows creep across the floor. She pulls her feet closer to her chair, as if the shadows will pierce her as they disappear under the table. She wants to believe the man she married means well and accepts her for who she is, but as she picks up the glass of wine she thinks about how much has changed since college. She was happy, bubbly, willing to try new things.

When Alexander asked her to wear slacks instead of jeans, work dresses instead of flowing summer dresses, to wear her hair up, back, or down, she was willing to try those things not only to please him but to see how they felt. Somewhere along the line it changed. He commanded; she gave. She prefers the comfort of flowing skirts; he feels they're inappropriate. She hasn't worn jeans for a year because of how he'd raised that eyebrow, questioned her taste. She's become afraid to do nearly anything without getting his input, worried she'd be wrong, concerned he'd not approve.

Valerie pours herself some more wine and climbs the stairs to the second floor where she shuts herself in the bathroom. She pours an overwhelming amount of lavender moon bath gel and slips in as the white scented bubbles form around her.

"I'm still here," Valerie says aloud, afraid she's slipping away. She closes her eyes and pictures the Valerie she wants to be. The image is hazy, lines missing, fuzzy around the edges.

Marriages require compromise, Alexander has said. But they also require growth, she wants to respond now. She was a girl; she needed to grow up. But she also needs to maintain some sense of herself.

She's merely a head and a hand with a glass of wine when Alexander appears. She opens her eyes in response to the opening of the door. She will say something to him, she thinks. She will tell him how badly he made her feel. She opens her mouth to speak, but Alexander allows the drawing to unfurl from his fingertips.

"What's this?"

"Don't get it wet," she waits for him to pull it away from the bubbles.

He examines it like an appraiser. For the first time, she has the desire to roll her eyes at him. "I started to tell you before my soup nearly poisoned you. A student's…"

"It wasn't that bad," he interjects with annoyance in his tone.

"I didn't say it was."

He stands up, dropping the sketch carelessly on the sink. "A student didn't draw that."

Valerie huffs out a breath which causes him to glare at her. "If you'd stop interrupting me, I'd tell you who drew it."

"I'll leave some salad for you. Don't forget, dinner with colleagues tomorrow."

Valerie cranes her neck to see the sketch. The beautiful art is still in pristine condition, no fingerprints, no watermarks, no creases from Alexander's careless hands. The parchment had been delicately tucked into a pocket in her purse. She wonders how often Alexander goes through her things.

11

"It's a four hour flight from NoLa to California, add the traffic from the airport, Claire and I walk into the house about 8 or 9pm. My father's pacing. My mother's sitting, feigning reading. She jumps up first, before my father can set in on me.

'Jackie!' She rings her small arms around my neck. 'I'm so glad you're home.' She kisses my cheek; I kiss hers, hug her hard.

'Momma, you're looking good. You don't age!'

'Oh, Jackie, stop it.' She pulls Claire in for a group hug. 'My babies are home.' She takes our hands and leads us into the living room. 'I have mint tea and fresh lemonade, what will it be? There's some leftover chicken. Anyone?'

We refuse. My father wants to start, I can tell. He's stopped pacing and stands in front of the fireplace, hands on his belt, like the cop that he is. Absent is the gun, the radio, but hands as if they were there. But who will he start on first? I'm betting it's me. My mom sits back down in her chair.

'I don't even know where to start,' he announces. 'This family is going to hell.'

'Oh, stop it.' My mom waves her hand at him. 'We are not

going to hell.'

'This one,' he waves his hand at me, 'then his sister follows in his footsteps. I blame you for this,' he points to me.

Claire sits on the arm of the living room sofa. 'Oh, Dad stop. Jack is not the reason I'm getting married.'

'Then why, explain. Explain to me why this can't wait until you graduate college?'

They say the cop is the last to know when his own family goes awry. He has no clue that Claire is pregnant. I look at my mom. I don't know if Claire told her or not, but she knows. She sits there, her eyes down. I step over to Claire, put my hand on her shoulder.

'Dad, don't freak out. Okay?' she starts.

'Oh, geesus, what the hell is it now?' He raises his voice, raises his hands, starts pacing.

We're all silent for a moment; it's got to be Claire. I look down at her as she gathers the courage. 'Dad, you're going to be a grandpa. Wouldn't you rather your grandchild have a father?'

He stops mid-step, glares at her. He's clenching his jaw, the muscles flexing so hard his whole head seems to shimmy slightly. Claire's eyes are clouding up. My mom's still sitting, eyes closed, she's taking deep breaths. Then, suddenly, she jumps up. 'A baby!' She curls around me and hugs Claire. 'A baby is always a blessing. Maybe you'll have twins.' I know my mom doesn't say that to drive my father insane, but my father rolls his eyes, throws his head back, and chokes out a cough or a snort.

I think he wants to go after Danny. Mom won't let him leave the house if he tries, but that's what he looks like he wants to do. Drive over to wherever Danny is, and if Danny's smart, he's hiding tonight, and wrap those thick hands around his neck. He drops his hand to his side, watches my petite mother fawn over my dainty sister. He gives up that ghost and turns his attention to me.

'And you. What the hell are you going to do?'

I step back and wave my hands. 'I'm here for Claire's wedding, then I'll leave if you want.'

'I don't want you to leave. I want you to take that money I

gave you and pay the damn tuition. What'd you do with that money? Where the hell have you been for the last six months?'

'I have your money.' I pick up the backpack. I don't know how much is there and I hope to god it's not covered in coke. I dig in the bottom, bring out the stacks of cash.'

'That doesn't look like ten thousand dollars,' he argues.

'It's enough. I'll get the rest.'

'Stop it,' my mother yells. 'You can't argue like that in front of a pregnant woman.'

There's a silence as we all sit there and look at each other.

'It's late. Why don't we all go to bed, and we'll have a fresh start in the morning.' My mom says, hoping it'll dissipate by morning, but my dad takes this statement as serious. He'll start again, calmer, at the breakfast table, but he'll work his way up.

I stash the cash back into the bag and head off to my room. My mother walks Claire to hers, and we all leave my dad standing there.

I'm lying in my bed, too stressed to work myself into a full jonesing. I don't want to leave the house, don't want to call anyone, but I lie there unable to sleep, hands behind my head staring at the ceiling, wondering how I'm going to hang here.

Claire taps on my door. After all these years, I know the difference in the taps. She slits the door, slips in.

'You okay?'

I shrug. 'Not as bad as I thought it was going to be.'

'So, what do you think will happen in the morning?'

I smile at Claire. She's so cute with her little freckles. 'Tell me about Danny,' I say.

'You met him.'

'Once or twice. You love him?'

'Yeah,' she says defensively. 'I wouldn't get married if I didn't.' She rests on the chair across from where I'm lying. 'You think I'm doing the right thing?' Her little voice is nervous.

'Claire,' I turn on my side to look at her. 'Girl, you've always made better decisions than me. Why are you asking me?'

She throws my t-shirt at me. 'What are you going to do?'

'I don't know. Guess I'll go back to school. Give that cash to the school, see if they'll let me pay them for the rest.'

"No. I mean about how you're going to get through.'

I nod, know what she's talking about. 'I'll do it, Sis. I'm going to be there for your wedding, won't let you down.'

'You have a plan?'

Now I laugh out loud, too loud. We both look at the door, hoping we didn't send up any smoke signals to let my father know we're awake.

'Yeah, I plan to sneak out and check out that leftover chicken. How about you?'

'Let's do it.'

Before the family gets up in the morning, I'm out. I make my way down to the methadone clinic and sign up. I ask them for the lowest dosage, but they insist on the highest, promising to wean me down as soon as they can. This is how these clinics work. They make their money from the government; methadone is an opiate replacement; a therapy for addicts. I've known people who were on it for two years. The clinic only gets paid if they have patients. The longer they have those patients, the longer they stay in business. It's not about cleaning up the addict. It's a business.

As long as I'm on it, I won't use. But it's still a drug. Some addicts sell it to dealers who will swap it out for crystal meth or pot or god knows what they got in their bag of tricks. Some of that dealing happens right out in the parking lot. This will help me get through to the wedding on Saturday and then Monday I'll see if I can find a real rehab, a real detox. At least, with this, I can operate through life. I'll still be sick, especially for the first few days until my body gets used to the change, then my body will start craving that. It won't want to let go of that either.

I'm walking up to my house. It's still quite early. Mom might be up making breakfast, Dad's probably outside for his morning swim. I wanted to be here in time for breakfast, get back before they knew I was gone.

Then, parked a few houses down, a blue town-car. The guys get out of the car, make like they're going up to the house when they see me, wave, come over before I get up to my house.

'Jack, my man, is that you?' Carl's the local drug dealer. An addict's best friend. 'I heard you were back.' His friends hang back. They're dealers, muscle, protection. Whatever or whoever they need to be.

I give them a nod of my head.

'Dude, you ain't got a minute for your friends?'

'Yeah, I'm late. But hey, how you doin'?' I pound his hand.

'I'm good, man. Hey, what do you say, want to come on over later, a little party?'

'Can't. Dad's on me.'

'You're fuckin' twenty-one. He doesn't have you anymore, right?' He elbows his friend.

'Yeah, well, you know how that goes. I'll call ya,' I say as I walk away.

He's eyeing me, watching me walk away, smile gone, serious. 'I'll be waiting, Jack.'

At this moment, I have no intention of calling him. But he knows if I start hurting, he'll be first on my list. My fingers will start dialing before my head starts thinking.

Mom's in the kitchen cooking when I walk in. 'Jack, honey?'

'Yeah,' I pop my head around the corner, walk around the little island and give her a good morning hug. I know she got up, poked her head in and didn't see me, probably got worried I wasn't coming back.

'Honey, got some eggs and bacon. Gotta fatten you up a bit. All that heavy food in New Orleans and I bet you were eating like a bird.'

I don't say anything. She knows I wasn't eating anything except whatever drug came in pill form. I am thin, damn thin, pale. Skin looks like shit. Addicts never know how bad they really look to others. It's all the lies those drugs tell us, after we start avoiding mirrors.

'Where's Claire, Momma?' I kiss my mom's head, which she leans in to.

'Your dad's out on the patio. Sissy's in the bathroom sick.'

I'm on to my mom after all these years; this means go talk to your dad and leave your sister alone, but I do the opposite and head down the hall, knock lightly on the door.

I hear Claire retching from the hall. 'I'm busy,' she says.

I click the door slightly open, 'you decent?'

'About as decent as you on one of your binges.'

'Oh, yeah, those hormones are kickin in big time!'

She's sitting on the floor, trying to hold her short hair back at the same time she's puking in the toilet. As she starts to retch again, I sit on the floor behind her and hold her hair for her.

When she finishes, she says, 'I'm sorry.'

'What's wrong?' I ask.

'Morning sickness.'

I nod as if I understand.

'You don't have to be in here.' She doesn't look at me. I don't look at her face. I rub her back, between her shoulders. This is what she's always done for me.

'And miss this? No way!'

She chuckles.

'Besides how many times have you done this for me.'

'True.'

Claire seems so young, so delicate. I know we're the same age, but somehow she seems much more innocent than me, so much younger. I feel like had I been here, she would have been safe, wouldn't have gotten into trouble. Maybe it's stupid, but sometimes addicts take the world on their shoulders. We're so certain that we control little parts of the world, just like we're certain we can control our own need for that drug.

Claire starts breathing a little more normally. She sits up straight as if she's testing her own body, seeing if she can trust it to move away from the toilet. She reaches up and hits the handle to flush away her morning crackers and tea.

'You okay?'

'I think I'm good for now.' She starts to push up.

I get up from behind her, let her have time to freshen up as I wait in the hall.

'Jack.' I hear my mom calling me. I walk out to where she can see me. 'Honey, leave your sister alone, get on out there and make peace with your dad.'

Is that what she calls it? Strange term for the storm that'll be pouring out on the patio at any moment. But I listen to her. I cross the living room and push open the door. Before I'm even through, my father's motioning for me to shut it. As if the women aren't going to be able to hear through the glass.

Dad's been working in the yard; I see his bucket of weeds next to the patio. The pool skimmer on the side of the pool. Now he's just standing there as if he's thinking of what he could do next. I come out and sit down. I'm expecting him to unleash. Where the hell have you been? What have you been doing? Or else, he'll start slow and it'll build.

He has his hand in his pocket as he turns to me. He's straight to the point. It is one of my dad's best qualities. 'What's the plan, Jack?'

'I went to the Methadone clinic today.'

'You know that shit is prolonging the problem.'

I hang my head. How many times have we had this conversation? 'But it makes getting straight bearable. I gotta get straight for Claire's wedding.'

He looks through the glass door at Claire and my mom. I see that snarl in his lip. He is not happy about that impending wedding.

'You're not straight on that shit. It's still opiates....'

'Dad, Dad, I know, I know. But I can't do anything about it until I get to rehab.' I feel like I mean what I say, but in truth I only half mean it. My brain wants to mean it, but my body, the cells that need those drugs trick me all the time. Some parts of me know this. But they are not the parts that win very often.

'Claire wants me here for her wedding. If I go cold turkey, I'll get sick. You know that. I'll go to rehab after.' That's the hard part right there. My body starts rebelling the minute it hears rehab. Out here, I can do what I want, go back to Carl or any of those fucks that sell the shit, and get what I seem to really want. In there, no. I'm locked down, locked in, and no drugs whatsoever no matter how much pain my body is in. And let me tell you it is pain. That drug is like a freaking worm in your veins; there's little tentacles in every cell, and getting clean is like pulling it out a little tiny shitty piece at a time. So, why go back and do drugs again? Because, it seems, it's never completely out and your cells, somewhere, hiding deep inside of you, want, want, want more. It tells you, you can just do a little, you can control it now. A person who has never been addicted has no idea the lies the drugs tell.

His lip curls up again as he looks through the glass. Claire slides open the door; her color is better now. 'Mom wants to know if you want to eat out here or in the house.'

'Out here is a good idea; it's a beautiful day, going to be hot later.'

Claire goes back in as my phone rings. I look at it. It's one of Carl's soldiers already. I turn it off. By the time I look up, my father's reading me. He blows out a deep breath. He has no idea the fight I'm dealing with, brain, body, guilt, 'friends.'

'Not in front of the women.' He says as if our conversation is a big secret that my mother and sister don't know about.

They bring out our plates already made, then go back for the juice and glasses. Dad and I sit, waiting until they are seated before we eat.

'We should talk about the wedding.' My mother, bless her big damn heart, brings up the topic.

After breakfast, Claire and I do the dishes. I hand her my phone, 'keep it for me.' She knows I mean keep it from me. I'll also not leave the house without one of them with me. This helps. The guys won't approach me, and they certainly won't come here. I gotta get through this week; it's going to be a hard-damn week. I spend most of it in my room, sometimes I go to the bathroom to throw up. I hate methadone. It's a shit high that's supposed to help you get clean, it's like giving a dying man life-support; it's just delaying the inevitable. The addict will eventually go back to using or end up in rehab. I'm hoping that I can talk myself into the rehab or have one of them force me right after the wedding. Not sure how long I'll last on this shit.

Each day that passes, I spend more time in my room. No one likes this, but I get snappy the more my body is away from the real drugs it wants. I try to spend the early part of the day with them, running errands or doing whatever needs to be done.

The wedding will be a small family and close friends' event in our yard. Mom makes the calls to get that done: the tables, chairs, umbrellas. It's supposed to be damn hot. The food will be easy, catered with two people serving. Claire picked out a white dress, my mom goes with her; but Friday, her final fitting, she wants a man's opinion and asks me to go.

On Saturday morning, I'm up at five to get the methadone so I can be back and help set up, be there for the wedding that will begin in the early afternoon. I come out of the clinic and one of Carl's guys is there. He buys the methadone or trades it – it's a way to get the addicts hooked again. He'll give them twenty bucks for it. The guy will think he can go without it one day, but he'll be calling for something or stealing someone else's before the day ends. Sometimes the addicts will take that money and get some crystal meth, but one dose isn't enough, so the same story: they'll beg, borrow, or steal by lunch time.

'Jack,' he sees me before I get in the car. 'Dude, what's happening?' He comes over and pounds my fist. 'I heard you were back.'

'Just got back a few days ago.' If I act friendly, it'll be easier to get out of here, I think.

'Carl said he owes you some.' He hands me an envelope of coke.

'Nah, he's mistaken. He doesn't owe me anything.' I try to refuse it.

'He does, take it. It's a gift.'

'Really, dude,' I say, 'I'm trying to stay clean.'

He nods, 'totally respect that, guy. Totally gotcha. Just put it in your back pocket and forget about it.' He puts it in my hand. No addict, no matter how clean, is going to throw that away. They're going to lie to themselves, put it in their back pocket and pretend they're going to forget about it. How many times have I done that? I tell myself I'll throw it away once I get out of the parking lot. I don't. I tell myself I'll toss it in the trash outside. I don't. I tell myself I'll bin it in the house, but when I walk in Mom and Dad are awake and in the living room; I'm afraid they'll see it. I go to my room. I tell myself to flush it down the toilet. And I stare at that little baggy as if it's a war. It is a war. It is a fn war. I feel like I'm alone in the world with this damn fight. I cannot force myself, no matter how hard I try, to walk across that hall and dump that shit down the toilet.

I hear something from Claire's room, push it deep inside my front pocket. She's awake, moving around, but I hear something else too. I hear sniffling or coughing. I think she's getting sick, so I go out into the hall and tap on her door. I open it a little before I hear her say come in. I walk in and she's sitting on her bed, wedding dress held against her. She's sniffling, softly crying. I rush over to her, 'What is it? What is it?' My head goes to bad places, she's sick, injured, Danny's not coming.

She shakes her head.

'What's happening? You okay?'

She nods. 'I just... don't... know....' Her voice comes out in spurts between soft coughs and chokes as she tries to hold back tears.

'What, honey?' I sit on the bed next to her, put my hand on her shoulder. 'What don't you know?'

'If this... is ... right? Am...I.. doing the .... right.. thing?'

It's hard not to chuckle. My sister is such a little girl. I know it's not right to say. My sister is a woman, and I know that, but when I look at her, sometimes I see that sweet high school sister who sometimes had the world by the balls and didn't know that she did.

'Well, let me ask you this. Pretend you're not pregnant. Pretend that you've been dating Danny for a year or two and that he asked you because he wanted to because I'm pretty sure he did, regardless of that little bun in the oven there. So would you want to marry him?'

She thinks about it, I see her eyes darting around as if she's trying to imagine that situation. 'Well, if we'd been dating a few years, and I'd finished college, then yes. I see us together.'

'So you took a short cut,' I say. 'You're taking a different path toward the same end.'

She thinks about that. 'You know, you're a little smarter than you look.'

I laugh, 'let's hope that's true.' I hug her.

She smiles, softly punches my arm.

I take her dress from her and hang it up on the back of the door. 'Why don't you go back to sleep. Mom's got this all handled, you get some beauty rest for your big day.'

She shakes her head. 'No, I can't sleep.'

'Okay,' I say, 'then just rest.' I urge her down on her pillow and pull the blanket over her.

'I won't be able to sleep.'

'You don't have to.' I turn to leave her room. She's already closing her eyes by the time I get to the door.

I want this day to be good for Claire. I want it to be everything she wants it to be. I walk out into the living room. My parents are watching workers set up the tables, umbrellas.

'It's going to be a damn one hundred degrees today,' my father announces.

'It'll all be fine.' Mom pats his arm.

'You know she'll drop out of college, she'll never finish,' my dad throws up his hand.

'Hey, hey.' I walk in. 'Claire's got enough to worry about today. Don't make her any more nervous than she already is.'

My dad nods, inspects me. He's trying to see if I've used anything more than the methadone. My mom has managed to feed about eight pounds on to my thin frame in the last week. My skin isn't as pale or broken out, but his cop friends will be able to tell I'm rehab bound again.

'Why don't you go get cleaned up,' he says to me.

I go back to my bedroom, strip off my clothes and spread out. No one will be arriving for hours; I have time to sleep too before I have to do anything.

*

At the wedding, Danny's nervous as hell. Danny's not as tall as me, but a healthy-looking guy. He's studying automotive technology and business at college. He's already got a little side business going for himself. Although he owned up, faced up to my dad pretty quickly when they were dating and after Claire broke the news to him; my dad is not a warm and fuzzy person, and I think Danny's still nervous that my dad might hurt him. And here he is at the wedding with my father's cop friends. I don't think he's sure he's actually going to make it all the way down the aisle and out the door to their weekend honeymoon in Monterey.

There's seventy or eighty people in and out of the house, on the patio, hanging out in the back, in the living room. Claire's college friends, Danny's friends, his parents, their friends, my parents' friends. I don't have any friends these days. I suppose I could have called some of my art school friends, but I feel alienated from them, never really bonded with them anyway. There was even a girl I was hoping to meet before I left. I tell you, when drugs get you, everything else is out the window.

Claire's two closest girlfriends come out first. Danny is knees-knocking at the back of the yard in front of the minister and his two friends who are standing up for him. My mom sneaks in on the other side, takes her seat; she was helping Claire get ready. When Claire comes down the aisle, she must be the most beautiful thing I've ever seen. She's holding her shoulders back and her head high. She's holding that bouquet in front of that tiny little baby bump that no one but her notices. Her short hair is pinned back, the dress is white and silky, and she has a little veil that seems to float on top of her head. Her cheeks are pink. She looks like an angel. I look over at my mom whose eyes are filling up. Claire looks so much like my mom, such beautiful women inside and out. I sit there and think how fn lucky I am to have these two beautiful people in my life. I glance at my dad who walks Claire down the aisle. It's not often I see that man hold back an emotion that isn't anger, but I see it there now, raw and close to the surface. They must both feel like they're losing their daughter, their child, their only good child. I drop my gaze to the grass. I suppose they put all their hopes into Claire after I turned out to be the epic disappointment of their lives and this is why her not finishing school, why her getting pregnant is so hard for them to accept.

I bite my lip, feeling my own loss. I watch Claire, my only cheerleader, marry a man who's going to take her away. Now, I really feel like I have nothing, no one, lost. This is a certain end for me too. Claire's always been there for me, been the buffer between my parents and me, more specifically my dad. She helped me hide things in the beginning, was my cheerleader when I tried and tried and tried to get clean. She'd reword dad's angry statements, so they sounded loving. She'd reword my worthless statements to him, so they sounded valuable. And now she won't be there anymore. I start tearing up myself. I don't even hear what they say to one another. Claire's voice is low and whispery, and I'm trapped in my own self-serving thoughts. I want to bolt. I want to run out of that wedding, but know I have to stay. I grab onto my chair and hold myself down from running away. I grit my teeth and bite my jaw. I can't hear what's been said or where they are in the ceremony. They exchange rings and I'm praying, holding my breath. Oh god, just let it be over, let it be over before I throw up from my own sick nerves.

And then it is over. After they and their wedding party retreat down the aisle, I half jog behind them. I get to the restroom and throw up. I rinse my mouth out, brush my teeth and straighten my hair. I'm in a suit, and I feel too hot, too uncomfortable. I take the tie off and undo the first few buttons, hope to hell my dad doesn't give me a hard time about this. I come out and there's a line waiting. First in line is a young woman I know only as one of my dad's cop friends' daughters. I hold the door open for her and smile. She's got long dark hair and her dress is too low cut for this wedding, but it's looking good on her. She smiles at me.

I walk back out into the main room, fans are blowing, and the doors are open, people meander in and out, get food, drinks. It'll go on like this for a few hours. A few hours, I tell myself, I can handle a few hours.

I do what I can to appear social and, at the same time, try not to engage in conversation. I stay as far away as possible from my dad's cop friends; they all know my history. Although some of them catch me anyway, 'hey, how you doing, Jack?' I smile, nod, move away.

I stick close to Claire and Danny; he and I end up in the same corner occasionally, both of us trying to avoid awkward social conversations. I met him once or twice before. The little bit I talk to him tonight just adds to the idea that he's a good man. No drugs, very little drink. He says he's too nervous around my family to drink tonight. He's got a plan to open his own business. They're both going to try to stay in school. They've got a plan for help with the baby. It all sounds good.

He taps my shoulder, 'hey, look, watch.' Claire's talking to someone she doesn't like very much. I can tell because she curls her nose just a bit and the smile is forced. 'See the way she curls her nose? She does that when she has broccoli on her plate too,' he chuckles. I can tell he loves Claire. Really loves her. He would have asked for her hand sooner or later, baby or no baby. Of that, I'm certain. They are lucky, I think. However the hell it happened, they're lucky they found each other and ended up together. I wonder, as I look down at the carpet, try to avoid eyes, if I'm ever going to find that. Am I ever, I wonder, going to clean my shit up and find someone who I love more than life itself?

He walks off to save her from that conversation.

I'm watching him and Claire head for the makeshift dance floor on our concrete patio. He holds her close and they whisper like new lovers.

'Hi,' a voice says from the side. I half turn toward the voice when I see it's the beautiful girl from the hallway.

'Oh, wow, hello.' I stupidly stumble over myself.

'You're not drinking,' she says.

'Nah, Dad doesn't like it.'

'Even though you're 21? You are 21, right?'

I nod, 'Cop father, you know how they are.' I laugh it off.

She nods, her eyes dart to whom I suspect is her father. 'Oh, yeah, I know how they are. Hey, you got a quiet place we can go?'

I wonder if she means what I think she does. Then she answers what I haven't asked.

'You got a den, a pool room, someplace where it's quieter and there's less people?' We have the den, but it's mostly my father's and he doesn't like us in it. So I suggest the garage where there's a foosball table tucked into the corner and a radio. She follows. My father keeps the garage near spotless. There are a few boxes stacked in a corner, and his car takes up one spot, but there's plenty of room. I pull out the foosball table.

'Seriously?' she says.

I chuckle, 'We better look like we're doing something out here.'

'Ah, I like a man with a plan.'

That's not really a plan; it's a cover. And that's pretty much all I'm capable of, one minute at a time, and at the will of any other stupid person who wants to suggest something. I dip my head. She pushes my chin up.

'Why you always lookin' down?'

'Keeps me outta trouble, I guess.'

'Got some chairs?' She's looking at the plastic lawn chairs my father didn't bring out for the wedding. I take them down, unfold them.

We sit down. I let her lead. I'm not great with people, especially one on one, and I'm not as brave with pretty women as I pretend.

'So, you got anything?'

I look at her, start to say, like what? but there's a look in her eye that tells me, she's heard about me, knows my history, and she's hoping I got something good to give her.

'Ah, no.' I feel the need to fill in, so I add, 'Yeah, I'm kinda tryin' you know to stay clean.'

I see in her face she loses all interest in me. 'You must have something left over, hiding, you got some oxy's or anything? Your parents got anything?'

My mind flip flops to that small white dose one of Carl's guys forced on me. She can see on my face I've just latched on to something and starts smiling again, wiggling in her seat, and moving closer to me. I think, yes, I can get rid of that coke. I'll give it to her. I won't be tempted. I lie to myself much more than I lie to anyone else. If it were that easy to quit, addicts wouldn't stay addicts, would they? I rush to my room, return, and hand her the baggie.

'Nice. Good shit.' She reaches her finger in, rubs a little on her gums, offers it to me. I shake my head. 'You sure?'

She dips her pinky finger with the longest nail, painted fire engine red, in. 'You first.' She pulls it out, shoving the coke covered undernail near my face. I sit there for what seems like forever and I'm trying to shake my head back and forth; no, I don't want it. But staring at that little bump of powder on her finger, I want it. I want it more than I want her, more than I want anything in the world. But somehow I refuse. I feel like a loser piece of shit though. I feel like less than a man in her eyes. I think, what is she going to tell people? I know this is all stupid shit running through my brain, worthless self-defeating self-talk, but this is how my brain works, and from what I hear, a lot of addicts feel the same.

She snorts it, throws her head back. I watch the release in her face, can almost feel the rush of her endorphins through her head, her body; when she looks at me again, her eyes are already glassy, and her smile is loose. She reaches over with her hand and pulls me close, kisses me hard. 'That's freaking good shit, Jack. Are you sure you don't want some?'

I nod, but I keep kissing her. She pulls away, sticks her finger back in the bag, waves it in front of my face, makes like she's going to do it. She kisses me again, then sticks her finger in my mouth. I want to pull away, but she holds my head in place with the other hand and, in all honesty, I don't fight that hard. Her tongue is in my mouth; her thick wet lips are on mine, and then that sweet, sweet feel of x starts flowing. It wasn't just coke. My body can tell almost right away, it's cut with other shit. But I don't even cuss Carl out in my head. It's like a blip of a thought between what the hell is she doing and oh my god that feels so good.

The door opens and there's a voice. We don't even pull away that quickly after we hear, 'What are you doing?'
When we do, we look calmly over to her father who stands there. She's done something with the bag; I don't know what. I'd like to say I'm afraid we've been busted, but that stuff is strong, and considering I haven't used in a week, the effects on me are instant. She leads me out of the garage by holding my hand. We pass her father and she tells him, 'Calm down.' And I barely see him. He's just a tawny blur as we pass.

I can't tell how much time has passed or what happened. I remember Claire kissing my cheek, Danny shaking my hand and me trying to act normal because I think no one's noticed a thing. I'd been sitting in the same spot on the couch since god knows when. I don't know what girl I was with or where she went.

When everyone is gone, my father grabs my arm. It doesn't hurt, but I'm on my feet. My mom kisses me and I think he's just going to put me in my bed, but I'm in the car and he's making that face, that horrible square, eyebrows thick, eyes slit, disappointed, wants to murder me look, and says, 'You're going to rehab now.'

It's for the best I go now. I'd been on the phone with Carl within the hour looking for the next kick. But I don't think that then. I'm protesting by the time he walks me into the hospital detox wing. He's called ahead and they're waiting for us.

'If you step out of here before thirty days, I will arrest you.'
I relent.

12

Fallbrook is in San Diego County and, as the Avocado Capital of the World, boasts nearly thirty thousand residents. The height of the season's festivities includes the Avocado Festival where nearly everyone wears similarly themed t-shirts. Fancy dinners with family or friends are held at The Oink and Moo. Valerie's high school graduation dinner celebration took place at The Veranda in the best dresses they owned. San Diego is casual. She thought all of California was this casual, flip flops at the supermarket, short shorts in the city.

In college, they all wore t-shirts and jeans. Alexander helped bring her professional game to another level. She loved that he cared enough to be honest, to advocate for her, and encourage her. As a young woman, new to dating a professional attorney, Valerie readily ate up his recommendations. He chose her dresses or advised her to wear long earrings with her hair up, a necklace with her hair down. He proposed colors, styles, and took her shopping when they were to meet his colleagues or his family. The excitement of this new lifestyle intrigued her, and she believes it is his confidence in her which she fell in love with.

She appreciated his input and thought that's what it was: suggestions to help her make good first impressions.

While she'd grown used to his continued prompting, it did occasionally wear on her. When he does this, she reminds herself that he has her best interests at heart. So, when the text messages come nearly every hour, she keeps this in mind.

"Black dress."

"Blahnik pumps."

"6:30pm."

"Mastro's."

"Change of time, 7:30."

"I'll send a car."

Once a month or so, they have dinner with Alexander's colleagues. For tonight, she's familiar with one of the couples, but the other couple, whom Alexander refers to as close friends, she's never met. While his company holds two large parties a year, it's impossible to meet everyone.

She straightens her hair, brushes it back, and spritzes once more with smoothing spray. She applies lip liner and tint and tucks them neatly in her matching Blahnik bag. There were parts of herself she wanted to leave behind. The girlish silliness, the insecurity, but there are parts she values. This is their struggle, she estimates, he's become too used to giving her direction and not listening. She likes her hair loose and free, the natural waves bouncing around her head; she loves seeing her Nan and making jokes. She wants to eat on the patio in the spring and wear cheap sandals to the beach. There is room for all parts of her. She can dress for his dinners and be casual other times. They just need to talk.

As the car arrives at the restaurant, she has convinced herself she's being silly. These are unimportant things, she thinks. No one argues over hair or food. She's being too sensitive.

Mastro's' large dining room is packed. The open seating, without benefit of walls or dividers, allows the level of conversations to become nearly deafening. White tablecloths and suited servers are everywhere.

The hostess takes her name and begins to lead her to a table in the center of the room where she can already see Alexander and one of the other couples laughing over a glass of wine. Alexander smiles and waves, excuses himself and meets her halfway. He leans in. She thinks he's going to kiss her, but he whispers in her ear. "What are you doing? Why is your hair...?" He splays his hand open. He kisses her and glances back at the table, placing his body between them and her. "Do you have a clip or something with you? Slip into the bathroom and put it up." He nudges her toward the ladies' room.

The bathroom is amber lit. Dim. Her reflection surprises her in this light. She doesn't see Valerie at all. There's a spirit of someone she thought she wanted to be. Classy, well dressed, but she misses the girl she used to be. Is this what grown up life is all about? Leaving your old soul behind, thereby creating a new person? She wonders if Alexander was once like Jack. Did he leave his face unshaven, have the enthusiasm of youth, enjoy the beauty of life surrounding him? Somehow, she doubts it.

Tears sting the back of her eyes. A dry lump forms in her throat. There's nothing wrong with her hair or her dress or that soup. But Alexander always finds something.

She pushes her little black purse onto the green marble vanity and searches for a clip. A single bobby pin reveals itself. She puts it between her teeth and begins to twist her hair around her finger, bringing it into a tight tornado that will wrap around itself and hopefully stay fastened.

The door stretches open and Celia nearly passes her. Stops, backs up. "Strays? Don't you hate it." Her short hair is down, dark except for the light streaks framing her face. "I may have a pin or two." She drops her purse on the counter and searches vigorously. She discovers two and smiles as she pulls them out. She sees Valerie's moist eyes in the mirror. "Oh, hon. Don't worry. It's hair, nothing to get upset about."

Valerie nods, accepting the pins. "Thank you."

Celia pats her shoulder and walks on.

At the table, Alexander takes great pride in standing and pulling out her chair. He introduces the new couple Thomas and Thea. Thomas is late fifties, early sixties, an executive at the company. Thea, his wife, is maybe thirty. She says she's from the island of Kauai originally, met Thomas and moved here for him. She giggles coyly, places her hand tenderly on his shoulder and fingers the diamonds around her neck with the other hand. "He stole my heart," she giggles again.

"And she stole my wallet." Thomas roars with laughter. "Just joking, Kitten."

Her smile doesn't waver.

Celia rejoins them, winking at Valerie and tilting her head toward Thea, then pats Barry and points to the wine. He pours her another glass then fills Valerie's.

"What do you do?" Thomas leans in so his voice can be heard over the dinner crowd.

"I'm a teacher."

"Kindergarten," Alexander answers before it's asked.

"What do you do with the rest of your day?" Thea asks, "Isn't Kindergarten like two hours a day?"

"It's four. Right?" Celia chimes in.

Valerie glances from one to the other, "No. It's a little more than six hours most days."

"Private school," Alexander explains.

"Must be nice to only work a few hours. What do you do with the rest of your day?" Celia picks up her glass and waits for an answer.

"There's planning..."

"Coffee with friends and shopping," Alexander interjects with a chuckle.

"You'd get along great here with my little Kitten."

Celia winks again and wings her eyes toward Thea, smiling.

Valerie's had these conversations before, but Alexander's response is new. She doesn't appreciate it but lifts the corners of her mouth as she reaches for the wine. The dinner is mostly uneventful, and she doesn't mind the loudness, even if it means she misses most of the conversation. Taking Thea's lead, she keeps a smile pasted on her face.

As the night crawls to a close, the crowd thins and the restaurant offers a lull in the roar of conversation. Thomas leans into Alexander. "You've made a good choice here in Valerie," he says, then adds in a near whisper, "much better than your first wife." His voice remains low and deep; with the clink of glasses, the chatter of patrons, the music that rises even as the conversation dies, Valerie is not certain she heard correctly.

As they leave, the sky appears midnight blue against the city lights. The warm day has turned into a chilly night. Valerie waits as the valet brings Alexander's car. She reaches for the heat as Alexander pulls into the light traffic and heads for the freeway. "Did he say something about a first wife?"

Alexander chuckles. "Don't pay any attention to Thomas. He had too much to drink."

"So, he didn't say anything about a first wife?"

Alexander doesn't respond; he carefully merges onto the 101 Freeway and joins the thousands of others who have spent Friday night out in downtown Los Angeles.

"Alexander?"

"Valerie, I'm driving here."

Valerie sits back. She glances out the front window, but she's not seeing the traffic. The sky is blue and turning black, to their left is the water, the beach, and remnants of someone else's sunset. In Japan, the sun is rising, and other couples are watching the start of a new day.

"I guess," she says softly, "I thought you could multitask, talk and drive at the same time." She glances out the window to her right; the darkness of the city is dotted by apartment lights, headlights.

"Wow," he says so loudly it echoes in the car. "If that's not passive aggressive then I don't know what is."

The silence that follows reveals the thumping of her heart against her ribcage. She has never felt so angry at him; she's also never felt so mute. She grew up with discussion, not arguments. Issues were dealt with openly, not by hiding secrets. The thought of an argument with Alexander intimidates her. She feels she'd lose before it even started. He needs to be right. It's the lawyer in him, perhaps. He will throw case logs and statistics at her. They've debated, sort of, over the dining table, round versus oval, the couch sectional versus one piece, and the paint. That wretched beige paint that covers nearly every wall. "Statistics show that a neutral color allows more choice in decoration, it cuts down on how many times new paint is needed, it's calming to the eyes, and fades well. In fact," he added, "one study by the Realtors of America found couples who have a neutral color live longer, happier lives."

Preference for warm colors probably has an equal and effective argument, but she was unprepared for the debate. When you're young and in love, you tend to give in to preserve harmony. Regret it later, maybe. She doesn't care about the paint, still. It's the point of his need to make all the decisions, have the last word, and now - evidently - keep valuable information from her.

"Fine," he says. "If you're going to pout like a child, I'll tell you that I was married for a very short time before I met you. She was a damn nightmare. And I do not want a repeat performance of what I went through with her."

Somewhere out there, a couple is climbing into bed. Somewhere out there, a man is pulling his wife close, and he's saying, I love you more than anything, and he means it.

A tear forms in Valerie's eye and she wipes it away before Alexander can see it.

*

Valerie waits at her station in the cooking class, apron wrapped around a t-shirt and jeans. She doesn't care about the cooking class. She is here today only to get out of the house and away from the silence that thickened like a wall between her and Alexander.

"Alone again today?" the teacher smiles.

"Yes, I…" Feeling more awkward than before, she wants to leave.

There's a rustling behind them as the door opens, slams against the frame, and everyone turns about the same time. Jack drops his yoga mat and trips over it, catches himself and then turns, half smiling, to see the whole class staring at him. "My bad, so sorry."

Valerie studies him curiously, a smile gathering unconsciously at the side of her mouth.

"The yoga studio is further down…" the Chef waves her hand, not yet disturbed by the interruption.

"Aw that, no. I always carry a mat with me. Never know when you're gonna need a stretch." He waves his hand at the abandoned mat and stretches his arms out to illustrate his point. He glances around the room, sees Valerie and starts toward her, "There. I'm with her."

The smile has stretched across her face as he takes his place beside her.

The Chef begins to engage the class; Valerie leans to Jack, a giggle in her voice. "What are you doing here?"

"I thought I'd save you from middle school flashbacks."

"Shhhh." The Chef makes eye contact, then turns away to begin handing out the list of ingredients. She waves her hand at the row of duck carcasses on the nearby countertop. "Today, we will make Duck a l'Orange."

Valerie's eyes widen. She pictures the feathered creatures swimming at the duck pond. "We have to…"

Jack glances from her to the duck carcasses stretched out on a nearby table. "Looks like there's Donald and Daisy and that one's gotta be Daffy."

"You and your husband will be much more successful if you actually engage your ears instead of your mouths."

"He's…a…"

"I'm just…"

Valerie and Jack look at each other and giggle.

"I can't do this to a duck," she whispers softly.

"Shall we cut class, teach?"

"How do we get outta here?"

Jack whispers, "just go with whatever I say. Lean into me," he puts his hand on her shoulder and pulls her into him. Jack raises his hand, "Ah, Chef." Everyone turns to look at Jack and Valerie. "The Mrs. isn't feeling so hot."

Valerie blushes. She covers her mouth and nose, coughs.

"I'm gonna take her to the doc's, so sorry to interrupt your class."

"Are you okay?" The young gay couple next to them move in.

"She'll be okay." Jack turns away, leading her quickly to the door.

"Go if you must," the teacher waves them away and turns to the rest of the class. "Go to the counter and select your duck."

They push out of sight from the class windows, then burst into laughter.

"Quack. Quack. Those poor little ducks. You did get a little pale before your cheeks got all red."

Valerie laughs so hard her eyes begin to tear up.

"Ah, look how cute you are, cheeks all rosy."

Valerie waves her hand at him. "Stop, stop." She takes a deep breath and another and starts to recover. "You forgot your mat." She reminds him.

Jack shrugs. "Eh, I'll get it later."

"Jack," a voice calls from the empty street. "Coming to yoga?"

He spins to see a woman rushing in the direction of the yoga studio a few doors down, yoga bag hanging from her shoulder. "Not today," he waves and turns back to Valerie.

"So what are we going to do, V?"

The street is near empty. Blockades at either end prepare the area for the farmer's market. A few vendors have arrived to set up their tables. The vans and pickup trucks full of their produce will take over the parking lot as they unload, and then clear the way for customers. But they have an hour or maybe more before the block is filled with color and scent, before the locals meander the fairway and families arrive with recycled hemp bags to browse through the new and unknown and hurry to their favorites for avocado honey, butter dates, or home grown mushrooms in addition to the seasonal fruits and vegetables.

"I'm a little hungry."

"I know a great place." He takes her hand and leads her to the end of the block. As they turn the corner, the street is busy with traffic and pedestrians. Jack leads her to a small group of people gathering around a food truck.

"Is this the place?"

"Have you ever had fresh, handmade pupusas?"

"Maybe years ago." Definitely not with Alexander who thinks food trucks are a mar on the city.

"You are about to have the greatest meal of your life." He turns to the window and calls, "Dos pupusas con ensalada de repollo."

In a few minutes, the young man hands Jack a bag and they turn to head back to the empty farmer's market. "There's usually some tables…" as they turn the corner, Jack points. "See, already set up."

As they eat, the market fills around them. Jack makes jokes and tells stories and they fall into a natural conversation of food, family, and friends.

"Thank you, Jack," she says sincerely.

"It's just pupusas. This is what they should be teaching in that cooking class."

"For getting me out of that class, for being… you."

"Wow," Jack pushes back in his chair. "I don't think anyone has ever thanked me for being me. That's pretty cool, V. Thank you."

They watch the yoga class pour out into the crowd of market goers, and then the cooking class. Jack and Valerie know it's time to go, but both seem too comfortable, even as they sit back with their bellies full and their conversation paused.

Valerie considers her afternoon. Shopping to avoid the inevitable or home to face the music, or lack thereof. She glances across the table at Jack who is smiling in her direction. "I don't think I've ever seen you in jeans, quite natural and becoming," he says.

The unexpected compliment pinks her cheeks and Jack smiles even wider. "Do you not get complimented a lot or do you blush each and every time?" He suspects the first is true.

"You look very comfortable in your sweats," she returns the compliment to avoid answering the question. "And I'm really glad I didn't have to see you in those yoga shorts."

His face twists and he shakes his head. "Those things are…" he chuckles and continues, "for other people, not for me."

They begin to gather their recyclable plastic trays and bamboo forks, bottles of water, and walk to the receptacles slowly.

"No veggies this week?"

"Not this week." She can't imagine, at this moment, even trying another meal.

"See ya next week?"

Valerie's smile widens and her eyes brighten at the thought as she nods.

"Hug?"

Valerie leans into his open arms, and raises her arms around him, whispers into his shoulder, "Thank you, again, Jack. You always brighten my day."

Jack holds on tight, inhaling her scent, glancing down at her shining hair, not wanting to let go. Then he rocks her, playfully, "You brighten my day too," as he places his cheek to her head.

He meanders through the farmer's market and she pauses at the entrance to the parking lot, watches him retrieve his mat from the Studio Grille where he exchanges a few words with the Chef. As he leaves, he glances over his shoulder, winks in Valerie's direction.

Valerie's lucky to have him, she thinks. Lucky to have a friend like Jack and, wishes for a moment, Alexander could be more relaxed, more fun loving and not so serious all the time.

Valerie arrives home with curtains and a quart of robin's egg blue paint. She stopped by a decorating store just for ideas, but excited about the possibilities, she launched into a design and purchased the items. By the time she pulls into the driveway, she resolves to start in that room. Alexander can have three beige walls, she thinks. She deserves to have a say and Nan deserves some color.

The house is empty, Alexander's car is absent from the garage. She takes his boxes, one at a time to the upstairs den and stores them out of sight. He can't complain if they're not in his way. She begins cleaning, wiping the walls and moving the shelf, opening the blinds, and then hauls the vacuum from the closet. When she shuts off the vacuum and turns around, Alexander stands in the doorway.

"Hey," is all he says to her.

"Hey," she returns.

"What can I do to help?" he offers as he walks in slowly, hands clasped behind him, head bowed.

Valerie glances around the room as he approaches her. He comes within inches of her, puts his face to hers.

"I'm sorry we fought, honey."

"Me too."

He pulls her close. "I know I'm hard to live with sometimes. I appreciate you putting up with me."

This is rare Alexander speak. She doesn't believe she's heard anything like it, maybe something close to it, but not quite like this.

"Thank you for apologizing."

He kisses her nose, her forehead, and hugs her not especially hard or warmly. When she tries to move closer to him, he releases his arms and backs up. "So, what are we doing in here?"

"Cleaning it up." She wants to say more but doesn't want to start another fight fresh from their last one.

"Okay, I'm in. Where do you want me?"

Valerie finds this different for Alexander too. Not only offering help but allowing her to choose what he should do. He's the take charge type. He's the type to give orders, not take them, so she struggles to find something specific to tell him to do.

"Well, we need to put the bed together and paint, but we should probably paint first."

"Paint?" His face stiffens to disagree, but he steps back and claps his hands. "Okay. Paint. We will go buy some paint."

She holds up the small can. "The sun comes in from here. We'll paint that wall. When the sun hits it, the room will become warm and inviting."

Alexander cringes.

"I saw it in a design magazine."

He nods. "Okay. Paint," he sounds painfully resigned.

*

In the cool evening air breezing across the living room, Valerie sits with her legs crossed elegantly on the couch reading a mystery. She searched the garage for some of her favorite books to place on the shelves of the guest bedroom, *Jane Eyre, The Madwoman in the Attic, Turn of the Screw* lean to one side; a photograph of her and Nan on the other. Among the books hid an unfinished title from Tana French she tucked under her arm for later.

While she enjoys the classics that leave so many questions unanswered, modern reads are able to transport her to real locations where all problems are resolved in three hundred pages. Alexander doesn't approve but tolerates this choice. He suggests nonfiction, even legal thrillers based on true stories. But she doesn't want to read about courts and lawyers. She wants to read about people and places, mysteries solved.

When Alexander walks in, she folds her legs, so he has room to sit. But he stands, waiting for her to glance up. Valerie, sensing this, puts down the book.

"My divorce papers." He hands her a manilla folder.

He doesn't explain, but sits next to her, waits for her to read it. It's clear he doesn't intend to say anything, so she flips open the file. Reading this file, she assumes, is supposed to answer her questions. But it's the short version, the legal version of a couple uncoupling.

There are no long written statements. No multiple page documents. There's a handful of papers, names, addresses, and reasoning: Irreconcilable differences. An agreement: a small sum of money Alexander paid to her. Date. She turns her head slowly to him. "You were still married while we were dating?"

He meets her eyes but waves his hand as if he's washing something away. "It'd been over for a long time by then. We just didn't file the paperwork."

"Were you still living together when we started dating?" She stands, flipping through the papers for more information, but the questions she needs answers to are not within these five sheets of white paper.

"Not as man and wife. We were getting the paperwork in order; she was looking for a place to live."

She drops the paperwork on the coffee table in front of her and backs away. She slips her hands down each arm, wiping away the disgust she feels. He was still married. She was, in some sense, the other woman. "You were still married. You were living together."

"Honey, don't be ridiculous. We just hadn't filed the paperwork. We were done."

"Did she know that?" Valerie says accusingly. How could she have been so foolish? How could he have kept this from her?

He stands, shoulders back, eyes narrowed. "What is wrong with you? Why do you have trust issues? It must have been something with your father."

Valerie points her finger, shock and anger choking off any rational thought. "Do not dare. My father was a wonderful man."

Alexander puts his hands up as if setting a limit, putting a wall between them in this argument. He steps back and takes a deep breath. "I am not going to argue with you about this. You asked about my wife. I gave you the file so you could have all the answers that you need. How dare you even suggest I would act without conscience."

"You gave me a file so you wouldn't have to answer questions." Her heart thumps so hard against her chest, she feels her breath leaving her.

Alexander's lip curls into snarl as he shakes his head. He turns and leaves, the slam of the kitchen door announces his departure from the house as does the car pulling out of the driveway, the screech of wheels on the street.

Valerie sits on the arm of the couch. Tears sting her eyes and roll down her cheeks.

13

Time spent reliving the past, questioning every movement, every word, is wasted time, but Valerie indulges, sitting on that armchair, losing track of time. She pushes herself into a more comfortable position on the couch, tears dried, inhaling calming deep breaths. Her mind wanders to the things she loved about Alexander; his take charge attitude, what she believed was his honesty; these things, colored now, carry a different meaning.

As she crawls into bed, she leaves the blinds in the bedroom open. The night sky is clear, the moon is waning, lending time for the stars to shine. She misses this, she thinks; the simple act of staring at the night sky dreaming. She wraps her arms around herself and pushes her face into her pillow. She misses a lot of things: Nan, her friends, sleeping in and staying up late. Her fresh tears turn to sobs as the unhappiness she's kept at bay bites into her soul.

She'd traded, not given up, traded, she thinks, her friends for Alexander, her sense of freedom for marriage. Not that he asked, but a new man demands your time and attention; a new marriage requires changes. But so much has changed, so much is different than she thought it would be. University study opened up a desire to effect change in school systems, and time spent as a teacher is valuable; and, even though the work is gratifying, it's exhausting; even though the children's smiles warm her heart, she pictured something else. Alexander suggested this job, this position; he knew someone who knew someone; it was close to the house they'd made an offer on.

In college, students trade roommates like they trade lunches. One girl goes to bed at 9 on the dot, the other is a night owl; someone likes loud music, the other prefers quiet. You talk to the RA, you pack up your stuff and move rooms, trade one human for another who better suits your personality. Sometimes it still doesn't work, but you deal with it. It's a short semester; it's a single year.

Before you live with someone, you don't know if they get up at the first bell of the alarm or laze their way into the day. Marriage is a process of learning what the other person wants, likes, needs. Her tears slow and she turns back to the night sky. Marriage is compromise, she thinks. Yes. It strikes her fast and hard and the tears stop. Compromise. Alexander needs to give a little.

When she finally falls asleep, it is with a quieted mind. A conversation, she believes, will help. He needs to be more open, less… the word barely escapes through her lips as she whispers it into the empty evening… controlling.

Daylight threatens the eastern sky as Alexander pulls into the driveway and parks. He doesn't want the rumbling of the garage door to alert Valerie of his return. The house is dark and he believes she's asleep, but where? If she fell into an uneasy sleep on the couch waiting for him, it could be troublesome. But entering through the back door, he finds the living room empty. He peeks his head into the guest room before listening for any sounds from the second floor. Alexander disrobes and showers in the guest bathroom, tossing his clothes into the washing machine before ascending the stairs quietly. He doesn't need another argument to begin before the last one has ended. But before Alexander crawls into the bed next to her, he picks up the remote. Annoyance grows as he watches Valerie sleep through the whirr of the blinds. He shakes his head and tosses the remote to the floor next to the bed and walks around, drops his body to the bed. When he hears her abrupt intake of air, he feels some sense of satisfaction; he lifts the blanket and lies down.

In a few hours, Alexander is up for his softball game. He doesn't wake Valerie, although while he's making breakfast, she appears. He pauses a moment and takes her in. She's beautiful, even in this sleep-deprived and robed state; he glances away feeling guilty. "Breakfast?"

"Sure. Toast?" She glances at the coffee pot, already brewing.

"No. I think we need to cut back on the bread. Summer's coming." He winks in her direction.

From the bread bag, she pulls out a single slice of wheat and pops it in the toaster. He pauses. "I said no."

"This is for me." She meets his gaze.

He returns to the eggs, flips the omelet, and offers, "Summer is coming for you too."

She stares at him soundlessly waiting for him to look up at her. When he refuses to glance back up, she says, "It is my decision to have bread."

He doesn't respond as he plates the omelet, cuts it in uneven halves and moves the smaller half to a second plate. He pours himself a cup of coffee and takes his breakfast to the dining room.

Valerie follows a few minutes later.

"No Nan today?"

"No. She has an event. Seniors only day at the Long Beach Aquarium and then whale watching."

Surprised, Alexander smiles in her direction. "Really?" He snorts out a chuckle, then asks, "I don't suppose you want to come to the softball game?" Fully expecting she will decline. Valerie had gone a few times when they were first married but has spent most Sundays with her grandmother. On those rare weekends she is home, she usually declines his invitation.

"Sure."

He wonders if the divorce papers scared her, reminded her that she could lose him. His smile widens. Not the result he expected, but one he will definitely use. "Dinner at my family's house?"

"Okay."

"Aren't you agreeable today."

Valerie offers her own little smile. "Marriage is about compromise," she says. "I feel I do my share of giving; I'm hoping that you will begin to see that and start to allow me some little freedoms."

He snorts, "I give you freedom. I let you paint the guest bedroom wall that wretched color."

"Maybe freedom is the wrong word."

Alexander glances up from his nearly finished breakfast, perhaps he'd underestimated the effect.

"I want you to open up a little bit. I want to be able to eat on the patio and have friends over once in a while. I want to be able to do some things that make me feel good, like you with your softball, and not have you comment on them, like me with this bread this morning."

Alexander drops his fork, stares at her a moment. He's analyzing. What is the best response in order to get what he wants out of the situation? All deal making is give and take, he thinks. He knows how to make a deal and have it appear as if the other party is getting what they want, but in reality his company appreciates he is able to bring them what they want for what little they're willing to give. It's all in the small details of the contract, not the wording of a single conversation. If they're hiring someone and the person wants moving expenses, the contract will read "truck rental." "Moving expenses" is too broad and undefined. It might include hotels and airfare, house rental, lease breaking. When they're merging with another business and the owner wants guaranteed employment for executives, the contract might read "attempted placement of all senior executive personnel." It does not mean they will still have senior level jobs or executive pay. Additionally, there's no time allotment attached. They could keep them on for a few months and then let them go.

Alexander reaches his hand across the table and touches hers. "Of course, honey. I haven't purposely tried to keep you from any of these things. I'm a bit of a neat freak, you know that. Patio dinners make me uncomfortable, birds, bugs," he adds a self-deprecating chuckle, "but I can be open, try new things." He picks up his plate, "you done?" and picks hers up with her nod. "In fact, I have an idea. Why don't we plan a summer party? When you've finished with your cooking classes, we'll throw a big event. We'll invite all our friends and call your Nan, too!" His tone borders excitement, "She can spend the night in that room, if she wants."

"Really?" This doesn't sound like Alexander.

"Absolutely," he leans over to kiss her forehead as she looks up at him. "I have only ever tried to make you happy."

Now that sounds like Alexander. She retrieves their coffee cups.

He wonders if she caught, "when you've finished your cooking classes." Deal making - know more than the other person. He knows she didn't attend last week; she left early feigning sickness. "Now, if you're coming to the softball game, get ready. I'll load the dishwasher."

She turns for the stairs. It was too easy, even she can see that.

He stands at the bottom step until he hears the shower; he flips open the phone and clicks a button. Relieved when it's voicemail, he says, "Need to cancel for today."

*

After the softball game, they dress for his family's dinner. He requests a dress and chooses the shoes he wants her to wear. They always dress nice for his family dinners. He wears dress pants and a collared shirt. She met his family once before the wedding for a similar dinner, and that's always how they've interacted, usually dinners, once a brunch for last Mother's Day.

Valerie knows why Alexander is so picky about his food: A chef and a full-time mother. When they arrive, his family waits in the family room, where there is a fully stocked bar, and plenty of seats around a wide screen tv. She wonders if his father invites guests over for Superbowl or playoff games; she can't imagine it's for a movie night. As Valerie glances at his mother, she can see a quaint book club with wine and chef-made snacks on a quiet Saturday afternoon.

Madeline is stiff and straight; she moves quickly, gracefully, and sits still only for dinner, or so it seems. So maybe the book club is a stretch. Her career as a court mediator ended soon after she met Arthur, their lawyer turned judge father. A few years after Alexander, they welcomed Theodore, and then more years later, Patricia, who is just a few years older than Valerie.

There are no nicknames here. There is no Ted or Theo, no Patty or Maddy, and she can't imagine the straight spined Arthur being referred to as Art. Therefore, Valerie is Valerina and never Val or her new favorite coming warmly from Jack's lips, V.

As they sit down today, Theodore teases Alexander. "How's corporate law going for you?" It's an old argument that began years before Valerie became part of the family.

"Just because I rarely see the inside of a courtroom, doesn't mean my work isn't challenging or exciting," Alexander argues. Words sparked passion at a young age. Language can be used to change meaning and thinking. He remembers his father's lectures about the language of the contracts winning or losing every case. "How's life defending criminals?"

"Alleged. Alleged. And very rewarding, my brother." Theodore's law firm deals with white collar crimes. It has proven, at times, to be very financially lucrative.

Patricia sits at the end of the table, sullen and silent. She has yet to graduate or get a job; the black sheep of this legal family. Her career will not be in law; she says she wants to be a journalist to which her father bristles and says, "She'll figure it out," and which Theodore responds, "Blogging about shoes isn't journalism."

"Are those last year's LouBoutin's?" she asks Valerie.

Valerie's surprise registers on her face as she answers, "I don't really know." Designer names mean little to her. Alexander bought these for her some time ago.

"Leave it," Madeline announces.

"Just making certain Alexander's taking care of his wife appropriately."

"Where's your husband?" Theodore bites out toward Patricia.

"Valerie," Madeline changes the topic. "What grade are you teaching these days?"

"Still kindergarten."

"Oh, haven't you moved up?" Madeline is forking her food around the plate.

"It doesn't really work that way," Alexander chuckles.

"Madeline," she still feels the tiniest bit uncomfortable calling her mother-in-law by her first name but feels the need to add to the conversation. "This is wonderful. How did you learn to cook so well?"

"Cooking classes." Her eyes pinch in the corners as she sweeps her glance around the table.

"Personal lessons in her own kitchen with trained chefs." Patricia adds as her father takes her hand, smiles warmly.

"Every woman who wants children must learn to cook, Patricia." Theodore bolts his eyes to his sister.

Sitting around the table, Valerie feels like an outsider. Not just this time, but every time they are here. Maybe that's why she doesn't make more of an effort to come. It's as if she's only ever in on half of the conversation, as if everyone is holding something back. She turns to Alexander and gains another level of understanding. She reaches over and takes his hand. He glances up and offers the first genuine smile he's given her all day.

*

Arches aching, Valerie kicks the shoes off the moment she's in the house. She picks them up, holding them by the strap as she sets her purse down on the counter. The softball game became endurable only because of the beautiful breezes sweeping over her. While she said hello to the other wives and girlfriends, they didn't include her in their conversations. Perhaps if she became more of a regular, but overhearing their conversations of acrylic nails, bleached hair, and their gossip about some woman who hadn't shown that day, she thought it best to keep her distance.

Family was family and while she couldn't imagine Alexander at her family table years ago with her mother rattling on Jeopardy about and her accountant father breaking into number sets, as he was apt to teasingly test Valerie's memory, his family seemed to poke at one another. She wondered if they even liked one another. While it wasn't a terrible way to spend a Sunday, she much preferred the loving company of her Nan and the complementary nature of Nan's friends.

Alexander grabs her arm in the kitchen doorway, pushes her against the wall and kisses her hard. He runs his hand over her body and lifts her dress, yanking on her panties. "I wanted you so much all day." He kisses her mouth, throat, works his way down her decolletage.

Valerie tries to readjust her spine which is hitting the door frame uncomfortably. Alexander reacts to her movement as if she is moving into him. He moans and pushes his full body against her, twisting his hand in her hair.

"Ow, ow, honey," she whispers, "honey, you're hurting me." She lifts her spine from the metal closure.

He pulls her from the door frame and pushes her against the countertop, her lower back catching in nearly the same spot.

"Honey," she drops her shoes and tries to leverage some space between him and her. He untwists her hair and goes back for her panties, pulls and spirals, there's a sound of a rip. "Honey," she tries again. "Honey," she says louder. "You're hurting me."

Alexander eases off, puffs disappointment into the air. He takes a deep breath. "Okay, sorry." He waves her toward the stairs. "We should spend the day together like this more often," he says as he follows her.

Once in the bedroom, he sweeps her into his arms, which causes Valerie to giggle, and sets her in bed. He kicks off his shoes and undoes the fly of his pants. She starts to sit up to pull the dress off, but he pushes her down and climbs on top of her, kissing her hard and long. He pulls her sleeves down, pulls her dress up, yanks the panties until they rip in his hand, and twists his other hand in her hair.

Alexander is sometimes rough, but this level of his taking charge in bed Valerie finds a little scary.

"Honey," she whispers. "Hon, a little softer."

"Some people like it rough," he moans into her neck as he pushes himself into her.

"And some people like it a little softer," she giggles.

He pulls her hair, "Say you love me."

"Ow... I love you."

He searches her face, tugs her hair a little tighter. "Say you love me like you mean it."

Valerie studies him for the smallest moment. This Alexander is new to her. This heated passion to the point that he's demanding and even hurting her is something she's unfamiliar with and she doesn't like it. "I love you." She wonders if those are the magic words that will stop it.

It doesn't. He drops himself on to her and wraps his arms around her, thrusting himself into her until he is spent.

14

"When my lawyer comes, he doesn't say much. We have a court date. Claire says hi. He doesn't tell me what to say or what to do or what might happen there, so I ask. He shrugs and says 'we'll see, sign here and sign this.' I know they'll be moving me. I learn more about how the system works from the inmates than I do from this guy.

For a moment I think about my dad, how he'd come home at night and sit on the couch, veg out on King of Queens or the Simpsons not speaking to anyone. My mom would work her way in with an iced tea or lemonade, sit next to him, rub his shoulders. He never talked about work and I think that thirty minute reprieve from real life was his landing time, where he would come out of dealing with people like I've become and the people I share these steel cages with, back into a semblance of normalcy of home and family.

This guy, I think, doesn't have that. It's all this all the time and he looks near dead. He's not much older than me, maybe 35, and he's burned out. I check out his ring finger, bare, no indents, no tan lines. The wrinkles around his eyes and mouth tells me he heads to the corner bar to throw back a few, but then he still takes the shit home with him, or he doesn't have the kind of home a person needs, filled with love.

I realize, not for the first time since I've come to Club Fed, I had that loving home and family the whole time and didn't appreciate it. Some of these guys never had that.

No one plans to become an addict. No one wakes up one morning and says, I think I'll spend my life face down in a pile of cocaine. We were just a bunch of kids fooling around.

Mr. Gonzales scoops up his papers and puts them in his briefcase, and he's muttering, 'okay, see ya.'

I put my hand out as far as I can, still handcuffed, and say, 'Thanks, Man, have a good day.' Can't hate a man for being unhappy. Maybe he thought being an attorney meant expensive business suits and powerful speeches in front of fascinated jurors. Maybe he had no idea he'd be sitting in front of thieves and junkies, most of whom haven't learned their lesson.

He glances up at me for the first time to see if I'm being snarky or sarcastic, then he reaches out to shake my hand and mumbles a bumpy, 'thanks, you too.'

A few days later, I'm in the brown and blue court room in my hazard cone orange jumpsuit, a few pounds heavier than the first time I appeared. I do look around the courtroom today. No one's there for me. It's a six-hour round trip drive, add traffic, and it's a full workday. I don't blame them.

The judge eyes me as the bailiff reads my case number. My attorney motions for me to stand up, and I do.

'We'd like to have this continued, Sir.' The attorney barely glances up from his paperwork.

The judge looks up over his glasses and waits for Mr. Gonzales to make eye contact. 'Do you have any suggestions of where Mr. Rose might be relocated until trial?'

The attorney pitches nervously back at the judge. He fumbles a bit with the paperwork. 'Sir, I didn't think that was an option in this case.'

'Does Mr. Rose have any previous criminal record?'

'No, Sir.'

'No previous drug charges, arrests, suspicious activities?'

'No, Sir.'

The judge pushes back in his chair. He seems to be waiting. I'm uncertain what is transpiring here.

'Sir, we request that the defendant be moved to rehab to wait for the trial.'

Rehab. I have not had good experiences with rehabs. It's either one of those state-run facilities where they put the throwaways of society, or one of those where they try to shove religion down their throats. I wonder if it's going to be better or worse than my cell, but I ain't got a choice in the matter.

Once I arrive, I believe it's Claire's campaigning that got me out of jail and into a rehab. It's not a usual state-run crap hole, but it certainly is not some posh retreat on Malibu beach. It is in the center of the city, near enough to the freeway to hear the hum of the traffic in a soft smooth monotone that tames the calls from the homeless below. From the barred windows, we can hear hookers shout out to potential johns; sometimes they fight with the homeless who ask them for freebies and, I swear, I think I hear them using. The stink of the city wafts upward into the windows, onto the tiny concrete patio: grime and exhaust, mixed with remnant aromas of crack. The concoction is sickening. I think that alone will stop me from ever using again.

Here, we have to get up in the morning and make our beds, then we shower for eight to ten minutes, appear at breakfast between 8 and 8:15 or we do not get fed, then we go to our chores or our groups. If we miss anything, we have to clean the bathrooms with toothbrushes or scrub the patio, the window frames, or the fryer in the kitchen, and it doesn't matter if they were done the day before; they are never completely finished. Sound terrible? Do we deserve something better? Hate this place? Hey, there's the door. And people do leave. People do fail, people break the rules and get sent back to jail.

At first, it feels like torture, punishment. It's like we're being trained, or rather retrained, to live a respectable life. They're breaking us out of our triggers, giving us other ways to handle our problems. As an addict, something doesn't go our way - we use. We get mad at someone - we use. The groups are the hardest part of this place. Seriously, I'd rather clean the bathrooms than to hear someone accuse me of something like showing attitude or not doing my chore to expectation or cheating on the work. But mostly they're right. And if they're not, we need to learn how to handle it because life is all about conflict and we need to learn to deal with it in a different way.

I don't share much, but at this rehab it's required. So they offer me options like cleaning the bathroom or scrubbing the filth from the patio. When I fire back and call this place a Nazi prison, that gets me hauled into the counselor's office.

I expect them to scream and yell. I expect them to threaten to throw me out, send me back to the feds. But they don't. There's a male and female counselor. One's a drug counselor, the other is a psychological therapist; they sit calmly with their hands folded.

'Where do you see yourself in five years?' the lady psychologist asks.

'I don't know.' I'm not ready for this question. I'm ready for a lecture. I'm ready for screaming. I'm not expecting this calm demeanor and conversation.

'Does anyone know what they'll be doing in five years?'

'Yeah' she says. 'I think most people have some sort of hope, some sort of plan. Bruce, what's yours?'

Bruce takes a deep breath; he didn't know she was going to ask him, but it doesn't take much to think about it either. 'Well, I hope to be married, maybe on our first kid by then.'

Then she says, 'I personally plan to travel to Ireland, discover my ancestral roots and look up some distant cousins.'

Then she looks at me again. 'How about you?'

'I don't know. It might be prison for me.' I lean into the calm space.

'What if it's not? What about after? What do you want in your life? You must want something.'

I sit quiet. I haven't thought about a future in a very long time. Sometimes now, I try not to think about the long road of prison time ahead of me. I try to imagine my life if I wasn't going to prison, or maybe after I get out.

'Say 5ish years, how old will you be?' she asks me.

'28ish"

'When you were a kid, what did you think you might have by that time.' The psych chuckles. 'I wanted to finish college before 30, but it took me longer than that.' She appears on the brink of middle age, some graying hair, laugh lines around her eyes.

'I guess, finish art school,' I offer.

She nods. 'Where do you live?'

'I don't know.' This whole line of questioning makes me uncomfortable.

'Well, near your family? far away? Some people want to move to New York. There's a big art community there.'

'No.' I answer quickly. 'I don't want to be that far away from my family.'

'Are you guys close?'

I almost respond yes, but I pause. We're not. So, I sit back again and shake my head from side to side. 'No.' And then I get choked up. 'I nuked it.' I start bawling. 'I fucking broke the whole family apart. I mean I think Claire and my dad still talk, but my mom died and my father threw me out forever and... it was on me.'

I rock backward when I realize how much I hate myself for the shit I've put my family through. This is the pain. This is why I use. The guilt and the pain of the things I've done to others. I've put my family through hell. And I start hungering for it now, for escape, my cells are screaming like billions of hungry open mouths begging for satiation.

Every day they bring me back and ask me these questions and more. Where do I want to be? what do I want in my life?

Sometimes, we get off track, start on one of these side roads until I start screaming out in pain, metaphorically speaking.

After a few weeks, I ask her why she's doing this to me.

'Jack,' she says. 'you have some very deep fallacies living in your being. Some drug addicts are abused, neglected and they use to drown that pain. Some addicts create their own pain and live on that. When someone is in pain and they drink or use drugs, it widens those gaps in the brain that remembers that pain. So next time they think those thoughts, the pain feels deeper. If they use again, the gaps widen again. Think about this, Jack. Have you ever hiked?'

I shrug thinking we are suddenly off track again, 'Yeah, when I was a kid.'

'So, when you hike a new path, it's all overgrown and hard to get through. But the more you hike it, the easier it gets. The brush gets beaten down, the trees get clipped back, the path becomes more dirt than grass. True?'

I nod. 'Yeah. that's true.'

'The same thing happens when you're thinking about your pain, the more you go back to it, the easier it is to access and roam around in. Then, when you think about that pain, and you drink or use drugs, that path gets wider. The next time you visit that pain with alcohol or drugs, that path gets even wider. Soon, you don't remember the small little path as it was, you remember this wide barren dirt path.'

I visualize this path in the woods, my buddies with me, ripping down more trees and bushes, pushing aside rocks, widening that path until it's a clear trail to hell.

Some people here lineup for phone privileges, want to call family, friends. I don't call my family. I don't want to bug them. I think it's just more painful for them to be reminded of me than just to forget me. And I don't recall the last friend I had who wasn't using or supplying. This is all hard for me. To be alone here without anyone on the outside. And this place is hard. They don't shove religion down your throat; they give you big doses of reality.

People call you on your shit daily. We sit in groups and people say, 'you're blaming,' 'you're not being honest,' 'you didn't finish this.' Every time you're dishonest with yourself or others, you're up at midnight scrubbing the toilets with a toothbrush.

It feels like they're trying to trip you up, they're pushing you to leave, escape, use. Then one day, I'm sitting in that hot sun on that damn concrete patio, on a time-out like a child, pouting like a five-year-old for spouting off at someone, and I realize that is exactly what they're doing. Every time I get angry, every time I feel treated unfairly, every time I feel hurt or confused or scared, I feel my cells scream for drugs. This is how I handled everything in the past! They are hitting every trigger point, my anger, my exhaustion, my sense of unfairness, all in an effort to round off those points. The real world doesn't give a shit if you have issues. They're not going to walk around on eggshells for you - and they shouldn't have to. I have to exist in a world with anger and disappointment and with people who will treat me according to their own issues, and I need to learn new ways to handle problems. It's like I'm hit with a lightning bolt from the clear blue sky and I leap up out of my seat. I feel, for the first time in so long, elated.

'Jack, sit!' Someone orders me from the window.

I turn and smile at the face I can't see, 'thank you, brother,' I say for the first time without sarcasm or annoyance.

A few months pass by with me doing the work with a passion, like my life depends on it and for no other reason than I want to learn to live a different life. When I go back to court, the judge says, 'Mr. Rose, if you find that you can do this program and keep yourself clean, I might see my way clear to reduce your sentence.'

I nod, not really getting it. Still convinced I'm in for ten years.

'Mr. Rose, I'm offering to reduce your sentence from ten years. I'd do more than nod if someone was offering me a new life.'

I meet his eyes. This man's serious. And he's right. It slaps me hard across the face: Hope. I don't even know when I felt it last. I wake up from the g'damn blanched world. I may yet have a damn chance at a real life. His face contorts slightly as he sits there waiting for something more from me. His nostrils flare and his eyelids turn red and twitch.

I step closer to the cheap wooden table among this thick hardwood on every other side of me. It doesn't seem to fit in this place. The wood of his judge desk, of the doors, and the walls, all good thick oak or something, dark wood, and then this cheap desk for cheap defendants like me. They probably had some nice wood table in here for the defendants and their attorneys and some shithead like me broke it up, ruined it. Maybe more than one. Because sitting on this side is a bad place to be, and bad people sit here. So, I think: Where do I want to be in five years?

'Judge, sir. Thank you for everything.' And I'm sincere, too. 'I think that had I never been arrested, I'd be in a much worse place, maybe dead or something. And for a while, I thought, good I'll rot behind those bars. But there's people like you and my sister,' I look at the public defender and he's not even paying attention to me, but to his paperwork, I won't include him, 'That care. And those people at that rehab, they care. I never knew people would care about someone they didn't know about someone like me who never helped anyone but himself. So, I am g'damn appreciative of you and whatever you plan to do for me. I plan to stay clean. I'm going to try. And if I don't, I hope you put me in a jail so far back and deep that I never see the light of day again. I'm going to work that program, and I'm going to be a mechanic, or something. My brother in law offered me this job, so I'll start studying....'

'Okay, okay, Mr. Rose. I don't want your whole life story. I just wanted to know you were taking this chance seriously.'

'Thank you, sir. Yes, I am, and I thank you.'

I work the program like a kindergartener learning their ABC's for the first time and earn a family day. I tell the counselors I don't want to bug my family. But they insist. I write a letter first, too damn scared to hear the sound of their voices on the phone – as if Claire's soft, sweet, 'hello?' in answering the phone will break me into a million little pieces that no one will be able to reassemble.
I keep the letter vague:

Claire,

How are you? I hope Tommy and Danny are good, and too. I love and appreciate all you've done for me. They have a family day here. I know you guys have done a lot, but the counselors think it'll be good for you to come, and it'd be great to see you.

It takes me three days of writing and rewriting to get this damn little piece of trash. I want to see them, but I'm also afraid to. I'm supposed to ask my father to come, but I don't even want to try. I tell the counselors, let's take it slow. And I don't budge on that.

I figure Claire is busy and I won't hear for a while, but I get a letter three days later.

'Yes! When? We miss you. Why haven't you called? Your attorney doesn't give me much information. We miss you so much and hope you're doing well. Love, Claire, Danny, and Tommy.'

She signs all their names, but then she lets Tommy write a T on the bottom. There's a folded paper behind this one and I open it up. Tommy has drawn me a picture of dinosaurs. At least, I think they are dinosaurs, purple and green, with a red tree, as best I can make out. I tear up, take it to my room and tape it to my wall next to my bed.

Family day is a few weeks away, but I write her right away and tell her the date, and I hear back immediately. She wants to know if she can bring Tommy, if there's anyone else she should tell or bring?

I say yes to Tommy and I don't know to the rest. Part of me is afraid my father will refuse, the rest of me is afraid he'll actually come. I'm not sure I can deal with him yet.

On family day, Claire, Danny, and Tommy come. Tommy is climbing all over me while Claire is trying to get him to calm down; there's cheap burger patties sweating on an old grill and hot dogs that might even be edible. Danny brings us all plates and we talk as if I wasn't in a jail enforced rehab and that this is just a Sunday lunch at a BBQ place. After we eat, there's ice cream, but before the ice cream there's 'the talk.' This will be my first time, but the others warn me about it.

'Imagine,' Diego, my roommate, said, 'getting your tonsils pulled out without anesthesia or pain killers. That's what the ice cream is for after, to dull the pain.'

I'm not sure what goes on in these, but I find out when we go in with my two assigned counselors and sit down. They give Tommy a basket which has crayons, toys, and play-doh to keep him busy. He sits at the coffee table in front of us as the counselors begin.

'This meeting works as sort of an after-all intervention. Interventions are when families sit around and tell the person what they've done, how they've changed, how you've missed the real person they used to be. It's used to get people into care. Since Jack came to us under other circumstances, this is an after-care intervention. He still needs to hear these things.'

Claire looks hesitant; she gives me a look of pity as if she's pulling out the pliers and knows it's going to hurt but going to do it anyway.

'My real brother has been gone a long time and I didn't even realize it until I was sitting here today with you. We were actually able to sit and have a conversation and laugh over stupid stuff. Do you have any idea how long it's been?'

I keep my eyes on her face as it struggles to keep from puckering with emotion.

'You were fun and smart and artistic, and you always had something nice to say. But that stopped at some point, maybe slowly, or maybe not because I was going through my own teenage stuff, but I do remember sitting at the table with you just being silent or sulky, and I didn't even realize it was happening. Sometimes I tried to talk to you, to ask you what was wrong, and you always said, nuthin', which I didn't really believe but I thought it was just teenage stuff. But you drifted further and further away. Dad realized first you were doing drugs and tried to get you help, you said you'd go, then you ran away, you didn't stay, or you'd stay clean for a while, never really completely coming back to you. I thought when I brought you back from New Orleans I had my brother back, but I didn't. I just had his shell back. I missed him so much. I missed you. I see now how much I was missing. I need you; we all need you so much to stay clean and sober and become a real part of our family again.'

Danny rubs her shoulder and Tommy twists to see her face reddening as she tries to hold back tears, then Tommy stops coloring and climbs up on her lap and rubs her cheeks. He turns to me. He looks straight at me because that's where his mother was focused when she started crying. He points his chubby little index finger at me and says, 'Stop!' with much more force than a two-year-old should be able to manage.

We all chuckle, but it's a weak and unexpected chuckle. But he's right. She's right.

'Jack, what do you have to say to your sister?'

It takes me a moment. I breathe deeply more than once to center myself so I don't cry;

I buy time and think about a response, then I sit forward and look at Claire.

'Thank you for being my sister. The powers that be, whatever they are, must have given me you for a reason. I have received a break here, the biggest break of my life, and I can only promise you that I will try to the best of my abilities. I've learned a lot here about myself and how to handle the world. I've dredged up the shittiest, oops, sorry, don't say that word, Little Man. I love you and Tommy,' I look at Danny who is watching Tommy's hands on his own. 'And you too, Danny. Thank you too for being who you are for taking care of my sister and giving us this wonderful little man here.'

I sit back and take another deep breath, relieved that I think the hard part is over.

It's not an easy thing to see the pain you've caused your family. It's worse because I know I caused them much, much more than

I'll ever understand. The hope and the disappointment, the lies, the dishonesty. Before, I felt like I was trying, but I realize now I really wasn't. I was buying time, not doing the right things, thinking I could control it and that my family didn't understand me, didn't trust me to handle my shit. When, the whole time, they knew the shit was handling me. I will never remember all the heartache I've caused them. It's a damn miracle that any of them are here now. I have to be thankful for that.

My father may never forgive me. I may never see him again. Watching your child become a zombie can't have been easy. Even apart from him being a cop and the pride that goes with that, I became his saddest case, his worst nightmare. But I have to be thankful for what I do have, and for the moment that is Claire, Danny, Tommy. Maybe someday my dad, maybe not. I have to let him decide.

There's more to this meeting. I didn't want to eat the ice cream after, but I did because I didn't know what else to do. Tommy was all over that ice cream and I let him eat half of mine too, which suddenly boosted my worth in his eyes as he hung on my neck and jumped up and down on my legs.

It was near dark as they left. I'd felt guilty for keeping them so late when they have a long drive home and work in the morning. I stretch out in my bed that night, stare up at the ceiling.

'Feeling guilty?' Diego whispered in the darkness.

'A whole lot of guilty.' I said.

'Eh, means ur growin' up!' He rolled over and I suspect went to sleep.

I imagine there's some truth to his statement. I couldn't sleep and I felt bad. When my insides feel bad, I start craving drugs. I know I have to short circuit that – that's what this rehab has taught me – so I pick up my notebook and make a list of all the things I have to be thankful for. I work backward from today, the visit, the court, and yes even getting arrested because that is what got me here. Without that, I wouldn't have reason or motivation, or most importantly, this wretched, hard as shit, rehab to help me heal these wounds I've caused to myself and to others.

While we're using, addicts think people don't notice their bs, and they learn to operate on a different program than most people, or so I assume. Addicts live without rules, without expectations, they don't live within the confines of society and, after a while, we forget how to live and take care of ourselves properly, let alone live in a world with other people. This isn't only an addict problem, but it is one of them. And this program, all the rules, the chores, the family days, and the punishments are pushing us to live a real life in the real world. It works for those who work it. We all find our own way to deal with it.

For me, I track that gratitude list. I think of my sister. I focus on that little man, Tommy. And I'm studying for that job Danny offered me.

I need to live a different life because I spent far too much time not living but escaping. And sometimes my veins still ache for a needle. I'm not sure why because I understand it's complete poison, but once it's in there it calls for more for a long time. I think that's one reason they keep us so busy and on a schedule here – so we don't have time to focus on those aches. Stay busy. Keep focused. Be thankful.

I did this for almost a year. Claire came as often as she could, but my father never did. Even though she never told me so, I knew she'd asked my father to come. I understand that, in some sense. I had to accept it. I'd caused him a lot of pain, a lot of disappointment. I can't control other people; I can only control me. I can hope that someday he'll forgive me, but I can't hold it against him if he doesn't.

I did write him a letter, as per the program requirement:

> Dad,
>
> I understand I've caused you innumerable amounts of pain. What I can remember is probably not the worst of it. I've let you down. I've let myself down. But I am trying to get it right. I am sorry, but I don't expect

your forgiveness. I only hope someday the pain I've caused you lessens and perhaps you can find it in your future to make room in your heart for me once again. I will not bother you. I will not write you again. I will not come and see you unless you tell me it's okay. I intend to respect the boundaries you've set. I only wish I had done that sooner.

I want to tell him I'm clean, but how many times have I told him that? I want to tell him this time is different, but they are just words I've used before.

I send it, but he doesn't respond. And I need to respect that. Maybe, someday.

When I go to court, I think the judge is not going to remember me other than a name on the file he has in front of him, but when it's my turn I stand up. I'm wearing a crisp blue shirt and khaki pants, thanks to the donations at the rehab. The shoes are a tad too tight, but they're black and look good.

'Mr. Rose.'

'Yes, sir.' I stand at attention.

'You are looking better. Seems like you've put on a little weight.'

I smile because he does remember me, and I have put on at least 20 lbs. I needed those pounds. And maybe more.

'How's the program going?'

'Very well, Sir. I've been clean for 13 months,' (including the jail time) 'and I've done all my steps. I've secured employment for when I'm released, and I intend to continue to attend meetings.'

'That is genuinely nice to hear. The counselors are calling you a success story.'

'Thank you, Sir.'

'Mr. Rose, I feel confident you will be an upstanding citizen of our society. You will find and keep a job, stay clean, and get tested when required. Your attorney has papers for you to sign. And, you have a few more weeks at that rehab. Correct?'

'Yes, sir. With your approval, I go home at the end of the month.'

'Mr. Rose' he eyes me over his glasses. 'I wish you much luck and don't take this the wrong way, but I do hope I never see you again.'

I'm so happy, I want to bounce out of these too tight shoes. 'Yes, sir, and I hope to never see you again unless it's under far better circumstances.'

When Danny and Claire come to pick me up, I'm quiet the whole way back.

15

"He doesn't listen, sometimes I don't know whether I should continue to even try." Over a much-needed lunch with Lucy, Valerie vents.

Lucy curls her lip. "Men never listen, but you have to try. I think that's the story of all marriages. It's only when you stop trying that the marriage is over, don't you think?"

Valerie shrugs. "I guess. And then what about the stuff he doesn't tell me. Lucy, he was married!"

"Some people are very embarrassed by their mistakes, especially with what you've told me about his family?" It's not a question, but Lucy makes it sound like one.

Valerie can't point to one mistake he's admitted. "Should marriage be this difficult?"

"You're asking the wrong girl now. I don't know any marriages that are easy. They have rough patches, you know?"

Valerie nods, feeling Lucy is right. She doesn't remember her parents having a rough patch, doesn't remember any serious issues or either of them being unhappy, but she was a child.

"It's the marriages that can survive those that are the ones that succeed. I mean, as long as there's love, right? I mean if you don't love the man..." Lucy chuckles to herself. "I would not put up with half the crap I do if I didn't love Kent with all my stupid heart and soul."

They wend their way back from their break to their classrooms to prepare for Parents' Night. This is the night at West Oaks when the school invites the families into a spotless and carefully crafted salesroom. The teachers lay out the best and most creative projects, decorate their classrooms with appropriate aids, and brag about the children - generally and individually. They will tantalize parents with previews of adventures for the following year. This is to encourage parents to enroll for the next school year. Gala tickets go on sale tonight. Posters with scenes from pseudo-50's memories adorn walls all over the school and each teacher is required to mention the gala and the benefits the proceeds will serve. Not just the pay of teachers and administrators, but the community outreach and scholarship, which is really the hook to any of these events.

Valerie doesn't like the salesmanship of Parents' Night. She feels it should be an honest night shared with families, failures as well as accomplishments. When the last parent leaves at 9:30, she sits down and takes a deep breath. She props her feet up as Lucy pops her head in, "Girl, I need a glass of wine after that!"

Valerie realizes how much she's missed having Lucy to chat with. "Have a seat."

"Oh, gosh no, girl. I'm going to do the clean up in the morning, I'm so tired." Lucy yawns as she waves to her friend.

Valerie wonders if she, too, can leave the clean up, paper cups, paper plates scattered from the offered refreshments, until morning. There's a tap on her open door. "Did you forget something?" She hopes Lucy has changed her mind.

"I did." Jack says.

Valerie drops her feet to the floor and sits up with a start. "I thought it was Lucy."

Jack steps in, "I'm sorry."

"I'm fine. Just startled." Valerie stands up, giggles at herself.

"Did Claire and Danny forget something?"

"No. No. I wonder if I can steal you away for a little bit. I want to show you something."

Valerie pauses. She glances at the time and pictures Alexander climbing in bed; he'll be asleep whether she gets home at ten or eleven. Some of the faculty go out for a glass of wine or a late supper. If Lucy had asked, she would have agreed. There doesn't seem a reason not to go. "Yes. Sounds good."

"Are you sure? You hesitated."

"Yes. I'm just tired."

"Nice." He smiles. "Meet me behind the old library as soon as you can."

*

The streets are near deserted as the darkness closes in on the older part of town. There are no streetlights behind the library; the parking lot borders an alley that is shared by homes. The main streets, in front of the library and to the north are mere steps away and well lit. Valerie pulls in, stays in her car until she sees Jack's backlit gait moving toward her.

She pops open the door and stands; the bright lights of the main street become more apparent, the noise of a crowd sounds not too far away, and the discomfort of the area skitters away.

"What are we doing here?" she asks.

"Wanted to show you something, come on." He walks close to her, gliding them behind another building which leads to the well-lit back parking lot of a darkened restaurant. Cars are lined in rows, hoods open, people meander the lot, glancing in the cars, leaning over the engines, pointing out paintings and emblems.

Jack walks toward a vintage Jaguar, one of the few with the hoods closed, and points out the paint, spots, claws and, on the hood, the eyes and face of a jaguar, the teeth shining from an opened mouth on the very front end. On the window is the "Before" photo of the old gray paint job. In the slot next to it is an old Model T with hot yellow and orange flames fading into a burst of a single color toward the back.

"I did these," he says quietly.

Valerie pauses and allows her eyes to linger on the details of each. "You painted these?"

Jack nods shyly. "A few more too." He touches her elbow to guide her down the row of cars. There's another covered with sugar skulls, culminating in a horrifying ghostly skull on the hood. "This is my favorite," he whispers. She leans down to see the color and beauty of the sugar skulls morph slowly as the movement of shapes pushes toward the front of the car and then completely change into the shadowy figure appearing to force itself through the metal. Jack leans down next to her, watching her face, the movement of her eyes as they sweep slowly over his work. A spark ignites within him as he thinks, she gets it.

"This is amazing work, Jack." She touches his hand as they curl toward the car.

"You work your magic on little souls, I work my magic on these."

"Back off that car, man." A guy in a leather jacket and jeans with his hair slicked back comes around and surprises them.

"Hex!" Jack says. They pound fists and half hug. "My friend, V."

She reaches her hand out to shake his, but Hex forms her hand into a fist and pops it against his own.

"You racing tonight?"

"You going to let me drive this?"

"Hell, no." He slaps Jack's shoulder, sees someone else he knows and saunters off. "Later, Jack."

"Where's my driver!" A man yells through the crowd and jumps out toward Jack. He's slim and short with a moustache and goatee.

"Sam, this is V."

"Wonder of all wonders. She's real!" He moves toward Valerie with open arms.

Jack places his arm between them, chuckles and turns Sam around. "Let me catch up with you in a minute."

"I get it, I get it." The guy clucks his tongue and waves his finger at them before walking off.

"Sorry about that."

"It's okay. Thank you, though."

He touches her elbow and begins leading her in the opposite direction toward a group of picnic tables near a food truck.

"Are you racing tonight?" she asks as he sits opposite her.

He nods. "Yeah. I am."

"Is it dangerous?"

Jack seems to waffle, but says, "Nah. Not really."

A couple of teenagers start their way. Valerie sees the young couple coming, and Jack turns as they reach him. The young man high five's Jack's waiting hand and the young woman climbs over the bench and sits next to him. "Hi," she says.

"Is this her?" The young man shakes Valerie's hand.

"V, this is Brian and Shell."

"You are so pretty." The young woman, maybe 16, wears glitter blush with her hair short and wild. "You the one who's got Jack all happy and singing at work?"

"Alright, alright, shut it down." Jack laughs out loud. "It ain't nothing like that."

"Sure as shit is," Brian snorts.

"V, don't let these kids freak you. They're messing with you."

"Hi," Valerie says. "Shell, is it?"

The young woman shrugs and something on her jingles; her earrings dangle, bracelets on her wrist, and a gold belted chain around her waist. "Michelle, Shelly, Shell. Bri says I'm hard like a shell, but I'm pretty too, you know, like one of those opal ones that looks like a rainbow in the sunshine?"

Valerie nods. The girl is completely adorable.

"How do you guys know Jack?"

"After school program," Brian laughs.

"Just stop messin' with her. What are you guys doin' here

anyway? You get busted here, you'll be back in Juvi, you want that?"

As Brian explains to Jack that they're leaving, Shell whispers to V. "He has a whole group of us at the shop, lets us help him out, teachin' us stuff. And he really does sing. I want to work on motors, but Bri wants to learn to paint like Jack." She giggles in a way that only young girls can.

Someone turns the music up, and Shell jumps up. "Ooooo, dance."

"I'm not dancin', go dance with Jack." Brian catches Shell as she throws herself into his arms and forces him into a twirl.

"He ain't got no moves. He's an old man." Shell teases when she rounds back toward Jack.

"Old... no moves... I'll show you. V?" Jack unrolls his arm toward Valerie.

Valerie takes his hand and they move away from the table, and try to mimic Brian and Shell, spinning, twirling, then Brian plants a big kiss on Shell's lips and turns toward Jack and Valerie waiting expectantly. Jack turns to Valerie, smiles, traces her eyes, her cheeks, her lips with his gaze before turning back to the teenagers. "Go on, get on home."

The teenagers burst out in laughter as they wave and head off in the opposite direction.

Jack chuckles as he turns back to Valerie who looks a little flushed. "If it's okay, I'm going to walk you back to your car now."

"Sure."

They continue to hold hands, almost absentmindedly, as they walk out of the parking lot and down the alley. "I hope you don't mind. The race will start soon, everyone gets pretty silly." he shrugs as they approach her car, "Truthfully, it's not exactly legal and I don't want you to get into any trouble."

She untangles her fingers from his and reaches for her keys from the small bag strung across her body. The car beeps and Jack reaches for the door. In one last gesture for the night, he opens his arms and asks, "May I?"

She moves into his hug, encloses him in her arms. The night air has chilled, and the sounds in the distance are muffled. Neither of them moves to release the other as he breathes in her scent, somewhere on her coconut lingers, shampoo, body lotion, he's not certain. When horns sound from the street, Jack knows they are for him. He loosens his grip and gazes at her as they slowly part. Valerie releases her arms but doesn't remove them completely. She meets his gaze, breathing in his scent. His lips move as if he might say something, but he says nothing. He pulls her in again for another hug, his face to hers, wishing she was single, wishing she was his, and wishing he could kiss her.

His warmth and tenderness feel good against her body. The dancing and laughing, friends, and now the cool night air at her back, makes her feel closer to him. She inhales deeply. He's fresh and his skin smooth, his facial scruff prickles her face, and she giggles involuntarily. She feels warm in ways she hasn't felt in a long time. The chill is chased away by the heat rising from her navel and spreading outward.

The horn sounds again and he releases her. He wouldn't offer his mouth to hers without asking, without being certain it was okay. He takes her hands, encouraged momentarily to ask, then he feels that ring on her finger. His courage falls away as does his hands on hers.

"Good night, V."

The warmth in her throat causes her words to sound like they're melting. "G'night, Jack."

He exhales slowly as he backs up; the sound of her words in the night stir him; his thoughts turn to the race feeling empowered. He knows he will win.

He closes the door after she slips into the seat. The car starts, there's a last smile, a last wave, and then taillights as she pulls out of the parking lot.

She turns away from Jack, away from the race. Her energy draining. Hand on the steering wheel as she turns, the sparkle of light on her diamond wedding ring. "Damn," she says to no .one, "damn, damn, damn."

*

In the morning, Alexander taps her shoulder. Her eyes flutter open. He's fully dressed and standing next to her. Something is wrong. The light in the room is off, the scene is strange. She shakes off sleep, thinking it might be a dream.

"I thought you didn't come home." He half chuckles. "I was just about to start calling people. What's your friend's name, Lucy? Did you girls go out?"

Valerie pushes herself up. She's in the living room, on the couch, fully dressed. "No. I mean, yes, but..."

"You must have been out late."

Valerie shakes her head as she sits upright. "It actually wasn't that late." Still wrapped up in the warmth and daydreaming of Jack, she sat for just a moment to kick off her shoes and replay the night in her head. "I just sat down for a minute."

"You must have been exhausted." He kisses her head and stands up. "I'm heading out, Chicken Lemonato with forbidden rice tonight. 30 minutes on low."

Valerie nods as she starts for the stairs. She pauses at the open door of the guest room. The light bleats through the luminous sheers and glows against the blue wall. The other walls are still real estate white and could use a less bright eggshell or cream. They'll need a bedding set, she thinks right before her eyes settle on Alexander's boxes; the ones she moved to the empty closet of his den are back again and piled, not so neatly, under the window. He's placed an open file on one of the shelves and a discarded photo frame on another. She pulls the door to a close and starts up the stairs.

16

Dressed in yoga pants and tennis shoes, Valerie slips out of the house when Alexander is out jogging. She has no plans for cooking class today. She's going to surprise Jack at the yoga studio, repaying the favor of getting her out of class last week. There's a giggle in her throat and a spring in her step as she bounces on the curb next to the studio. Peeking through the glass door, only a few people have arrived, and Jack is not among them. She waits, moving around people who come for the class.

She stands so she can see the entrance to the cooking class, just in case Jack plans to surprise her again. It's five minutes to ten and he hasn't arrived. She steps inside the building and peeks into the classroom.

"Hi! Are you new to yoga?" the receptionist greets her.

"No. Well, yes. I'm new. I'm looking for my friend Jack. Has he arrived yet?"

The girl checks her list and shakes her head. "You're welcome to wait inside."

Valerie signs in and grabs a mat from the basket and gets comfortable in the back of the class. The music is soft, there's the scent of grapefruit essence in the air, candles burn behind the yoga instructor. He folds a blanket and sits on his mat. "I see some new faces," he smiles towards her and to another practitioner, "welcome."

Valerie spends the first few minutes of class waiting and hoping, but finds that the meditation, breathing, and movements require all of her attention. She took yoga classes in college, but it's been a while. Some of the poses are harder than she remembers and, when they are finished, she is glowing, not only with the shine of sweat but peace has worked its way into her system, and she feels good.

As she leaves, she crosses her arms and walks toward the cooking class. She misses Jack but wonders if she should miss him this much. She glances back to watch the others exit the yoga studio; maybe he's coming to the next class. She thinks she understands what he meant now, when he said he had to get zen with the world. The yoga class left her feeling light and trouble-free in some sense.

The farmer's market is open, the day is mild, and the cool breeze dries the sweat on her arms. Tummy purring for nourishment, she steps toward the tent which houses HomeBoy Bakery to select a chocolate croissant.

"There you are," a woman from her cooking class approaches her. "We were hoping everything was okay."

"Yes, thank you." Behind the woman who's name she doesn't remember, she sees Alexander heading for the Studio Grille. She grabs the bag from the clerk's outstretched hand, jogs over to catch Alexander at the door.

"What are you doing here?" A crooked smile hides her momentary panic.

"What is this?" Alexander's Saturday casual is khaki pants and a button up shirt. T-shirts and shorts are for exercise and softball. All other activities require presence, proper dress. You never know who you may run into.

"Croissant. Want some?" She holds up the bag, which he takes from her hand. "I thought I'd surprise you. You said there was a farmer's market." He gives her a peck on the cheek. "Thought we could pick up whatever you made in class today and you can remake it tonight. This way the recipe will be fresh in your mind."

Valerie smiles nervously.

"Valerie, what are you wearing?" He gazes down at her yoga pants, hoping they won't run into anyone he knows.

"There's a yoga studio down further. I thought I might try..." She allows the sentence to die as Alexander's head swivels toward the market.

"So, what'd you make today in class?"

"Uhm, vegetables… " Valerie decides to come clean, tell him she's missed the last two weeks. He takes her hand and leads her to the nearest trash can, drops the bag containing the croissant in, and steps toward the center of the market fairway. "I hadn't even touched that."

He glances down at her and back at the trash bin, chuckles, "Good." He wiggles her hand to regain her attention. "Vegetables and what?"

"Salmon and a grilled vegetable salad," she snipes. The recalled recipe served as the first official meal she'd made for him as man and wife. The first official meal he'd scoffed at. At least then, he tried to be polite.

They are choosing tomatoes as a familiar voice calls her name.

"Miss V! Miss V!" Tommy runs toward her. Her heart skips, Jack and Alexander will meet for the first time. Beyond Tommy's fast little legs are Danny and Claire. "Hi, Miss V. How are you doing today?" Little Tommy mimics a taught greeting.

"I'm fine, Tommy. How are you?"

"I am so sorry." Claire catches her breath as she puts her hands on the little boy's shoulders. "Tommy, don't run off like that."

"It's no problem. It's always a pleasure to see families outside of school." She runs into kids and their families on a semi-regular basis. Alexander glances at the couple and down at the little boy. "This is Alexander. Alexander, this is Claire, Danny, and this little bundle of energy is Tommy."

Alexander nods, shakes Danny's offered hand. His gaze sweeps over Danny's Saffarri t-shirt and casual shorts, then to Claire's breezy blouse and shorts. "Nice to meet you," he offers in return.

"I'm so happy we ran into you. Since you and Jack and Tommy have become such good friends, we wanted to invite you guys to a barbeque next Saturday."

"That is sweet of you to ask." Her heart pounds a little harder at the mention of Jack's name. But as she looks up at Alexander, he's turning back to the tomatoes and has heard only part of Claire's invitation.

"We'll have to check our calendar," he glances at them over Valerie's shoulder.

"I'll let you know but thank you for the invitation." Valerie doesn't want them to be offended by his clearly dismissive action. She ruffles Tommy's hair and smiles, genuinely happy to see them.

"Sounds good." Danny picks Tommy up.

"Nice seeing you," Claire calls sweetly as they head off toward the fresh orange juice.

"You too!"

"They are one of the families from your school?"

"Yes." Valerie doesn't like his tone.

"I guess it's not as exclusive as I thought." His tone drops to seriousness, "Why is he calling you Miss V and not Mrs. Graham?"

"There's another teacher with the same last name. The admin didn't want the students or other faculty to be confused."

"I think we have everything we need." He makes the final selection of vegetables without her.

*

Once home, Alexander sets himself up at the dining room table with work while Valerie cooks. The first and last time she made this, he thought the fish was too plain and the vegetables overcooked. She adds more garlic to the salmon and watches the vegetables carefully. In some way, she wants to prove she can do this. Everyone makes mistakes once in a while; she feels she may not need cooking classes, but a chance where he doesn't balk or judge.

When she brings the plates in, he announces, "I just talked to Mr. Stewart. Starting Monday, the kids will call you Mrs. G."

Valerie's mouth hangs open for a moment, before she realizes and forces it closed.

"This smells great."

Getting five-year-olds to understand a name change is not easy. There are only a few months left of the school year; she'll let it go until fall semester begins. However, she's grown to like Miss V. She doesn't offer this to him, she doesn't want to try to explain a five-year-old's brain to Alexander. Maybe, what he doesn't know won't hurt him.

She glances from the food back to him. This must be what he thinks when he doesn't tell her things, like his first marriage. Maybe not knowing about the yoga class and cooking class won't hurt him either. Maybe not knowing about Jack, their just friends anyway, won't hurt him.

"These cooking classes are really paying off." He mouths another forkful.

"I actually made this for you before."

"And see how much better it is now when you make it right?"

Valerie drops her gaze. There's something hard and dark building within her. It's annoyance, anger, defiance. Any one alone presents a problem; together they grow spiny and sharp, dangerous to soft, round marriages.

"I'd like to attend the barbeque. I think we should get to know some of the families from the school."

Alexander chuckles. "You want to go sit outside while some amateur chef tries his hand at giving us e-coli? No, thank you."

Valerie glares at him. She takes a deep slow breath. "I can't say I ever thought about it that way."

"That's why you have me." He glances from his phone to his paperwork, unaware or unconcerned with his wife's current mood.

"It's good for me to interact with the family. It'll give me more insight on the children. I'll make certain not to eat any meat."

Alexander pierces her with his gaze. Her eyes drift to her untouched plate of food and she picks up the knife and fork. "This is good," she says triumphantly.

17

"Danny and Claire offer me a room in their house, but I feel I'm intruding. I get up and go to work with Danny the next morning. In that little spare time the rehab gave me, I read books on car repair. In theory, I can do anything that needs to be done. But besides changing oil or checking the water levels when I was a kid, I haven't done much to cars. I promise myself if he wants me to scrub the grease off the floor, I'll do it. He shows me around the garage, bigger than I imagined, three bays for mechanics, another with a paint station. Then he points out a couple of cars and tells me, 'go to town.'

Seems he picked up an old Judge, and a few others at a Police auction and they are all mine to do with whatever I want. I start right in on that Judge, plan to strip it and rebuild it from the frame up.

At first being out is scary. I'm afraid I'll misstep, run into someone, mess up, so I don't go anywhere, except where they go. I don't want Claire or Danny to worry about me the way I've made my parents worry most of my life.

One day, after work, I tell Claire in a nearly asking tone, that

I'd like to go over to the art school. I want to see if I can finish the last class or two and finally, after all these years, get my degree. Claire looks at me and, for a moment, I see my mom. I'm worried because I can't read the look: her eyebrows come to a peak above her nose, then flatten out and she blinks.

'What the hell, are you asking for my permission? You're a grown man. I think it's a great idea. Get your ass out and go.'

I laugh, and she laughs. So after work the next day, I go over and see the counselors. I have to make up the semester. This means, I have to work every day from 8 to 5 and spend the rest of the night at art school, 'plan to be here until 10pm every night, Mr. Rose.' The counselor looks at me like she doesn't think I'll make it a month, but it sounds like a dream. No more hours to myself! Right after work, I head straight over to art school. There is no time for me to get lost or think about anything else.

I love the work. It's nearly like lockdown. I'm kept busy from sunrise to sunset. I find myself local meetings and I find myself a local sponsor. I get up even earlier than Danny, so I can get in a meeting before work.

I ask Danny if I could have the old room in the back. Whatever this auto shop used to be, there's a little room in the back. It has a bathroom, but no shower, so I tell him I'll build a shower. And that's how I spend my weekends.

It's a plan. I like it. I live it.

I earn my degree, but no graduation ceremony, which I really don't mind. But Claire buys me a hat and takes a picture of me with them.

When school is done, I start working with the afterschool program, putting in more hours at the shop, I start working with the racers, painting their cars.

Claire and Danny think I'm working myself to death, but I tell them, it's all cool, just keeping busy.

I find my own place. A little place on a concrete plot that no one wants. It's two rooms and a bathroom. An old forgotten shop of some sort. No one wants to pay to make it livable. With Danny and Claire as co-signers, I put down a deposit. I spend my extra time making it livable.

One day, Claire asks me to go with her to pick up Tommy. 'In the spring,' she says, 'I'm going back to finish my education. I want you to pick up Tommy. So I want you to come with me a few times.'

I agree. They've done so much for me that I would do anything for them, and Tommy is my little heartsong. Love that little man so much that I could spend every day with him and never get tired of it.

Then I see the teacher. She's wearing a dress and dancing in the yard with the students. There will be some sort of show and the children will sing and dance, and she's practicing with them. The kids are all over the place; they can't remember the steps and they are messing up the song, but she just keeps smiling and keeps singing and putting the students back in line. As she's twirling, her hair is all free and loose, and she's got a smile that makes the sun want to rise.

Claire sees me gawking with a goofy look on my face.

'Uh hmm.' She fake clears her throat. 'She's married, Jack.'
I chuckle. 'Don't worry, I don't have the time or the inclination for a relationship.'

18

Spring Sundays in Huntington Beach are unpredictable in the best possible ways. The whole week might be hot, then Sunday will surprise residents by raining. A breezy week might be blessed with a stilled and sun filled seventh day. This particular Sunday seems intent on covering all bases. The numerous accidents on the 5 Freeway doubled the travel time, and Valerie reaches Nan near noon. The sun fades as she pulls into the parking lot and a light mist falls as Nan slides into the car. "Let's get movin', my dear. I'm starving."

Valerie leans over and kisses her cheek. "How was your week?"

"Drive first, talk later."

Their view at the restaurant overlooks the beach. Through the window, the waves crash furiously against the rocks and sand; the gray sky thickens as they order soup, bundles of bread, and hot tea.

"There is never a bad time for a good cup of tea." Nan holds the steaming cup to her lips.

"Think it'll storm?"

"Oh, no, it's just making threats. We don't allow storms down here in Huntington. We'll call the mayor! Get our lawyers involved." Nan drums her hand down on the table lightly.

Valerie laughs. It occurs to her why she likes Jack so much as she watches the ocean waves. Jack has the humor of her grandmother, the gentility of her father, and the positive energy of her college years.

"What's that smile for?" Nan winks.

"You are in rare form today, aren't you?"

"A little stir crazy, I think. Haven't done much lately. Tired."

Valerie reaches for her hand. "You okay? Everything okay?

Nan smiles softly as she watches her dear granddaughter across the table. What will happen to the poor girl when she's no longer around? "I'm old, honey."

"Not a day over 45, I'd say." The waiter returns with their bread and soup.

"Oh, someone's looking for a good tip. Keep talking like that honey boy and you'll get it too!"

Valerie turns red with laughter.

"Will there be anything else for the lovely ladies?"

"Oh, he's good." Nan chuckles.

"No, thank you."

Nan circles her spoon in her soup, lifts it to her mouth and blows. "Spill it." She blows on her soup again. "Usually you're full of stories; today, you're a little bit quiet."

"I'm letting you go, you're on a roll."

Nan curls her finger toward herself signaling for Valerie to speak.

"I dreamt of my father. He walked into my backyard and handed me a feather."

Nan pauses mid-spoon-to-mouth and smiles. "He was a sweet man."

"Then I woke up. There was a feather next to my glass and Alexander took it out of my hand and threw it away."

"He did not!"

"He scolded me like a child. I felt humiliated. We argued. He didn't come home until five a.m."

"About a feather?"

"No. He was married. When we were dating, he was married to someone else. I had no idea."

Nan drops the spoon in her bowl and shakes her head.

"The last couple of weeks…" Valerie pauses to gather her thoughts.

"Or years?" Nan gazes at Valerie sympathetically.

Valerie sips her tea, glances out over the ocean; her eyes become glassy.

Nan reaches across the table and takes her hand. "What are you thinking, my dear girl?"

Valerie sets her cup down. "I feel like I wasn't as upset as I should have been when he didn't come home. I need to have a talk with him. I didn't realize how many things I've left for him to do and decide."

Nan withdraws her hand, sips her soup from the spoon.

Valerie turns her attention back to the willowy woman. "You disagree."

"You can't blame yourself for the way he acts, honey. I hate to see you do that."

"I don't think I am. If I have an open conversation with him, he'll…" Valerie doesn't finish the sentence.

"Change?"

When Valerie hears it aloud, it doesn't sound quite right.

"Honey, I understand why you chose Alexander. He was smart and confident, he swept you off your feet and offered you a different life. These are not bad things, but if he's hurting you then you can't let him do that. That's not what people who love each other do to one another."

Valerie nods. "I'm going to talk to him, Nan. If he loves me, he'll understand that some things need to change."

Nan takes bread from the basket and dips it in her soup. "Eat, honey. The soup is good."

Valerie picks up her spoon and watches as the clouds begin to clear and a circle of light appears on the tumultuous waves.

"Told you, someone called the mayor."

Valerie smiles. Nan's always been able to cheer her.

The threatening storm has passed, and Nan's condo is bright and airy. The patio door stands open and a gentle breeze sifts through the sheer curtains. Valerie sits at the dining table and gazes around the room. It's seafoam green with touches of the beach everywhere. There's a painting of starfish on one wall, shells found on the beach on the shelf below. A mermaid figure on the opposite bookcase, and a picture of Valerie, her mom, dad, and Nan on the coffee table. Valerie is three with chubby legs. She sits on her dad's lap, next to her mother, with Nan behind them. They are at the beach sitting in folding chairs huddled under a sun umbrella.

Valerie moves to the couch to take a closer look at the photograph. It's faded with age, but the frame is new and snow white. She picks it up and studies it as Nan comes back in.

"Nan," she says, "who took this picture?"

"Your grandpa."

"Do you miss him?"

Nan nods slowly. "I talk to him nearly every day."

Valerie rests her head on Nan's shoulder.

"Valerie, I'm going to ask you something and I want you to be completely honest with me." Nan looks at Valerie's face. "Are you happy?"

Valerie is slow and thoughtful in her answer. "Not much right now," she says quietly.

"Your grandpa and I were friends during high school. He dated a lot of girls. Bad boy." She snickers as she pats Valerie's arm. "I was crazy about him, but I went out with other boys just so he didn't think I was waiting around for him. When he finally came around, I never let him get away with any silliness. We had our rows, but damn I loved that silly man."

Valerie smiles at Nan's memory. "Were Mom and Dad friends before they got married?"

"Don't get me started on them." Nan stands up. "Now, let's go for that walk you've been promising me." They get up and head to the beach on a hunt for more shells.

"Your dad pursued your momma. He felt they were meant to be together. But your mom felt she could do better. She went away to college for a year, dated the jocks and the brainiacs and became quite the social butterfly."

"Really, Mom did?" Valerie never thought of her mother that way. Her mother spent the last years of her life in a wheelchair. Her heart not strong enough to pump the blood to her extremities; her legs and arms too weak to support her.

"When she came home, she'd had enough of the big life as she put it. She signed up at the local college and gave in to your father. But, oh my goodness, she put him through the racks. Your father tried so hard."

Valerie remembers her father as a kind and gentle man who tried to make the people around him, his wife and daughter, happy.

"I think your Mom loved him from the very start. She just didn't know it or didn't want to admit it. Love scares some people. You know what I mean?"

Valerie nods.

"Honey, it doesn't matter where the people start or what ups and downs they go through. If they love each other, they want to make one another happy. And you have to be happy or your no good to anyone. Not yourself, not your kids." Nan leans down and picks up a shell, examines it and drops it in her bag.

"Like Mom, after Dad died." Valerie slips the bag from Nan's arm, watches Nan as she turns back toward the beach, the wind blowing her hair. Losing Nan scares her more than anything. Without Nan, she'd only have Alexander and that not only makes her sad, it frightens her.

When Nan turns back to her, Valerie forces a smile. They walk back to Nan's condo, wash the shells in the sink, and find places on the bookshelf and side table among her collection.

As Valerie drives home, she considers her wording to Alexander. He has always taken control, made decisions. His criticisms are new, hurtful. But, also, maybe she is changing, growing. She can explain this to Alexander. But will he listen and understand?

She's still deep in thought as the song on the radio fades into the voice of a news reporter: "Still no suspects in the high-speed race on Friday night in Santa Clarita which resulted in a vicious accident. Police are investigating this as an illegal street race. The car in question, flipped on its side, had modifications that street racers have been known to use."

Valerie's heart pounds. She nearly hyperventilates as she white knuckles the steering wheel.

19

Valerie welcomes the children at the kindergarten gate on Monday morning. She must see Tommy's face, Claire's countenance. If they show, their body language will tell her everything she needs to know. She has no way to get in touch with Jack, no phone number, no address. It would be inappropriate to ask the office for the family's records for personal information; they'd ask why she needed it. But she must know if he's alright.

It's the skip of the little blonde boy and his mother's smile which signals Valerie all is well. Had something serious happened, they may not have shown up. If Jack had been injured or worse, she'd be able to read it in their postures, their eyes; she's relieved as she greets them.

She's confident, when Thursday comes, Jack will reappear.

But Thursday, Claire arrives at the kindergarten door with Tommy at her side. Valerie's surprised as she walks toward the door. "Tommy forget something?"

Claire waves her hand, "Probably, you know kids. But I wanted to give you the information for Saturday. If you and your husband are able to come."

Valerie glances over the postcard with the address, date, and time.

"Nothing special, just family."

"Thank you. I'd love to come."

"Great!" Claire offers a genuine smile.

"My husband has a previous commitment."

Claire waves her hand again. "Don't worry. Jack'll keep Danny company and we girls will chat. It'll be nice to have another woman to talk to after hanging with those two. Cars, cars, cars. It's all they talk about."

Valerie chuckles.

"Uncle Jack is going to paint a Ninja Turtles car for me."

Valerie laughs. "Aren't you a little young to drive?"

"Yeah," Tommy nods his head in a big sweeping motion. "But he said he'll do it when I can drive, when Mom says yes. Mom has to say yes."

Claire smiles. "Someday, little guy. Someday a long time from now."

"Does Jack bore you with all his car stories?"

Valerie shakes her head. "No, saw some of the paint jobs he's done. Where is Jack today? Doesn't he usually pick up Tommy on Thursdays?"

Claire's face instantly changes as she draws her eyebrows together and her lips thin. "Oh, that brother of mine. I could just…." She glances at Tommy. "Uncle Jack hurt his knee helping someone…" she whispers the rest, "in a race!"

"He's okay?"

"He'll live. This time." Claire bites her lip.

"Unless Mom kills him for being naughty." Tommy's kicking his shoes into the floor.

Both of the women laugh.

"Where do they get such things?" Claire winks as she and Tommy turn to leave. "See you Saturday."

Valerie likes Claire. Their conversations have been few and

limited, but the petite woman is sweet and genuine. She and Danny work hard and want the best for Tommy. Tommy is confident and spirited, the signs of a well loved and well-adjusted child. Sometimes it's easy to tell when there is trouble in the family. The child acts out at school or becomes withdrawn. Valerie has even noticed that Tommy has calmed down and become more focused, which is a natural part of maturing through kindergarten for most children.

Valerie turns her attention back to the next five and half hours she'll have to herself. She spins around the class, checking desks and walls for any needed changes or cleaning. She sits down on one of the hard-wooden children's chairs, her knees up to her chest. An overwhelming loneliness catches her off guard and she swallows sadness. She feels the need to cry.

She shimmies her shoulders, trying to shake off the feeling. "Be happy," she whispers as she lifts and marches over to her desk to check her reminders: "Coffee. Dry cleaning." Her mind wanders to the empty guest room, half finished. New sheets, a comforter, shells. Valerie inhales and exhales deeply. Shopping can fill some of those empty hours.

Reclaiming the room, she moves Alexander's boxes to the still empty closet in his den. At the home store, she chose a Tiffany blue bedding-set because of its hint of seafoam green. It matches the Robin's Egg blue on the wall and will remind Nan of her own color scheme, making her feel more at home. She adds a shell sculpture and digs more of her books out of the boxes in the garage to make the shelf look fuller.

When she finishes, she sits on the bed, curls up her feet and calls Nan.

"Hi, honey!" Nan's excited voice pops through mid-ring.

"Hi, Nan. Do you want to come for a visit this weekend? The room is all made up and you can spend the night."

"Oh, honey, that's sweet of you, but I'm going to stay here this weekend. Is everything okay?"

"Yeah." Valerie grows quiet.

"What's wrong, my girl?"

"Just missing you today."

"Aw, my sweet girl. You're always in my thoughts and prayers. You could spend the weekend here. My guest room is for you and you alone, you know that."

She's only used it once or twice when Nan wasn't feeling well, much to Alexander's dismay.

"Yes, thank you, Nan." Valerie considers using it more often.

"See you Sunday."

"Yes." She stands up and backs out of the room; the room is bathed in an afternoon glow. With the creeping darkness gone, now it just feels lonely and unused.

Without much thought, Valerie orders dinner from one of Alexander's favorite local restaurants. Mahi Mahi with lemon and capers, asparagus, and white rice. Alexander's usually home by 6:30, no later than 7, unless he calls. By 7:30, no Alexander and no call, she re-packages the dinner, recorks the wine.

Valerie starts upstairs when she hears the hum of the garage door, then the kitchen entrance open and close. She stands in the entryway as he lifts the lid on the reboxed food before glancing up. "Looks good. I thought you might forget again."

"You usually call if you're going to be late."

He tilts his head to one side, examining her. "Late meeting." He pours himself a glass of white wine. "I was actually in the area today, stopped by to surprise you for a late lunch."

"What time did you come?" She re-enters the kitchen

"2. Don't you finish at 2?"

"Most days 2:30, but Thursdays it's 1:30. The kids get out early." She studies him. In all the time she has worked there, he has never stopped by. It was a chore to get him to the Gala last year and he refused to attend the Holiday Show, even when all the other spouses came. While he's familiar with her schedule in a general way, he's never expressed an interest in the specifics unless she had to run an errand for him, "Can you get to the copiers by 3? Pick up the dry cleaning before they close at 5?"

"That must be it." He sips his wine. "Mmm. Nice choice" He glances at the restaurant packaging again. "Don't you use that time to prep for the next day? Isn't that what the extra time is for, grading, paperwork, whatever else kindergarten teachers do?"

"Sometimes. I usually get in early and do most of it then. And I do have four other days a week to work as late as I need." She swallows. "Is something wrong?"

He chuckles and moves toward her, pulling her into his arms as he sets the wine down. "You are so cute." He kisses her head and searches her face. "I'm just wondering how my wife is spending her time these days." He's smiling, but there's a serious intent in his eyes. It unsettles Valerie. "You seem distracted lately. Forgetting dinner. Showing up to a cooking class in yoga pants. It's a little off."

"I only forgot dinner once," she says.

"Or twice." He backs off, leans against the island. "So, what did you do today that I couldn't find you?"

"Follow me." Valerie leads him to the guest room, pushes open the door.

He walks in all the way, picks up the shell sculpture from the shelf and holds it carelessly as he plants his eyes on her. For a moment, there's a look on his face as if he might crash the sculpture to the floor. He's not angry, but there's something in his countenance she finds alarming. "I get it now. My wife is readying for an unwelcome guest."

Valerie crosses her arms, tears trickle from her eyes. "Your wife is... lonely. I'm lonely." she simpers. "I don't have many friends. All I do is work and run errands for you."

Alexander's face drops into something near sympathy. He discards the sculpture onto the bed and beelines toward her, hugs her. "Aw, don't cry honey. We can find you more things to do and you can skip your nan's this weekend. We'll see my family. You should hang out with my sister, Patricia."

Valerie yanks herself from his arms. "I tell you I'm lonely and you want me to skip seeing my only living relative to befriend your sister who hates me?"

Alexander chuckles, "she doesn't hate you; she treats everyone like that."

"I'm going to see Nan." Valerie stands her ground, willing her tears to stop.

"On Sunday, we will have dinner with my family. If you want to see your Nan, go on Saturday."

She starts to protest, "the barbeque." But it occurs to her that he remembers, and that is what this is about. He wants to interrupt her plans.

"I'll go early on Sunday and be back in time for dinner."

"You can give up your nan for one Sunday. Come with me to my game, hang out with my friends, and then we'll go see my family. Fair is fair."

"Fair?" she asks without much conviction.

"You see your grandmother every week. How often do we see my family? Once a month? Once every other month? You can make this sacrifice. One day without your nan or go on Saturday."

Valerie crosses her arms. "Honey, we need to talk openly. I'm unhappy. Some of the things you say are hurtful."

Alexander rolls his eyes. "You knew who I was when you married me." He softens, reaches for her shoulders. "It is not my intention to be mean. I'm honest. You know this."

Valerie sighs out a breath. "But I don't think you need to be so harsh. You take away my croissant, insult my cooking."

"Do you want to be fat? Do you want me to lie to you and tell you your cooking is better than it actually is?"

She shakes her head, glances up at the ceiling. Her words are not coming out right. "It is my decision if I want to eat a croissant. And you seemed fine not telling me you were married."

He pulls away, tucks his hands in his pockets and fixes her with a glare. "I decide how my wife represents me. I married a slim woman for a reason."

Tears restain her cheeks. "We just need to talk openly." She tries to put her hands on his arms, and he backs away. "Marriage is a give and take. I need you to give me some space, give me..."

He snorts. "I've given you more than you've ever had."

"Why were you late tonight?" Her voice shakes. "Why did you decide to make me wait without calling?"

"Don't question me," he sneers.

Valerie cries. "I am trying to have a conversation with you. I'm trying to solve some problems. Please help me."

Alexander turns in place, feeling trapped. They still stand in the beige hallway, stairs to one side, guest room to another, kitchen behind her. "In the hallway? Problems are not solved by arguing in a hallway. And you do need help, that is clear. I'm going to make an appointment with a psychologist for you."

He moves around her to go to the kitchen. Valerie's cries turn to sobs. Her chest aches, stomach knotted. She doesn't know if she should follow him, but when he reaches for his phone with his back to her, she knows the conversation is over.

She locks herself in the upstairs bathroom, fills the tub with water and Jasmine Surrender. By the time she climbs in, her sobs have subsided to whimpers. The light disappears from the window frame, her skin wrinkles and prunes, and the water grows cold. Small noises move outside the door. The bedroom light flickers under the door, then scurries away.

She hears Alexander's soft snores as she opens the bathroom door. They'll get louder the longer he sleeps. They'll peak about two a.m., before he mumbles himself into a new position. The even breathing will return. She slips downstairs, makes herself a cup of tea. The yard is bathed in moonlight. Something about the quiet beauty is haunting. A movement on the back wall catches her attention, a rat scurries into the shadows. She shivers.

20

"Street racing is another way of feeding my addiction. I figure that out too late. When I lose control, the car spins, and flips, and I panic, trying to undo the belt. My kids are there, the teens I mentor, my friends; I thank the powers that be that V is not. It's a terrible thing to watch someone you love die, can't let that happen to her.

And it's fine in theory, when I make her go home just in case something happens; I always think nothing's going to happen. In the years I've been racing, only one or two people were hurt, and no one died.

But this car's flipped. I'm stuck with the seat belt cutting into my groin, and I can't get out. One of the kids crawls in with a knife.

'Get outta here,' I yell. I can smell the gas leaking and I won't be responsible for anyone else's death, especially a kid.

He hands me the knife and backs out. I can't hear anything, even though I know people are shouting at me.

I cut the belt and writhe out. I get far enough away, and the kids help me up.

'My car!' the owner screams. He paid me a good amount because he knows I win. But shit happens, and he knows that too.

'Look, we're not going to be able to move it before the cops get here. Get your girlfriend, go home, get your pjs on, check the movie listings on tv. When the cops show up, you tell 'em you watched the movie, went to bed, and your car is on the street. Take 'em out, and when you can't find it, lose your mind.' He knows the drill. Cops aren't fooled, but they got nothing on him.

'Shit, shit, shit!' he screams.

'Dude, you hear me?' I grab his shoulders, give 'em a shake to make him focus. 'Hearin' me, man?'

He nods, grabs his girl, and they are gone.

'You kids, too, out. Home. No one was here.' Most of them skate.

My leg's cut up and my hip is killing me.

'What about you?' Bryan waits. He's one of the kids I scooped up; he was heading straight for juvi, but I got him straight, got him to help me out in the garage, and his friends too.

'Help me to my car.'

Bryan and Shelly take to each side like crutches, walk me down to my old Pontiac Judge. Their own ride is just a block away; they scurry to it.

I sit there for a moment. The street is empty now. It's past midnight. The sirens blazin' in the distance. And I think of V. Had I not gotten out, everyone would've left. There'd be me and the overturned car on an empty street, hell and gone from any help.

I decide then and there the high I get from street racing is not worth it. It's not worth losing my life and definitely not worth losing V or worse. I pause my panic, push down the anxiety.

I try to imagine how she'd find out. If I died, maybe she'd never know how I felt. I try not to let that thought settle. But I do think about it and think about her. I keep telling myself we're only friends. Friends. Friends. I drive that into my skull. Getting involved with a married woman was not my plan and it's not good for my sobriety. But I can't let her go.

I can still bring the business to Danny and not be one of the street racers. Stay far away. Sometimes they ask me to come watch how their car performs so I know what modifications it might need, but that just gets me going and my body wants behind that wheel. I'll have to put my foot down, have to say no.

Maybe I need to do that with V, too. But I can't. Nothing's happened, I think as I picture the way I held her that night. Pulled her in my arms and didn't want to let her go, smelt the sweet scent of Jasmine on her skin, coconut on her hair, saw the way the moonlight hit her eyes and for a moment, stars sparkled in them. We can be friends, I tell myself. I can do that.

I drive home, peel off the jeans, wipe the blood from my leg.

Put a hot towel on it. No meds. All roads lead to drugs.

Spend the rest of the weekend at Danny's, can't be alone with all thoughts and no movement; those pathways in my brain that lead to trouble start pounding like they're hungry. And if bad things gonna happen, I gotta plan to stay clean.

Claire takes care of me, bandages, antiseptic, ice. She's not too gentle either. She's mad. She tapes me up, drops an ice pack on my knee.

'Damn, Woman,' I say.

'Oh, did that hurt?' She sneers at me, bumps my leg on purpose as she walks away.

I jump in pain again. 'Come on, Claire,' I chuckle. 'Girl, gimme a break here.'

'Going to race again? Are you?' She comes back at me. 'Learned your lesson yet?'

'Learned, Woman, learned. I'm out!' I raise my hands in surrender.

Claire walks into the kitchen, puts the first aid kit away.

'That's one mean woman you got there,' I look over at Danny who's sitting in his easy chair watching all this go down.

'Better quit while you're ahead.' He glances up, makes certain Claire's not in hearing distance. 'Your lady there?'

'No.' I whisper. 'She stopped... I showed her and made her

leave.'

Danny knows. He knows a little. He sees me come in every day, happier and happier, knows something's going on. I tell him it's just a lady friend, as in friend, but he guesses there might be more. We don't mention any names, but he figures that out too when Fridays come and I'm acting like a goof and he hears me say, Tommy, V, and I did this, or we went here. He's on to me.

Claire returns with some juice, slides it across the coffee table next to where my leg rests. I watch her slow and cautious like, afraid she's going to hit my leg again. 'Who you guys talking about?'

'No one.'

Claire looks at me, leans over close to my leg.

'What?' She stares at me steely eyed. The woman is all kinds of mad at me.

'Honey,' Danny tries to call her off.

'You're not allowed to talk right now.' She points at him. 'What is going on? Who are you guys talking about?'

Neither of us say a thing. She reaches over to me, tries to grab my phone. I hold on to it, then she smacks my leg and grabs it out of my hand when I recoil in pain.

'Oh my god,' I yell. 'You are one mean…'

She looks at me, points her finger.

'Beautiful, loving creature,' I change my tone.

Danny nods behind her. Raises his eyebrows.

Claire's searching my phone. She sees a picture I took of Tommy, V, and I at the duck pond; she raises her head slow, looking at me like she's going to leap over the coffee table at me.

'Honey,' Danny stands up. 'Honey, calm down. It's not our business.'

'Tommy's teacher?!'

I lift my leg off the table and move it away from her, I cover my head and look through my arms. She's going to kill me. The whole time I'm laughin'. I'm stiff and in so much pain, I can't do anything else but laugh. The woman is gonna kill me. And then her husband.

'Wait, wait,' I say. 'Please.' I'm holding my hands up between her and me because she has my phone and I'm pretty sure she's aiming for my head. 'We're just friends. I swear. Just friends. We've hung out with Tommy between us the whole time. I swear, Sis.'

I don't offer that I brought her to the races. I've put the woman through enough.

'She's married, you know?!'

'Absolutely. Nothing else happening. Being straight with ya. She's just a really nice person.'

Claire sits down, looks at the picture and smiles at Tommy's round little face between V and me. 'You swear? Nothing else?' I point to the pictures, tell her to check my messages, none. 'She is really sweet.' She hands my phone back to me.

There's a lot that night that I don't say to my sister. I gotta sit with my feelings. I gotta talk to my sponsor. I gotta get to a meeting. And most of all, I gotta get my head straight before I mess up the last three and a half years and end up back in prison for screwing up my probation. Tonight would've done it. Had I been caught out there in that car, would have been sitting in front of that judge again and it would not have been a happy reunion.

I push my head back on the couch, count my blessings. Claire. Danny. Tommy. That judge. 3 years, 6 months, 22 days. V.

And I take a deep breath, blow it out nice and slow and close my eyes.

21

There's a thing married couples do after an argument where nothing gets solved. Sometimes each sees the need for another less heated conversation; they make up and move forward. Some couples move around like the other is not there, as if they are ghosts existing on different planes. Others, sooner or later, pretend it never happened, and life begins, not anew, but again.

They move through Friday somewhere between ghosts and again. He kisses her in the morning, and she prepares his pre-made dinner in the evening. On Saturday, she leaves while he is jogging, not in an effort to sneak out like a coward, but with no plans to attend the cooking class. She's given up on that one, but she'll have coffee at a local shop and buy something to take to Danny and Claire's barbeque.

She suspects Alexander will be ready to make up tonight. It's Saturday. She will have been gone all day and he will be waiting with dinner, wine, and then their usual Saturday night sex. She jitters nervously at the thought. He'd been so rough last time, she ached for a week.

By the time the farmer's market is beginning to close, Valerie hustles to the bakery for a Dutch apple pie and half dozen cupcakes; kids, she thinks, will appreciate the handheld prize of a blue coated, cookie monster inspired sweet rather than a slice of the more adult dessert.

"Danny, you remember Ms. V,"

"Valerie," she offers as she shakes his hand.

"And this is our neighbor, Harris. His little girl, Anna, is running around here somewhere with Tommy."

Jack's absence looms large as she takes the seat opposite the men.

"Lemonade? tea? something stronger?" Claire points to the bar where pitchers of lemonade and iced tea sweat next to a bottle of wine.

"Lemonade is fine. Thank you."

Danny leans over and pushes the chips and dip toward her. "Jack made the dip, it's super spicy, be careful. He thinks jalapenos are too mild, so he threw in a habanero."

"Don't tell lies," Jack appears through the patio door, limping. "It's a serrano, not a habanero. Two completely different peppers. This man," Jack makes eye contact with V as he tilts his head toward Danny, "just can't handle a little heat." He leans over and half hugs Valerie as he sits next to her. "Good to see ya." He passes the lemonade from Claire to Valerie as Claire pulls a chair closer.

"You okay?" The day suddenly seems brighter as Valerie motions to his leg.

Jack starts to nod and opens his mouth to speak, but Claire interrupts. "Oh, you haven't seen him, have you? You know what this numbskull did?"

Jack turns to Claire, "Tommy's playing trampoline on your bed."

"And you didn't stop him?"

"Did I ever stop you when we were kids?"

Successfully sidelined, Claire slaps his bad leg and jumps up. Jack cringes then laughs, "It barely hurt," he calls behind her as she runs into the house.

"You better stop messing with her Jack, she's going to get you good." Danny chuckles.

Harris picks up his drink. "You racing, Jack?"

"Street racing is illegal, and I'm a good boy," Jack smiles before he turns to Valerie. "I may have gotten a little injured in a car accident which may or may not have happened around some other people who may or may not have been involved in some sort of race which I know nothing about." He winks. Then he leans in and whispers. "That was my last race, hand to..." he raises his hand, looks up, down, and at the empty chair to his left and smiles to himself.

Tommy and Anna dart for the pool, cherry bomb into it. Claire raises her arms, then shakes her head as the water splashes over the edge. She sits, eyes shifting from the kids to Jack. "If he even thinks about doing it again, he's toast. I'm going to throw his body on that grill right over there."

"Yes, Ma'am." Jack leans over to Claire and kisses her cheek. "Promise, Sis. I'm done. Love you."

"I don't know how you do it Valerie." Clare watches the kids as they get out and jump back in.

Valerie smiles, "Do what?"

"Twenty little Tommies every day all day."

"That's quite an accomplishment," Harris follows up. "One afternoon with Anna and I'm napping on the couch before dinner."

The day is typical for spring north of Los Angeles, warm and bright. The scent of orange blossoms waft through their yard; the patio cover is trellis-like and topped in new growths of pink and white jasmine. When the breeze billows by, an occasional bloom falls around them. Shade trees surround their pool, a weeping willow on one side, an old weeping cherry tree on the other. The scene is exquisite, Valerie thinks.

"It's not all day, only six or seven hours, and I have help."

"You have one aide!" Claire laughs. "I can barely handle one child."

"She has a gift." Jack gazes at her admiringly.

"I don't know about that. I think it's easier when they're in a pack," Valerie chuckles.

"Do you want your own some day?" Claire leans in.

"I do, someday." She feels, for the first time in a long time, that she is being listened to. "I love kids. The kindergarteners are fun, and kids are all different; some whine, some scream, got the shy ones and the energetic ones."

"Yep, there's Tommy!" Danny interjects.

"But it doesn't turn you off?" Harris asks. "I have a friend who's a teacher. After a few years, she said, no way!"

"They are so excited about learning something new. When they finally can sing that whole ABC song, or draw a butterfly, their eyes light up. Pure joy. I definitely want the opportunity to see my own child light up like that. And one of the best things," she adds quietly, "they don't worry. You know what I mean? They're not worried about passing or failing, they're not worried about first grade or Christmas. They live every day…"

"In the now," Jack finishes the sentence with her.

"Yes." She points at Jack.

"Jack?" Harris calls, "You?"

"Me. Oh, yeah, I want like ten!"

"May they all look like your wife!" Harris jokes.

Danny lifts his glass and says, "Now there's something we can agree on."

Laughter fills the yard, rounds back and hangs onto the flowers above their heads.

"I'm going to get the grill started here." Danny excuses himself and Harris follows.

"Do you want more?" Valerie asks Claire.

Claire's eyes track the kids around the pool. "Maybe someday, after I finish school."

"Is that why Jack picks up Tommy some days?"

Jack sits up, "Didn't I tell ya? She's finally finishing her degree.

I'm so proud."

Claire blushes. "I guess we both took the scenic route. Tommy! Anna! There's towels." She pulls out her phone and flips through it. She turns it toward Valerie and Jack.

"No. No." Jack tries to push the phone away, but Valerie sees the photo of him in a graduation cap standing between Claire and Danny. "Put that goofy picture away," Jack blushes.

"You should be proud," Valerie says.

"Time to go help with the grill before that man of yours burns everything." He limps over to the radio playing soft music near Danny and Harris, he turns the station, and then clicks the volume up; Louis Armstrong's "What a Wonderful World" competes with their chatter.

Claire smiles. "He gets so embarrassed, but he should be proud. He worked hard for that."

Valerie feels welcomed, included. "You both should be proud of the work you put in. And you have that gorgeous little boy, a beautiful family. That's quite an accomplishment all on its own."

Claire eyes Tommy. "Being a mom is pretty amazing. Exhausting," she turns back to Valerie, "but amazing."

Tommy is in the middle of the pool when he first sees Ms. V. He squeals and launches himself through the water, climbs the clacking aluminum steps, and runs, dripping wet, to throw his body toward Valerie.

"No running." Claire calls. "Towels!" Claire tries to catch him.

"I'm so sorry."

Valerie leans forward and hugs him.

"Tommy, you're getting Ms. V all wet." Jack calls over the grill.

Danny hustles the towels over, wrapping Tommy in one and handing the other to Valerie.

"It's perfectly fine."

Claire ushers Tommy into the house to dry him off as Harris follows with Anna. Danny moves back to the grill, playfully nudging Jack out of the way. They jokingly argue about who is burning what before Jack turns to Valerie. "Come on over in the sunshine," he calls. "You'll dry faster over here."

He changes the radio station while he and Danny have another exchange, "you don't know music,"

"Me? you're the one that's tone deaf."

"Oh, no, here we go!" Danny backs away from the radio, his hands in mock surrender to Jack's choice.

Hozier's deep throated, bluesy tune plays as Jack reaches for Valerie's hand, "Don't listen to him, V. This is the best music in the world." He places his hand around her waist, "May I have this dance?" And while he and Valerie fall into a natural rhythm with their bodies next to one another, Jack calls to Danny. "Grab your old lady and get out on the dance floor."

When Claire returns, Danny drops the spatula and pulls her to him for a dance. Valerie and Claire laugh as the men spin them around.

"Look at him, Dan's got some moves," Jack says.

Tommy appears and runs toward the pool; Claire breaks away to stop him.

Jack watches V seemingly enjoy the activity. Tommy struggles with Claire, Anna rushes out of the door, cupcake in hand, laughing devilishly as Harris chases after her.

"Cupcakes?!" Tommy gives up the struggle for the pool and races back to the house.

Valerie turns back to Jack. It's nearly like De Ja' Vu: Dancing with her father. The high school play. Singing with her friends at 2am next to a closed dorm pool. Being here with Jack feels like all the best times she's missed so much. She feels more at home in this moment than she's felt in a long time.

Sweat glistens down her face and pauses on the side of her mouth, her lip trembles. Jack hasn't stopped gazing at her. He's found something in her arms. The music's playing, the scent of jasmine surrounding him, and that bead of sweat working a trail from her cheek to her lips. He feels her gentle intake of air. So much of his life was lost, wasted; he doesn't want to lose anymore, doesn't want to miss one more minute of bliss. "Can I..." he begins to whisper, but a shadow falls over them. Their dance stops mid-step. Jack's head snaps to the man who stands strong and straight, an inch or two taller than he.

Jack releases Valerie straightens his spine, and shoves his hand out. "Dad."

Valerie notices the resemblance. Thicker, older, with a serious countenance.

Although it seems the whole place goes quiet, the kids run and scream, Harris chases them, and the music plays. Claire stands apprehensively in the background, and Danny closes in to say something.

His father glances from Jack to Valerie and back again. "Street racing, more tattoos, and I'm guessing that's not your ring on her finger."

"Dad!" Claire gasps from behind him.

"You're batting a hundred, still, huh?"

Jack drops his hand. "Sorry, V, Danny," Jack edges around his father, offering a quick hug to his sister before he disappears.

"No, Jack, wait. Dad!"

"Dad," Danny says, "This is Tommy's teacher, Ms. V."

Valerie watches the older man's face shift slowly from anger to regret and moves away before he can offer an apology. She pauses near Claire, "Thank you for the invite."

"I am so sorry," Claire sounds out. "I am so sorry."

Jack's Judge purrs to life. His face stiff with sadness. His phone in one hand, gear shift in the other. Valerie opens the passenger door and slips in.

"Are you okay?"

"I'm sorry for that. My dad..." He's embarrassed, averts his gaze.

"Forget about that. Are you okay?"

He shakes his head, grips his cell phone. "I've called..." he faces her now. "I've tried my sponsor. I'm sure he'll get back to me."

"Can I stay with you until he does?" The pain in his eyes, the sallow look of his skin, she's worried for him.

Jack half smiles. "You don't have to." But it would help.

"I want to. You've listened to me a lot. You've been a real friend and I want to be that for you." She reaches out and touches his wrist.

Jack nods. "Okay, follow me. I need to get out of here."

Jack's place is a small building surrounded by a slab of concrete. Wood and tools to one side brag that it's a work in progress. There's a semi-circle of fresh dirt in front of a big window, a rose bush in a nursery container next to it. He stands in the open door, keys dangling from his fingers as she pulls her car in.

"I hope this is okay," he says as she approaches. "I didn't want to go out anywhere."

The place is small but clean. He has a small kitchenette and a table, his bed occupies what might have been considered the living room, a hall between the two leads to a bathroom and a view of paints and easel awash in natural light.

"I'm sorry, I wasn't… I don't usually have company. It's just me here." He releases a small nervous laugh before he starts to limp back toward the kitchen.

"What do you need?"

"There's an ice pack." He points to the freezer, lowers himself to his bed.

Valerie grabs the ice and places it gently on his knee as he pulls himself further onto the bed. "Here?" He nods and moves it slightly to the side.

"You're a lot gentler than Claire. That girl wanted to kick my butt clear into next week."

Valerie glances around the room, bed made, books line his dresser top, a dog-eared *Dante's Inferno,* a well-read *Modern Philosophy,* and a curled *Twelve Steps on Buddha's Path,* sit next to a small painting of a woman and a larger water color drawing of a wooden chair taped to the wall behind.

"But I'm done with it," he adds. "For real. I realized that it's just far too dangerous and I'd rather have..." he pauses, "other things in my life."

He takes a deep breath, touches her hand. "So sorry about my father. We ..." he pauses. He doesn't lie these days. Lying is a step away from using - at least that's the way it works in his brain. "We haven't talked since I got into trouble, since before then. I totally get it. I was such a bad kid for so long, he doesn't want to trust me. He has every right to be upset with me. But he shouldn't have taken it out on you."

"He was confused."

Jack shakes his head. "Maybe."

"He wasn't taking it out on me, he was just..."

"MAD!" Jack chuckles to lighten the mood.

"You didn't know he was going to be there?"

"I think Claire was trying to work some reunion magic. He's not ready." Jack looks thoughtful. "I have to accept that. He'll come around someday."

Valerie watches him as he speaks. She considers her own situation, accepting things she cannot change. "I'm sure he will." Valerie's words bring a smile to Jack's face.

"You are just a bright little star."

She tilts her head. "Not everyone thinks so." She glances back to the painting. "Is that your mother?"

"Ah, yeah. My mom. She was such an angel. It's not finished yet. Not sure I'll ever be able to capture her..."

"Her spirit?" Valerie finishes.

Jack stares at Valerie.

"And what's that?" Valerie points to the watercolor of the plain brown chair.

"It's a reminder of sorts." Jack thinks about his one-time friend Kiao talking about higher powers. "There's this philosopher who had a theory that we have all this knowledge before we were born, but we become confused in life, we make mistakes. Everything, he says, has an essence and a purpose. I thought it was a nice way to look at the human experience; we all make mistakes, and we all have an essence and a purpose. This human experience is all about learning and growing back into our full body of knowledge."

The thought circles them, leans them closer together as they study the simple picture of the complex idea. So much of life seems the same. So simple at first, then the complexity of the building, the understanding, the use.

"That's nice," her voice drops to a whisper as if anything louder will disturb the space.

The ice pack slips and they both reach for it, Jack pushes up from leaning back, rubs his hand up and down her arm, barely touching her skin. "Thank you for coming. It helps." He is breathy desire, squeezing his eyes closed and open again. Gratitude, he thinks. Thank you for your friendship, thank you for your presence. The waves of desire press against the winds of reality.

His touch is soft and gentle. Goosebumps raise on her neck, a desirous giggle trapped in her throat. Need fills those empty spaces within her, pinch at those lonely places. She inhales a hum, a long and slow exhale as she moves into his touch. A little tenderness won't hurt anyone.

When she turns to his face again, it is nearer hers. The swipe of his hot breath slides down her cheek, down the front of her dress, she turns into him, faint puffs of air reach his chin, his lips, and his lips part, start to speak, but his breath is lost. She watches his lips as he clears his throat, form the words, the question she knows he will ask, she wills him to ask.

He touches her face, "Can I.."

Her hand lifts to his unshaven face. She touches her lips to his; the kiss is unbruised gardenia petals. He sways her in gently.

*

The western sun lazes in the sky, warming the room with an aurelian glow as they settle in each other's arms, Nina Simone's booming voice radiates in bold acoustics from Jack's phone. He caresses her arm; she breathes in, reaches up to take his hand in hers, and cuddles into him.

"The light in this room is perfect."

Jack's voice is low and clear. "The morning light wraps around the window frame, gets me up and moving. The sunset is a bonus. When I bought this place, it was two rooms, one window over near the kitchen. I added the room in the back for painting and, because it needed more light, put all these windows in. Natural light makes you feel alive."

Valerie stretches up and kisses him.

"I know it doesn't look like much, but it's a good place to start."

Valerie reluctantly begins to unwind herself. She decided at some point not to go home tonight. Although she'd deny it's guilt, her reasoning is uncertain. She'll go to Nan's. "Will you be okay?"

"I am very good." His phone's blue light blinks, security in a message reminder. He'll respond to his sponsor who will be waiting, explain how life just got better and worse at the same time.

In the last remnants of sunset, they linger in a hug before she sinks into the car and hauls herself down the street, pausing at the corner. Jack waves from his doorway.

The freeway leads her to the safety of her grandmother's. When she arrives, she calls Alexander. He sends it to voicemail, his digital silent treatment.

"Alexander, I'm at Nan's. I'm going to spend the night here." She pauses, considers an apology or a proclamation of love, but clicks end call.

Knocking lightly at Nan's door, she doesn't expect an answer. She uses her key and tiptoes in. An owl night light glimmers near the sink; a sing songy television commercial leads her to the hall. "Nan," she calls softly so as to not frighten her.

"Valerie?" Nan throws her legs over the bed and grabs her robe.

"Did I wake you?" Valerie's eyes tear up as soon as she sees Nan's concern.

"Heavens, Honey, what's wrong? Are you okay?"

"Yes."

Nan holds her arms open and Valerie rushes into them.

"My poor, poor girl. Let's get us some tea and talk it out."

"No, no, Nan. You need your rest."

"I'll rest when I'm dead. Right now, I want to be with you."

22

Dark clouds rake the skies, threatening a spring rain to remember. Home is empty and cold when she arrives. Although she's early enough for the planned dinner at his parents' house, he has vacated without her.

She rummages through the refrigerator. Near empty. She didn't do the shopping; he didn't prepare meals.

She dips into a bath thinking of Jack, his gentle touch, the scent of his skin. The door opens, she jumps with surprise as Alexander walks in. A nervous exhale escapes her lips. "You scared me."

Alexander relaxes against the sink, crosses his arms. "Didn't mean to." They stare at each other for a long moment. She breaks the gaze and drops her eyes to the tub of cooling bubbles. Guilt nips at her.

"You seem relaxed," he offers.

"So do you."

He nods. "Seems like we needed a break."

She shoots him a glimmer of a smile.

"It's okay, honey. Sometimes, married people need a little

space. But we do need to talk, don't we?"

She kicks the nipping at her toes away and pushes herself up. "Yes," her voice whispers into the evaporating bubble bath.

Alexander tugs the towel from the rack, moves it closer to her. "I'll start the meal prep, you come down when you're ready."

The nip of guilt has turned into a gnaw in her gut as she descends the steps; meat is cooking on the stove, vegetables sliced on the cutting board. "You did the shopping."

"Someone's..." the thought catches before it escapes his lips. He must be constructive tonight. Win her over.

"Want to help?" Besides washing the vegetables, he hasn't asked her to help in the preparation. "I thought, maybe" he shoots a glance over to her, "you could learn from me, since you don't like the class."

She steps closer to him. He's wearing a t-shirt, apron over his khakis. He's beautiful like this, muscles rippling over his creations. "I have a confession to make."

He smiles knowingly. "The chef called," he glances up, before pointing to a dish.

"What..." her voice is lost in repressed panic as she hands him the clear glass dish she will stick into the oven at some point this week.

He watches the discomfort rise, her cheeks blush. He waits a minute longer, let her wonder. "She said you hadn't attended and mentioned that you were seen at the farmer's market with a man."

"How..." The word and breath sticks in her throat.

He chuckles. "I paid for the class. She must have seen us, didn't realize I was your husband."

"Yeah," her voice shakes.

"So, no more cooking class," he launches in. "That will make you happy, yes?"

"It's not that I don't want to learn to cook. That class was not the right fit." It sounds right, but somehow it still feels like a lie.

"What else?"

"I want to make some of my own decisions, and I want you to

not criticize me."

He pauses his preparation and fixes her with his eyes, that single eyebrow on the brink of raising. "Criticize? Suddenly, you are taking my efforts to improve our lives personally. I have only ever tried to give you what you wanted."

Her mouth opens and closes, opens again, closes again. She watches that brow as it relaxes in place, but her voice is gone; her thoughts a mass of crossed wires which doesn't allow a clear sentence to come out.

"I allowed you to decorate that room in that wretched color," he attempts a chuckle, which feels false. "Honey, a marriage is two people working together toward a common goal. There are bound to be little glitches here and there. We work through them. Yes?"

Her head dips forward, again she opens her mouth to speak.

"We wanted a nice, quiet life, yes? Haven't I attempted to give that to you? I ask for small things in return."

He glances up, points to another serving dish, which she will place in the oven at 350 degrees on another night of the week.

"We have a good life, don't we? I want you to look pretty for my events. Not that you don't any other time." He smiles at her, eyes the drying waves of her hair hanging over her robe, the sun kissed nose and forehead. "You're beautiful, honey, all the time. Maybe I don't tell you that enough."

A smile unconsciously graces her face.

"There must be give and take in every marriage. I give you as much as I can. I would greatly appreciate it if you don't go running off to your grandmother's when you're upset with me. Can we agree on that? We must talk it out, not run away."

Valerie hands him another dish, then another. The words waiting on her tongue become small and insignificant. Her complaints, somehow, seem petty. Alexander seems so reasonable. He gives her so much and asks little in return. The unhappiness mixes with guilt and thickens in her throat. Her eyes become moist. Maybe it's her, maybe there's something very wrong in her.

"This is nice." He washes his hands, dries them on the nearby towel. "It feels good. We should cook together more often." He wraps her in his arms and hugs her long and hard, like he used to, like he hasn't in a long time.

"Saturday is our company party. I want to buy you a new dress. Sunday is Mother's Day. I'd like us to have dinner with my family."

"But…" She releases her arms, wants to see his face, but he holds his hand to her head, looking over her shoulder.

"Honey, see, this is what I mean. You're being just a little bit selfish. You saw your grandmother this week. We spend, what, one day a month with my family? Doesn't my mother deserve to have her whole family there too?" He releases her and the space between their body chills as he pushes her hair behind her shoulders, kisses her lips. "Your Nan didn't raise you to be selfish, honey, did she? She will understand."

Valerie nods. Nan would never ask her to choose. Nan was and is always selfless.

23

Big round raindrops pour down most of the day. The kindergarteners are rambunctiously stir crazy and can barely sit for their afternoon song. Today, the parents arrive at the door with umbrellas and the children rush out. Claire waits until the parents are gone and steps in the classroom as Jenny says goodbye.

"Ms. V." Claire reaches for Valerie's arm. "I am so sorry about my father. He was terribly embarrassed."

Valerie shakes her head. "It's really alright, family stuff is…"

"Messy! Let me tell ya! Can I make it up to you sometime with a coffee, no brothers, no fathers, just us?"

Valerie smiles. It's obvious Claire knows nothing about her and Jack. "I'd like that."

Watching Claire work her way out into the rain, Tommy splashing in every puddle, she sits down, puts her feet up. Rainy days are exhausting. The children are stuck inside. Even though the teachers rotate the auditorium, the library, and music room, the kindergarteners have a lot of energy and no place to run it off.

There are wet paper towels in every corner, muddy footprints on chairs, and handprints on the walls.

"Straight jacket?" Lucy pokes her head in, shaking off her umbrella before folding it up and hanging it on the doorknob.

"Does it come with a foot rub?" Valerie laughs. "I sincerely think I can't move."

Lucy leans on a nearby desk. "They are wild on days like this. I hope it doesn't rain tomorrow."

"I might call in sick."

"Me, too. Let's play hooky and go to the mall like teenagers." Lucy lifts herself to sit on the desk.

"No gala planning today?"

"Not today, almost finished now. We can get back to our Thursday coffee dates."

"Sounds incredible," she muses. How much has changed in just a few months. She has no idea where she'll be on Thursday. Will there be a Jack by Thursday?

"How's things?" Lucy inquires.

"Just crazy." Valerie minimizes the truth with a chuckle. She doesn't have the energy or the confidence to confide in Lucy. They are work friends. Coffees on Thursdays, an occasional movie on a Saturday afternoon. Lucy warned her about being seen with "a father", warned her of the school ethics.

Lucy nods as if she understands. "Fight?"

"More than one." Valerie leans forward.

"Alexander called me Saturday, looking for you."

Valerie is suddenly alarmed. But then, calms herself. He wouldn't say anything which might be interpreted poorly. He has an image to uphold. "Saturday? I was…"

"Saturday night, not too late."

"I was at my grandmother's. He…I thought he knew that. He didn't even call me."

"It felt as if he was looking for information. Asked me if we were meeting for coffee on Thursdays."

"I always tell him where I am."

"I thought maybe he was wondering about that father you've

been seen with, like maybe word got back to him?"

Valerie shakes her head. "That's not…" she stumbles over her words and gazes earnestly at Lucy. "I'm sorry he called you. That must have felt awkward."

"Not to worry. Nothing my husband wouldn't have done if he was worried. You doing okay though? You know you can call me if you need anything."

Valerie stands up and hugs Lucy. "Thank you. I think I'm going to go home and soak in a nice hot bath with a warm cup of soup and make an early night of it."

"That sounds like heaven."

Valerie spends a few minutes cleaning and heads out toward her car. The rain has paused,
but the low hanging clouds threaten more. As she approaches her car, Jack's Judge pulls in the empty spot next to her.

"Hello," he smiles, climbs out of the car. "I didn't have your number, and there's some sort of two-day rule."

"Two-day rule?"

He reaches inside the car, pulls out a single rose. "It's been awhile, so I'm not sure of the rules, but my kids tell me it's important to call or text within two days or I've committed some sort of unforgivable sin."

Valerie smiles, takes the rose, glances across the parking lot at a few teachers who have paused in their doorways.

"Jack, can we go somewhere?"

Jack follows her gaze. "You name it."

"Some place…" She thinks coffee shop, park - all public places where they might be seen. "Private?"

"I won't assume, but you are welcome at my place any time."

"I'll meet you there." She touches his arm. After he drives away, she turns in the opposite direction.

When she arrives at Jack's, he's waiting with a cup of steaming tea.

"May I?" He opens his arms for a hug.

She moves in for the much needed embrace and raises her

head for a deep kiss. When they take a breath, she says, "Jack, we have to talk."

He takes a step back, offers her the made bed, while he stands, crosses his arms and waits for her to start.

But she says nothing at all.

"May I start?" Jack asks. "Thank you for being so warm and being there for me the other day. I feel like," he exhales a light chuckle, "you saved my life. Stuff with my dad runs deep, and I wasn't in a good place. Thanks for staying with me. And I hope you have no regrets, but..." he runs his hand over his unshaven face. "I will never make trouble for you. Whatever you decide from here on out, I'm on board. You're a special person, V." He reaches out and takes her hand.

Valerie inhales, bites her lip and stares at him. She starts to speak, but her voice cracks and tears trickle down her cheeks.

"May I?" He sits next to her, pulls her into his arms and rubs her back while her tears turn to cries. "It's okay. Whatever it is, it will be okay."

When she recovers enough to move her head from his shoulder, he reaches to his dresser for a tissue.

"I'm just not sure... I don't know..."

"V, it's okay. You don't have to know anything right now."

One hand on her back, he rubs lightly in small round circles. He reaches for the tea she set down and hands it to her. "Chamomile. Calming and comforting."

"You're so nice," she wipes her eyes with the tissue, takes the tea and sips. "Thoughtful. Were you always like this?"

Twisting his body to face her, he pulls his leg on the bed between them and shakes his head back and forth. He must see her face for this. Gage her reaction. Be honest and see if she can take it. "Not always. That's why me and my dad..." he pounds his fists together, "butt heads. But I'm trying. He's not ready and I can't force him." Jack takes a deep breath, the courage to continue. "V, I'm not perfect, but I will always be honest with you. I told you I am in recovery. I'm not sure you know what that means. But that thing you saw with my father -it's because I put him through hell for years. Up until a few years ago, I lived a selfish life, but I've learned life is about giving. I'm trying to make amends, do what's right. I've been clean for three and a half years. I go to meetings. I have not missed a day of work since Danny hired me. I do everything I can for my sister and her family because they gave me another chance. Those kids you met, Bri and Shell, I teach them and their friends how to work on cars so they don't end up like me." He reaches out and takes her hand, warms it between his. "I didn't plan for what happened between us, but I certainly don't regret it. I am sorry if it's messing with you. Getting to know you and spend time with you is a gift, it really is. Wherever you want to go from here, whatever it is you need from me, it's yours. And if that includes never seeing you again..." no matter how hard he tries, he can't complete the sentence.

"No," spills from her lips. Her head rocks back and forth as she holds his gaze. "I.." can't imagine going on without him? How can she mean that? Her eyes break down to his chest, his hands, and she takes both of his hands in hers. How can she feel this way? She leans in for a kiss, waits for him to lean in. When his lips touch her, the longing, the warming, the desire is instant and strong. She pulls him in, kisses his neck, feels his hot breath on hers and for the moment, she wants him more than she wants anything.

*

Walking her to the car, they can't seem to let go. "I want you to have my number, in case you need me."

She hands him her phone, "I'm a..." afraid Alexander will see it. "My husband..."

Jack nods. "No worries." He clicks through her phone, downloading an app. "This app," he points, "looks like a game. But..." he presses it, "it's a private text messaging. It won't make a sound, but a little white light will flash."

He pauses a moment, nearly enters the wrong number. He hasn't used that app since before jail. He hasn't dialed that number since before any of that went down, but the addict's brain never forgets some things. The bad things. He shakes it off and enters his phone number, then calls his phone. "No one will know." Something inside him blinks. His new life is completely open and honest. And this is suddenly becoming something else.

24

"**N**early a year and a half I fought the fight. Watched Claire get big and then shrink again. Watched this little miracle open his eyes and make his first sounds, grow from a little alien into a big, beautiful baby boy. It was the longest I'd been clean since I was fifteen. My family seemed, in some lopsided way, glued back together; same puzzle, different shape with the two new additions. I worried Danny was taking Claire away but, the whole time, she was bringing him in. I had a brother, a nephew. This beautiful little creature who counted on his mom for everything, so trusting and so innocent. It made me think about my own mom, how she was always there, how she must have loved and cared for me the way Claire was with Toms. That's magic, right there.

Dad started trusting me again, stopped checking on me all the time.

I was going to AA, not really doing the steps, not drinking the kool-aid, but it was keeping me clean with a new set of friends. That's the damned key right there. Show me your friends and I'll show you your future, one of the speakers said.

Little Toms just started crawling. We were at my parent's

house. It was around the holidays, not yet Thanksgiving; the weather was still warm and we were barbecuing some St. Louis Ribs while sitting out back. My dad was at the grill, Danny had little Toms on his lap feeding him his afternoon bottle and Claire had fallen asleep on the chaise lounge.

My mom tapped my shoulder and said, 'Jack, honey, go over and move the umbrella closer to your sister so she doesn't get a sunburn.'

Without question, I got up, moved one of the sun umbrellas. I was adjusting it, looking up at the blue sky beyond the red umbrella when my mom started coughing. She'd not been feeling great, a little congestion, a cough here and there, but this cough was different. It was deep and hoarse and wouldn't stop. I stood, foolishly, hands still on the umbrella, gazing at my mom. Claire woke, sat up, stared in the same direction. My father stopped flipping the meat and glanced over the grill. Toms woke up, started crying and Danny put him over his shoulder, patting his back. And Mom kept on coughing. When she'd finished, there was blood all over her hands.

She sucked in a wet gasp. For a moment, it seemed nothing moved. Not a cloud in the sky, not the ripple of the water in a pool. I'd swear a bee stopped in midflight. Then we were all up and running for my mother.

We poured into the emergency room.

At some point, Danny took Tommy to his parents' place and came back. It was two a.m. before we got any answers. And it was the C word.

When the doctor told us, we said: No. Absolutely not. Must be a mistake. She never smoked. She rarely drank. She wasn't around people who did smoke.

Before we left the hospital with a we'll-know-more-in-the-morning, they said three to six months.

My father stayed. He made us go home. 'Go make sure I shut off the grill.' Geezus, the house would have burned down if he hadn't. Danny had to work in a few hours, and he got up and went.

Claire picked up little Tommy and was back at the house with me in the morning. I'd sat stiff on the couch until she arrived. I hadn't checked the grill, but since the house hadn't burned down...

In the early morning light, raccoons fought over whatever was left on the grill. Barbeque sauce spread everywhere, dragged across the grill, table, concrete; looked like a crime scene. And then the real blood on the cushion and the ground near where Mom sat, nearly the same brown now as the sauce. I retched in the potted plant next to the pool.

We went back down to the hospital where my father hadn't slept. His partner and one of his friends had joined him. He tried to make us leave again, but we waited. Tommy crawling on the carpeted floor and Claire continually wiping his hands from the dirt.

When the doctor came out this time, he said one visitor at a time, and she'd be able to go home as soon as she was stable.

I was last in. 'My, Jackie. You can't let them bother about me. Your dad needs to go home and get some sleep; make sure he eats, okay? I have some potato salad in the fridge, and there's chicken in the freezer. Take that out for dinner.'

I caught her hand between mine and held it to my mouth.

'Momma,' my voice was a hoarse whisper, 'I can't...' But I didn't finish it. This wasn't about me. This was about her. I nodded and said, 'Okay. I will.

We had her through the holidays: one last Thanksgiving, one last Christmas, and one last New Year's. I didn't leave her side except to go to class. And when classes ended, I didn't leave the house unless she told me to go to the store with her grocery list. Claire did most of the cooking, people brought food over, but hardly any of us ate. I can still hear Mom's voice saying, 'go in there and eat. You're all getting too skinny. Look at you, John,' she said to my father. 'You are skin and bones.'

The second week in January, she passed quietly in her own bed in her own home with all of us around her.

I ate that stress and that loss and nothing else - didn't ask for help.

My father put one hand on my shoulder and one hand on Claire's after my mother's last breath. He mumbled something. To this day, I don't know what he said. My brain was already set on using. Eighteen, nineteen, however many months of sobriety gone before I even left the house.

I remember thinking if whatever the powers that be can take a sweet angel like my mother and not a piece of shit like me, there was something very wrong with the world and I didn't care to be a part of it.

I fell hard and fast.

When I showed up to my own mother's funeral high, my father threw me out of the house for good. I knew he meant it. And he had every right.

A few months later, my friends want to go party in Tijuana. Alcohol and drugs dirt cheap. Sounded like a freaking addict's paradise.

I had no idea my friend was planning on scoring a few kilos. When we were pulled over, the worst thing I thought was happening was a DUI, routine drug bust, they'd find some pot in one of my pockets, paraphernalia in the car.

But when they tore the car apart, when they carried me into that room, life as I'd known it was over. And I didn't care."

25

The dress is an off the shoulder, black, Gucci Bartolli. A hugging, slick midnight satin feel. Valerie stands in front of the mirror, feels exposed, concerned a wrong movement will leave her completely bare. Alexander sits on the bed in the reflection, gazing appreciatively, a smile so wide it's nearly eating his face. His eyes narrow as they run up and down her body.

"Come here," his voice is sex smooth. "I am going to enjoy peeling that off you tonight."

She gazes up at his smoothly shaven face. Tan. Chiseled. The thought of coming home, of him pulling at this dress, climbing on her with that dangerous look in his eyes again sends a spike into her spine.

He stands, running his hands up her body. "I have something else for you." He grabs a box from behind him, flips it open in front of her. Laid over black velvet is a diamond station choker with diamond stud earrings.

A year ago, she would've drowned in awe. Two years ago, she may have fainted. He's given her jewelry before. He's made fusses over her before. But this is over the top and for some odd reason it concerns her more than impresses her. "You shouldn't have." Although she attempts genuine awe, her voice shakes.

"No need to be nervous." He directs her to sit on the edge of the bed as he drapes the necklace over her. He's appraising her in the mirror, pulls her hair back behind her shoulder. "Stay here." He steps over to her vanity, picks up the hair spray and comb before returning to her. "I want this back," he says, "not slicked, but out of your…" He pushes the comb through her hair. It snags and drags across her scalp.

"Oww," she raises her hand and he pushes it away.

He sprays generously, and steps back to appreciate his work. "Perfect. Perfect. Do you have the new LouBoutin's on? You are going to wow them tonight." He kisses her cheek.

*

The Norton Simon Museum is a privately owned art collection in Pasadena, the galleries redesigned by Frank O.Geary and dedicated to Simon's husband. They offer a sculpture garden with a pond and brag twelve thousand pieces, less than half of which are on display. The galleries surprise with Rembrandt, Degas, and Monet as well as displays of Modern, Spanish, and Cubism.

Alexander's company holds their bi-annual galas at places such as The Space Museum, The Science Museum and, tonight, the Norton Simon by offering large donations in exchange for a few hours. The bar opens opposite the pond and sculpture garden, which is lit with sparkling globes and candles that float along the water.

The women wrap themselves in this season's designer gowns and the men don tuxedos. The curator's display features a room with distorted mirrored doors and frames placed next to various Picasso and Cubist paintings. Next to Picasso's *Woman with a Guitar* is a torso mirror, distorted to make the body twist and bend. A similar mirror is placed adjacent from *Woman Reading a Book,* the mirror angled on a downward slant, distorting different parts of the face and upper body. Popova's *The Traveler* is complemented by the appearance of a cracked and broken mirror coupled with colored glass. Meant for entertainment, the men and women pose and chuckle at themselves while enjoying the art.

Another gallery displays modern art under black lights with a 3-D projection of the solar system where the patrons of the night can reach their hands into the Milky Way and attempt to capture Venus or Pluto in their palms. Valerie reaches up just as Saturn rotates away.

They are in awe of the spectacular display.

"They must have donated a fortune," one of his colleague's whispers to Alexander and Valerie.

Alexander beams and, when the woman moves away, he leans into Valerie. "Our company closed a couple million-dollar projects thanks to me. That's why I wanted you to look especially lovely tonight. I believe the President of the company will highlight me in his speech."

They meander the galleries, spend time with couples, CEOs, some of whom Alexander pretends to know, and some he wants to become more friendly with. "Strike up a conversation with his wife" he says softly. She's at a loss when introduced to the couple but Celia and Barry join them, and the conversation moves more smoothly. Celia is practiced at this, bubbly and comfortable. She touches Valerie's arm. "Ladies' room?" She whispers to Marguerite, whom Valerie is supposed to friend, and winks, "Come on, women always go in groups."

The ladies' comment on each other's hair and gowns and click across the marble floors to the patio for champagne. Once on the patio, Marguerite leaves Celia and Valerie for her "oldest of friends."

The ladies work their way back toward the men, pausing again at the mirrors and paintings. Celia bounces and twists, laughs, and encourages Valerie to try. Valerie feels she is beginning to have a good time, feel relaxed.

"Did you see this one?" Celia points to Picasso's *Head of a Woman*. "It's said to be a portrait of his wife." Celia tilts her head from one side to the other in the mirrored door standing at an odd angle to reflect the patron and the painting. The drawing that resembles the shape of a horse head, eyes at odd angles with a slashed line with crisscrossed marks. "You must try this." Celia moves out of the way, then waves to someone down the corridor. "I'll be right back."

Valerie tilts her head to the left, her eyes line up with the eyes in the drawing and the long slash becomes a scar over her mouth. The x's zipping it to a close. It's an ironic smile sewn shut like a doll. She tilts her head to the right and the strangely angled drawing is head to head with hers, mimicking a frown, and in the mirror there are two of each of them. She hears Alexander's voice nearby. Through the slit between the mirror and the wall, she can see him still talking to Barry, one of the CEO's whose wife she was to friend, and another man she doesn't know.

"Your wife is the bell of the ball," one man says. Valerie doesn't know who is speaking, so she's surprised when Alexander responds. "Thank you." Valerie smiles, glances back to the mirror, head still tilting right, moving closer to the mirror, she becomes one with the painting, moving away, her head splits in two, one part horse's nostrils, the other scarred neckline.

"Very fuckable."

Her head pops up as her cheeks turn red.

"Did you have to put her in that? Every guy in the company…" the voice drops too low to hear the rest.

Valerie steps back, out of view, blushing from her forehead to her cleavage.

"That's the point, buddy."

She sees his elbow nudge one of the other guys.

Barry steps closer to Alexander, "Good idea getting our wives together. Mine can teach yours to be more social and yours can teach mine how to dress."

"We all love beautiful women…"

She can't tell if it's the CEO she met or the other man speaking.

"But we are a company of families. Alexander, children

represent more solid, stable relationships. Allows the company to know you are here to stay."

She tilts her head to see Alexander's face. She has a side view as he speaks, drink in hand, smiling, charming all who watch.

"Yes, sir. All planned. Valerie's spending the summer in cooking school," he chuckles, "she's not a very good cook. And she won't be returning to work in the fall. By next Mother's Day, we hope to be celebrating our first little Graham. The second should be in another year. It's best for children to be closely spaced."

Valerie leans forward. The voice carries the same tone as, "beige is the chosen color of designers," "the kids will call you Mrs. G starting Monday," "I want you to wear this." Affable, but unquestionable. No room for movement. No time for questions. The decisions have been made. She feels nauseous and pitches back, her head is tilted left, that slash across her mouth, the x's locking up the seam. No mouth. No say. She gasps for breath against the zippered mouth in the mirror.

"...he's sure. That's why he shops in the sorority section." The other man snorts in amusement of his own crude joke.

"There's something to be said for younger women, much more willing to..."

"You okay?" Celia's hand is on her arm.

Valerie shakes her head, then nods. "I..." She's burning up; her skin is red, her brow has the signs of sweat, and her eyes are stinging. "Just need some air." She backtracks, not willing to pass the men, around to the patio and then for the front door. They'd checked their summer jackets, but she doesn't care, doesn't need anything to keep her warm. The cool night air bristles against her angry body. She waves at the first taxi and he pulls up. As he pulls onto the freeway entrance, Valerie throws her shoes out the window to the homeless woman standing with a sign, "Will work for food."

The sound of a rip brings the driver's eyes to the rearview mirror. At the offramp, teenagers joke and laugh. She empties the

Coach evening bag of her keys, phone, wallet and tosses it out the window. The driver paces himself, eyes from the street to the rear view at regular intervals.

She tugs the diamond station necklace off. "You married?"

"Yes, Ma'am. Twelve years, four children."

She slips the necklace over the front seat. "A tip for your wife."

As the driver pulls into her driveway, he fumbles for the necklace, reaches it out the window at her. "No, no."

"Yes. Yes." She folds a fifty into his hand. "If you don't want the necklace, give it to someone who does."

The earrings picked off, one in the grass as the driver pulls away, one in the planter next to the front door. It's over. It's over. It's over. Zings through her brain and body.

She finishes ripping the dress and drops it in the hall. Still, after that long ride home with the air rushing at her face, her skin feels hot to the touch.

She yanks her dresser drawer to the floor, tosses the finery everywhere in search of her jeans, grabs a t-shirt, and her running shoes. Her overnight bag is stuffed with whatever occurs to her at the moment; it's a mish-mash of what she might need, what she can't live without. Never again. Never. Never. Never. Again.

In her car, she speeds toward the freeway. At a stop light, the little white light blinks on her phone, another signal blinks red; her phone is at 15%. She fishes through the car until a horn bleats behind her. She pulls over searching for her charger. Tries to check the message without it; the phone hiccups, stalls, and then shuts off. She tosses it across the car. Turns her little blue Toyota toward Jack's house.

I am done. Done. Done. Done. She turns a corner and nearly runs into a parked car. In the darkness of the unlit street, she pauses at the curb. Pain bubbles up, disappointment, embarrassment. I will not cry. I will not cry. Breathe. Breathe. It's okay. And when she's calmed down, she drives carefully to Jack's house. The lights are on, his car is in the driveway. She hesitates.

Through the kitchen window, she sees him. He measures the window, writes something, his eyes trace the frame, then down to the floor, up to the ceiling. His face is serious, thoughtful. He picks up the tape measure again, sees a car, moves closer to the window and recognizes it is hers. She waves her hand and his face brightens into a smile. The door flies open and he is there, reaching for the handle.

"I didn't mean to intrude," she says. "My phone…" She fishes for it on the passenger side floor and picks it up, "died. I forgot a charger."

"Completely fine. Whatever the reason, it's always good to see you. Come in? I probably have a charger."

"I was going to call…"

He rubs her arm as he guides her in. "Tea? You look like you could use some tea."

She blows out a breath, stops fumbling, "Yes, thank you."

He fills an old kettle with water and sets it on the stove. She glances at the kitchen table where he dropped the tape measure is covered in papers. He's made some detailed drawings of his house, a living room is to butt up against the kitchen, a dining room where the door is now. She turns around: he's moved the bed and replaced them with his easels and paints.

"You've been busy." She attempts a smile as he answers the kettle's whistle.

"It keeps me in a good place to stay busy. Besides, the other room gets the morning light. I love the first rays of the summer days sprawling over me." He rubs his hand down his chest. "Makes me want to jump out of bed." He's full of energy, happy.

He hands her the tea, makes a cup for himself. "No caffeine," he offers.

"You know, if you put the living room that way and dining room this way, it'll make for a pleasant entrance, don't you think? Then it'll leave you enough space in front if you ever want to have a yard."

He glances down at the rough plans. "You think so?"

"I'm sorry. Just thinking out loud. It's your house."

"That's okay. Have a seat?" He pulls out the chair for her.

"I'm heading to Nan's."

"The charger, yes." He leans over and searches a drawer, pulls one out and places it between them.

"I saw you called, just wanted to let you know I'd be going to Nan's for a few nights."

He nods, glances at her hand sitting on the table. "Everything good? You alright."

"Yeah," she says too confidently, then "I don't know.... Is it okay if we don't talk about it right now?"

"Absolutely. Whatever you're comfortable with." He sips his tea, tips the chair back onto two legs.

"Thank you."

"You hungry?"

She slides her head from side to side.

He uprights the chair, places his hand on the table. "Need a Jack hug? They're free with every cup of tea."

She giggles. "Yes, thank you."

Jack jumps up, takes her hand and she lifts. He wraps his arms around her fully and rocks her gently back and forth. "Rocking actually calms the nervous system."

She breathes him in, wraps her arms around him and is calmed, settled, feeling better. She rests her head on his chest, takes a deep breath and yawns, suddenly tired.

"Can I call my Nan from your phone?"

He pulls his phone out of his pocket and hands it to her. "I'll give you some privacy."

"No. It's okay." She holds onto his hand. Nan picks up on the second ring. "I'm sorry if I woke you."

"You didn't wake me, I'm waiting for Saturday Night Live to come on."

Valerie chuckles, thinks Nan is teasing her.

"I'm coming to spend the night. Is that okay?"

"You never need permission. That room is yours."

Valerie yawns again. The long day, the nervousness, and then rush of anger has exhausted her.

"You okay to drive?"

Valerie nods into the phone, yawns again. "Yeah. I'll be fine."

"Where are you?" Nan asks.

"Jack's."

Jack's face registers surprise as she smiles up at him.

"I tell Nan everything," she whispers.

"Oh, that explains the name on caller ID. Put him on, I want to ask him a question."

Valerie looks at the phone, then hands it to Jack. "She wants to talk to you."

He grimaces playfully, then takes the phone. "Yes, Ma'am."

"Don't call me Ma'am. That's for old ladies."

"My sincerest apologies, Senorita." He grins in Valerie's direction.

"That's better. Does Valerie look okay? Does she seem too tired to drive?"

He inspects Valerie playfully, opening her eyes, patting her cheeks. "I think with a cup of coffee, we can get her flight ready."

"Okay, put her back on."

Amused, he hands the phone back to Valerie.

"I read an article in Women's Day about this woman who got into an accident and was charged with tired driving. It's a real thing. I don't want you to have an accident, sweetheart. Maybe have a coffee, something to eat to wake you up. Unless you can stay with Jack? You're welcome here honey. But I couldn't bear to lose you."

She does feel tired. "I can get a hotel."

"I want to hear you ask him," Nan insists. "I don't want you driving around looking for anything right now. You sound really sleepy."

"Uhm, my Nan would like to know if it's okay for me to spend the night."

Jack chuckles. "Of course. Tell her," he raises his voice so Nan can hear, "On my honor, I will be a gentleman."

"What's the fun in that?" Nan titters. "Thank him for me."

"I will, Nan. I'll see you bright and early."

"Bring Jack," she says.

Valerie smiles up to Jack. "She wants you to come tomorrow. If, that is, you're absolutely certain I can spend the night."

26

Jack is nervous. He fusses with his shirt and questions the jeans. "I should have shaved." He raises his hand to his stubble.

"Jack, the best thing you can be is yourself. Don't be what you think anyone else wants." Her voice quiets, wishing someone had told her that years ago.

Valerie knocks and hears Nan's voice, "What are you knocking for? You have a key." She slides the ready key in and opens the door.

Nan sports clean white walking shoes with her fishnet shell bag hanging from her shoulder. "There were high waves last night; they'll be some good pickings if we get down there before the tourists do."

"Nan, this is Jack. Jack, my Nan."

"Ma'... Ms... uh, nice to meet you."

"Just call me Ruth or Nan." She waves her hand, winks at Valerie. "You didn't tell me how good looking he was."

Valerie grins.

"Love this little thing you got going here." She plucks his chin between her thumb and forefinger. "Okay, kids, let's hit the beach!"

Valerie and Jack follow Nan as she pushes through the sand toward the water's edge. Each find shells and holds them out for an approving motion from Nan as they walk along the shore. Valerie takes the fishnet bag from Nan's shoulder and places it on her own only to have Jack take it from her and toss it over his shoulder.

It's early enough in the day for the Pacific morning to be calm and serene; the wind is soft and the sun hasn't yet begun to heat the sand. Couples and families begin to show up, toss a frisbee and lay out blankets. Nan stares out at the ocean watching a boat in the distance. Some kids holler and point to one side; then they all pause to scan the horizon for dolphins at play. No one tires of the beach; each day is new and different, each sky precious and unique.

Nan watches as Jack picks up a feather and hands it to Valerie. It's long and tan, almost amber in the bright light, with white tips, an average seagull feather, but Valerie's smile widens and she pulls it close to her heart. The gesture warms Nan's soul. Her precious granddaughter will be alright.

"Lunch!" she announces and lifts her knees toward The Water's Edge Cafe. A simple coffee and sandwich shop situated on the sand between the parking lot and the beach. They offer a few umbrella'd picnic tables adjacent to their walk up window. Valerie orders three turkey and swiss on croissants, their menu is limited, and three bottled waters while Jack helps Nan climb over the bench to sit.

"So tell me about you, Jack." Nan pulls Jack down beside her.

"I'm an open book, what do you want to know?"

"Valerie tells me you're an artist."

"Yes, Ma'... Nan." He pulls out his phone and offers her photos of the movie studio and racing cars. Nan ohhs and ahhs and asks questions about this painting or that.

When Valerie sits with the food and water, Nan tears at the plastic wrap covering her sandwich. "Jack, have you ever had beignets?"

"New Orleans! Oh, yeah. Spent a little time at the blues clubs north of Bourbon street. You, Nan? Did you sow some wild oats there in your younger years?"

"Well, don't think the oats I sowed were that wild, but I've been there once or twice. What is that place on the waterfront? It's pink and serves the strangest chicory coffee." Nan squeezes her eyes closed trying to picture the scene.

"Café Du Monde! Do not like that coffee, but it'll get ya movin' after those late nights." He straightens up. "Not that my nights were that late, Nan," he winks.

"Uh-huh."

"You been?" Jack turns to Valerie, sitting across from them.

Valerie slides her head from side to side, a wide grin on her face. She's thoroughly enjoying watching them together. "What's a bay…"

"Beignet." Jack and Nan spout in unison.

"You haven't had a Beignet? We'll go. The three of us. We'll hop in my Judge and take a road trip. What'dya say Nan, you ready to take on Bourbon Street again?"

"Oh, honey. I have too much explaining to do as it is! Can't add anymore to my list. Take her, let her explain absinthe smoothies to St. Peter." Nan coughs and clears her throat, smiles with a twinkle in her eye as Jack pushes the water closer. "Hydrate," he urges.

After lunch, they walk along the beach toward Nan's condo. Jack rolls his sleeves, unbuttons his shirt and appears much more comfortable.

"Young lady," Nan beckons to some teenagers passing them by as she holds out her phone. "I know you young people take good photos, do you mind?"

The young girl frames the shot motioning for Jack and Valerie to move in as Nan stands between them. She clicks one shot after the other, waving, "closer, closer."

"I was going to make cookies for our guest," Nan drops her shell bag in the sink and glances at the butter, flour, and sugar sitting on the counter. "Completely slipped my mind. Valerie, do you mind?"

"Don't go through any trouble."

"Hush, Jack. We'll be on the patio." She grabs Jack's hand and leads him out.

Valerie observes them on the patio from where she stands. Nan chatters away and Jack does too. They are enjoying each other, which makes her feel good. They've talked about books and religion, shells and feathers and even families. "Have lots of kids," she said at one point, "so you can have lots of grandkids. They're the best part of all your hard work." She shot a look at Valerie as she said it.

Jack talked to Nan more in one day than Alexander has in the years they've been together. Valerie shakes her head knowing she's been wrong about so many things.

Nan and Jack's heads have moved closer together, their voices low as Valerie sets the timer and moves toward the patio.

"What's your plan, young man?"

"I don't know that I have one. Neither of us expected this."

She's not really questioning him, is she?

"Gotta figure it out. Otherwise it's not good for anyone."

"No, no, it's not." Jack's head sways slightly.

"Nan, what are you doing?" Valerie's tone is one of amusement.

"Nothing. Nothing. Those cookies done yet?"

"Almost. Why don't you guys come in so I can keep an eye on you."

"The gig is up," Nan says to Jack. "We'll be right in." Nan leans forward and Jack starts to stand. Once Valerie is out of sight, Nan grabs Jack's wrist, motions for him to sit back down.

"I don't want to see my girl hurt," she whispers.

Jack leans in. "I wouldn't do anything to hurt V," he whispers in her ear. "I love her."

Nan smiles. Jack takes her elbow, helps her up. She takes the opportunity to wrap her arms around Jack's outstretched forearm and allows him to lead her.

"Oh, my, what a day. I am plumb tuckered out." Nan shuffles toward her bedroom.

Valerie takes the cookies from the oven and cuddles up with Jack on the couch.

"This is beautiful," he nuzzles against her cheek.

"The view?"

"Nah, this moment." He pulls her closer, closes his eyes.

27

"Sunday night I sprawl back on my bed, enjoying the cool night air blowin' over me, enjoying the aftermath of a beautiful weekend. Get up on Monday, go to work, feeling like I'm walkin' on clouds. I get a message from my girl and pick up to text her back, but my kids show up after school, get them working on a car, Bri he's all up about learnin' to paint, but I tell them they have to work from the ground up, strip it, put it back together, body, engine, extras, and then paint. No shortcuts. Then Danny comes back, looking a little nervous, cops following him. He says, 'hey, Jack, these guys want to talk to you.'

'Yo, guys, come on back.' I'm cool, nothing can ruin my day, I think. I don't know how the street racing slips my mind, but it's not front and center. I think they're there to talk to me about a car.

'Mr. Rose, we found your fingerprints on a car.'

It hits me hard and fast and I freeze for a moment before I turn and chuckle. 'Which one?' I wave my hand toward the back of the garage; the bay doors are all open, there's like ten out there, two inside, one in the paint dryer.

'It happened to be in a car we found overturned on a street;

the unfortunate victim of a street race.'

'Damn, anyone hurt?'

The officer doesn't respond. He sees the kids pausing and watching in the background. 'Who are they?'

'Kinda my after-school program. I teach them how to work on cars, keep them off the streets.'

'Where were you the Thursday before last?'

'Thursday night? Probably here.'

'Midnight, Mr. Rose.'

'Then home, asleep.'

'How would your fingerprints have gotten in a car that was most likely used in illegal street racing?'

'I work on cars. So do they.' I think of Brian crawling in the car, giving me his knife.

Bri steps up. 'We were with him. Shell and I, we were hanging at his place with his girl.'

I cringe and the officer sees it. That's all kinds of bad. I don't want the kids lying for me. I don't want V involved in any lies.

'Mr. Rose? Problem?'

I lean into him. 'My girl is married. I'd rather not bring her into this.'

He nods, looks over at the kids. 'Looks like you've cleaned up your act. Right, Mr. Rose?'

I give him a slow, probably not very convincing nod. Looking at him I realize how far I've strayed from my path; how close I am to screwing up the last three and a half years of my life. I'm lying. Got my kids lying.

It messes with my head. I'm no good the rest of the day. I send the kids home, wait til Danny closes up, and follow him out.

I pull up at my house, feeling like shit. My dad's stalking my front door. Oh, fuck, I cannot deal with one more thing. Was just going to shower and change, head out to a meeting or ten, see my sponsor, but, no, Dad needs to have a chat right then and there.

He starts in before I even get the door open. He heard about everything. He knows about the race, he suspected about V. He asks, and I tell him 'ya.' I'm done with lying and hidin' I tell him fuck all and he's on me. 'You're supposed to be clean; you're supposed to be changed.'

'I am clean, Dad. I am.' I'm screamin', he's screamin', and neither of us are listening or even hearing one another.

He storms out. I'm shaking so bad, I pick up the phone to call my sponsor. But I start to dial ... you know who, don't you? I'm so far gone, I start to dial some number imprinted on some broken piece of my brain. But I stop.

It's that thing. That chase. I click the numbers on my cell slow and sure. I press my fingers on each one of those buttons and I keep my eyes burned shut until my sponsor answers.

28

Shadows flex around the kitchen thrown by the single shower of white light coming from above the island. Alexander and Valerie move around the edges: his hand, her face, his sardonic smile, the small sway of her head.

"I don't want to fight."

He moves in. "We won't fight. I know you overheard something, but it wasn't what you thought it was."

She hmmfs, "Okay."

"It was rude of you to leave early without talking to me, without saying goodnight to our hosts. Embarrassing for me."

She shifts her weight from one foot to the other, tilts her head and glances away.

"I want to ask you a question but, before I do, may I see your phone?"

She meets his gaze, eyes his outstretched hand suspiciously.

"Please?"

She slides it across the island to him. There's no use in hiding anything now.

Pressing a few buttons. "See this app?"

Valerie believes he's discovered the texting app but, when he turns the screen to her, it's a different icon.

"This is a tracking app. So, before I ask you where you've been, I want you to know that I already know. So, please don't make a fool of yourself by lying."

He glides her phone back across the counter. She slips it into her pocket. "If you know, then there's nothing else to say."

Alexander retreats from the light, leans against the counter and crosses his arm. He's a menacing shadow, an outline against the window. "It's important that you say it aloud, that you tell the truth."

She leans against the opposite counter. Another shadow, rounded and small.

"That's the only way we can move forward. I thought you were seeing someone. I just didn't think you were foolish enough to think you'd fallen in love with him."

"I'm not going to talk to you about this."

He chuckles. "We can fix this. I want to fix this. I'm not abandoning you."

For a single instant, the desire to win his approval blooms, but then just as suddenly wilts as she smiles in spite of herself. "We can't fix what I heard. We can't pretend I didn't sleep with another man. These things happened."

Alexander stands; the soles of his leather shoes pad the ceramic tiles quietly as he takes a few steps around the island, moving closer to her. She straightens and pushes away. Figures crawl counterclockwise at the edge of light.

"You misunderstood. Tell me what you think you heard, and I'll explain everything."

She scoffs. "I don't need an alternative explanation."

He advances, she retreats. "Is it that you slept with someone else? Would it make you feel better if I'd done it too?"

"Of course not!"

"No?" He laughs heartily. "You can do it, but I can't?"

"That's not what I meant." Valerie needs an escape. The guest room. The back door.

He nods, smiles warmly, laps in her discomfort. "Look, honey, people stray, it happens. Couples forgive and move on."

Tears sting the back of her eyes. "It's not supposed to happen. If you love someone, you don't have sex with other people. If I was in love with you, if you were in love with me…"

"Honey, don't cry," he opens his arms, shifts closer. She withdraws toward the other side of the island. He drops his arms. "There is a difference between making love and having sex." His voice is quieter but carries that same confident and persuasive tone. "There's a difference between loving someone and fucking someone else. You're young, honey, so young. And I knew it was a risk to marry someone so naive to the ways of the world, but you are so lovely."

"Stop it." Her voice is low.

"You stole my heart from the first moment I saw you. It was at that coffee shop, remember? You were gazing at the options, wondering what would get you through finals."

"Stop." Her tone gains strength.

"I wasn't giving you enough attention. I understand that now. You were lonely. You needed someone."

Tears streak her cheeks. "And you, were you lonely?"

"No, I was angry. You left. I didn't get even a mere mention in my boss's speech, so I fucked his wife."

"Oh my g…" Valerie's mouth falls open.

"She wanted it," he scoffs.

Valerie's tears stop. The clock over the stove tings tinnily at midnight. All her illusions dispelled; her shadow seems to slump in place. But the guest room door opens, closes. Alexander sniffs, shoves his hands in his pockets, and leans against the counter.

*

In the morning, Alexander knocks lightly on the door before starting breakfast. Valerie showers in the guest bath, pulling clothes from her closet, and hurrying back to the guest room to change. She waits, hoping he'll leave. When she finally turns into the kitchen, his newspaper is on the counter, his plate next to him, waiting for her.

"Eggs or waffles?"

She hesitates. "Not hungry," her voice is rough and flat, barely hers.

"There's coffee," he points. "Will you have time to do the shopping today? If not, that's fine. We'll order groceries, have them delivered." His voice is normal, his mannerisms, other than his breakfast at the kitchen counter, is routine.

She waits until he glances back to his newspaper before she grabs a cup from the cabinet and pours herself a coffee. She turns back toward the guest room.

"Valerie."

She pauses, glances over her shoulder.

"It's a rough patch. That's all it is. You don't throw the baby out with the bathwater."

*

Concerned about the app Alexander installed on her phone, she waits to text Jack until she has time, over lunch, to uninstall it. Just as she begins the text, Mr. Stewart knocks on the door of her classroom and enters without invitation.

"Mrs. Graham." He stutters, avoids eye contact, but then rallies and straightens his spine. "It's come to the administration's attention that you may be involved in an inappropriate relationship with a student's father."

She stands but offers no resistance; yet he holds up his hand as if to stop her.

"Of course, if this is just hearsay or gossip, nothing will happen. As a married woman, representing our school, it would be inappropriate for you to be seen around town with a man who is not your husband. We would have to… uhm… cancel your tenure here at West Oaks."

She imagines Alexander on the phone to Stewart, "There seems to be some gossip. Of course, my wife is just being friendly, she doesn't understand the implications…" He would lecture

Stewart on faculty/family interactions, rules and policies; he'd throw in, somehow, it would endanger the school's image.

"Mr. Stewart. I'm going to make your job easy. Consider this my last year at the school. In June, when the kindergarteners graduate, my time here will commence with them."

"Mrs. Graham, that is not..."

"Mr. Stewart, you are a weasel. Tell my husband, I said that."

His face reddens, he scoffs and turns to leave as the children come rushing back in with Miss Jenny.

After class, she picks up her phone to once again text Jack when Lucy paces in.

"Hey, girl. Didn't see you at lunch. You look tired." Lucy touches her hand to Valerie's shoulder. "You feeling okay?"

Valerie nods without conviction. "Lucy, if I need a place to stay tonight, can I call you?"

"Sweetie, what's wrong? Absolutely. You and Alexander fighting?"

"Something like that."

Lucy hugs her hard. "You call if you need me."

As Lucy leaves, Valerie begins to type a message. She pauses, needs to keep it simple. He is not the cause of nor the savior from her problems. She needs to sort this on her own. "Thinking of you. Hope all is well." She nearly ends it with "I love..." but back spaces and adds, "xxoo."

*

Valerie stands in the kitchen, leans over the sink and stares out at the expanse of green. Not even this view causes an inkling of doubt. She must leave. She must leave him. There's a strange sort of relief that rises from the decision, as if so much confusion has suddenly cleared. He won't be home for hours, she has time to make a plan, pack a suitcase.

The door opens, Alexander holds up a bottle of her favorite buttercream chardonnay. "Should we chill it, order a pizza?"

She gazes at him. The confident smile, the self-assured twist as he drops his briefcase, turns toward the cabinet for the ice bucket.

He's certain he can win her over, buy time to wear her down, talk her into believing she'd misheard, misunderstood, and that all couples have these problems. Not this time.

"Mr. Stewart came in to threaten me today."

"I'm sure he wasn't threatening you," Alexander's sanguine. "He's doing what's best for the school, and for you."

"Or for you?"

He chuckles sardonically. "There are many benefits to my position." He leans on the counter across from her, studying her profile. "And many benefits to being my wife. I got you that job. I can get you a better one," he exhales audibly, "or none."

"I told Mr. Stewart this would be my last semester there."

Alexander crosses his arms, watches her walk away. "Wait," he clicks open his briefcase, slips a file onto the counter. "I'm not sure you realize who you'd gotten involved with. Seems your boyfriend has a drug problem, some legal troubles. Good choice." He raises that eyebrow.

She clenches her jaw. "I'll be at a hotel." She spins away.

In a single, long stride, he catches her wrist, yanks her back toward him. "Honey," he squeezes her hand. "We can work this out. I can give you anything you want."

She jerks her hand free, straightens her spine and stands her ground. "Alexander, why do you love me?"

He chuckles, surprised.

"Seriously, what is it you love about me?"

His hand clips his lip as if he's trying to stop himself from laughing, then he drops his hands and focuses on her face. "You're beautiful."

She waits.

"Adorable when you're angry."

She nods. "Okay."

He laughs. "What do you want me to say? That's not enough?"

"I'm just really tired of playing these games with you." She turns for the steps, unconcerned that he is following. She's not afraid anymore. She pulls a suitcase from the back of the closet, throws it open on the bed as he watches.

"Honey, this is just silly. Stop this. People do not leave each other because they have a fight."

"I need some time, space." She pulls dresses from the closet, picks up a pair of shoes and tosses them into the suitcase.

"You're not going to him." His mercurial temper rises as he pushes the suitcase to the floor. "He hasn't even responded to your text. He got what he wanted from you and now he's gone."

She hadn't planned to run to Jack, hadn't planned to even see him until she was installed somewhere else. A hotel. A friend's. She wouldn't presume to move in with another man on the very day she left her husband.

"I'm going to a hotel," she whispers and reaches for the suitcase.

He grabs her arm, yanks her away from the inverted suitcase. She struggles free and jogs down the stairs. She can hear him kick something, punch the door as she bursts out the front door, purse in hand.

At the Holiday Inn, she tells them one night, then two, and before he runs the card, she says, "make it through Friday."

The young man runs her Visa through once, then twice. "Ma'am, seems this card has been canceled."

Weary, she hands him her ATM card; when that doesn't go through, she knows Alexander has canceled her cards.

When she returns to her car, she clicks Lucy on her cell.

Lucy answers on the first ring. "Hunneeeyy, come on over."

The little Toyota purrs to life as her phone rings in her hand. The caller I.D. reads an Orange County pre-fix.

"Mrs. Graham? This is Orange County Hospital, Ruth Pardonas has been admitted."

"Is she okay?" They'd left less than 24 hours ago. Nan was sleepy from the excitement of the day, but she seemed perfectly fine.

"Ma'am," the nurse's voice is smooth and comforting. "While there's no immediate concern, you should come as soon as you're able. She's asking for you."

Valerie bursts into tears, searches her glove box for napkins, then wipes her face. "She's okay. You're okay. Everything will be okay." She blows out a few breaths, drives mindfully toward the freeway.

29

The hospital is white and gray with an antiseptic stench wafting through the corridors. One nurse after another points and gives directions, but it doesn't seem like Valerie will ever reach Nan, elevators and check-in desks and more corridors. When she gets to the room, an air tent confines Nan's head and chest. The screens are beeping, lights flickering, with an array of lines and cords - Valerie can't get close.

"Are you Valerie?" It's the same voice from the phone. Seeing Valerie's face, she adds, "It's just to stabilize her breathing."
Nan appears to be asleep, appears to be breathing normally.

"We do need to talk, would you mind?" The nurse splays her hand toward a table. She drops a brown folder, sorts through papers as she invites Valerie to sit across from her. "Your grandmother is eighty. She's lived a long, good life. Although we're not supposed to say someone is dying of old age, that is what's happening."

Valerie tears up, glances over to the tent lightly sucking in and out.

"Her heart is slowing, blood not pumping regularly to her

organs, her body is beginning to shut down." The nurse's voice is warm as it recites words she must have repeated thousands of times. She's practiced. Firm, but comforting.

"How long does she have?" Valerie is expecting months, maybe she hopes to hear a year.

"Weeks?" There's doubt in the nurse's face. "Days?"

Valerie gasps, eyes watering as she tries to focus on the paperwork the nurse is placing in front of her. "Is there anything we can do?"

"No," the nurse is wearing gray, like the arrows on the wall that led Valerie to this room. "And more importantly, she doesn't want anything done. She signed a DNR. Do you know what that is?"

"Do Not Resuscitate." Valerie mouths the words without sound. She learned the phrase when her mother died from heart failure due to diabetes.

"That's the bad news." The woman pats her hand to bring Valerie's attention back to her. "There is good news, if you can understand it that way."

Valerie sits up and takes a deep breath willing to listen to anything good.

"Your grandmother doesn't want to and doesn't have to die here in the hospital. Since she lives in our senior housing, there are nurses who visit on a regular basis. But she will need someone to stay with her."

Valerie sniffles, wipes her eyes and nods.

"Are you able to stay there with her 24/7?"

Valerie responds without hesitation. "Yes."

The woman offers a warm smile. "This really is the best way to pass, surrounded by our loved ones in our own bed."

Valerie sobs out loud.

The woman pushes up and pats her shoulder. "You're doing the very best thing you can for her by being there with her."

"Yes." A soundless movement of lips. "I know."

*

In some ways, unstated and unacknowledged, Valerie has always known this place would be Nan's last home. The nurse/concierge at the door, the health care insignias on the staff's clothing. This is a place for people to spend their final years. Nan mentioned, in between conversations, everything is taken care of. All agreements made before residents move in. Valerie thought it was an aside, but Nan was preparing her.

Valerie drops the overnight bag packed days ago in the guest room. A quick glance tells her there's a dress, some jeans, tops, and shoes.

By the end of the week, Nan is stable enough to come home. The staff sets her up in her bedroom, a buzzer next to the bed. The nurse leaves an instruction sheet, phone numbers, the nurses' schedule, and do's and don'ts. It's the same list they've gone over every day at the hospital.

Nan sits and watches as the technician and nurse leave. "Are they gone?"

Valerie sits on the bed next to her, waits for the sound of the door clicking into the jamb. "I think so."

"Thank goodness. What buzz kills."

Valerie snickers in spite of herself.

"Top shelf over the refrigerator, bring me the See's chocolates."

"I don't think…" Valerie consults the list.

Nan slaps it out her hand. "I'm dying. Give me my chocolates."

Valerie agrees. What does it matter now if Nan has a chocolate? She returns promptly.

"You up for some gin rummy? Go get the cards."

By the time Valerie returns, Nan snoozes on the propped pillows. Valerie closes up the chocolates and places them on the nightstand with the cards. She adjusts Nan's pillows and pulls the chair close to the bed.

A loud knock and an even louder voice chiming, "Good morning," wakes Valerie. She jumps up and a nurse is making her way down the hall.

"Was it a rough night?" The nurse asks. They look in at Nan who is just opening her eyes.

"I guess for me."

"I'm here to check her vitals, give her any medications, and give you a break. Go shower, take a run on the beach, whatever you need to do."

Valerie bristles, "No, I'm good."

The nurse faces Valerie, her tone low and serious. "Do it for her if not for you. You can't be a mess while taking care of someone else."

Valerie opts for a shower before sitting on the patio with Nan's computer. She orders a pair of shorts, t-shirt and some extras from a nearby store. By the time the hour is up, Valerie has two cups of tea and toast ready.

Nan appears bright and chipper as she sips her tea. She's pale, but her eyes are sparkling.

"How are you?" she asks Valerie as if it's any other day, as if they're not sitting in her bedroom with a week or two left.

"I'm good, Nan. I'm happy to be here with you."

"Hmmm. And what's Alexander think of that?"

Time is too precious to retell that story. "I'm done concerning myself with what Alexander thinks."

"Do tell," Nan sips her tea and winks at Valerie.

"I think I married him for the wrong reasons. I think I was enamored." She remembers the coffee shop, the handsome stranger smiling her way. She and her girlfriends crowing when he passed the barista his platinum card and said, "for all of them."

"Well, I'm sorry if you're hurting honey."

Valerie moves the chair closer to Nan's bed, helps her set the tea on the nightstand.

"I'll be okay." There are so many things she wants to say. She wants to say don't die, don't leave me, but that would be unfair to Nan.

Nan smiles. "And Jack?"

Valerie sets her tea down. "I think he's gone too. It's just going to be me..." she glances over to Nan, "me and you."

Nan guffaws. "Don't start lying to me now, girl."

A solid silence passes between them as Valerie sits on the bed and grasps Nan's hand in hers, tears springing from her eyes.

"You're going to be okay, my girl." Nan brushes Valerie's hair behind her shoulder. "You've made a good decision, honey. You didn't get a chance to be on your own, to find out who you can become. You will get that chance now. And whatever you do, it'll be great!"

Throat throbbing from unreleased sobs, Valerie leans into Nan, hugs her.

"You won't be scared or lonely. You'll be on a brand-new adventure and I want you to enjoy it. Every minute of it. Do all those things you've ever wanted to. Eat crackers in bed and sing in the shower."

Valerie chokes out a laugh, even as tears fall onto Nan's shoulder.

*

Nan, Valerie, and Char play Hearts when Nan drops a card and says, "Go, fish," Char snickers, "We're changing games in the middle? Someone must be losing."

Nan's eyes have gone blank as she stares straight ahead at the wall, her mouth moving as if she's speaking.

"Char," Valerie whispers.

The small, older woman watches Nan. "It's getting close," she says sympathetically.

There's a hard knock at the door, followed by another quick and urgent sounding tap. It's too early for the nightly nurse visit; she suspects it's another visitor. Perhaps Walter or one of the other residents. Nan's friends and neighbors have stopped by with food, treats, flowers, and good wishes. The refrigerator is filled with Tupperware and the living room with flowers.

"Stay with her," Valerie whispers.

There's another knock before she reaches the door. When she

opens it, Alexander brushes past Valerie and turns around in the living room as if looking for something or someone. "You here alone?"

"I'm with Nan."

"Is your boyfriend here?"

"Stop it, Alexander. I'm here with Nan."

"How is Ruth anyway?"

"Not well."

"Sorry to hear that." Alexander approaches Valerie, takes her hand and smiles as he looks her up and down, shorts, t-shirt, socks. "You look so cute." His voice is tender, soft, almost as if he means it.

"Alexander, you need to leave." She drops her hand as he loosens his touch.

"Honey, come home. Let's put this behind us." He shifts closer, tries to meet her eyes.

When she doesn't respond, won't meet his gaze, he grips her elbows and pulls her close. "You knew who I was when you married me."

"Maybe I didn't know who I was." Denials won't help him hear her.

His grip loosens as he looks into her eyes. "Valerie," almost pleading.

"Let go of me," she says softly.

"You heard her!" Char stands in the hall with a baseball bat raised above her head. "If you leave quietly, you can leave with your balls."

Alexander releases Valerie. "I'll leave," he offers Valerie one last intense gaze. "I know I didn't do everything right, but I do miss you. I am willing to do whatever it takes. So, call me. Come home. Please."

Valerie says nothing.

He passes Char as he leaves. "Nice seeing you, Ruth."

Once the door closes, Char's arms give out and the bat slams to the floor. "Who's that asshole?"

"Are you okay? Where did you get this?" Valerie collects the bat from her, a smile gracing her mouth.

"Oh, honey, we all have them." Char straightens up and rubs her own shoulder. "I rang security, they'll be up in a minute. You okay, honey? Did he hurt you?"

"I'm okay." She hugs Char. "Thank you."

"I'm going home now. I've had my work out for the day. You come and double lock this door behind me."

When Valerie returns to the bedroom, Nan's cheerful. "Did you see your Mom?"

"Nan, what do you mean?"

"She said you look pretty today."

Valerie turns toward the empty space at which Nan stares.

"She wants you to be happy."

"I'll try, Nan."

"She said she likes Jack."

Valerie tries to smile as she cleans up the cards and places them on the nightstand, adjusts Nan's pillow. "She never met Jack, Nan. You did. You liked him, didn't you?" Valerie leans back in the chair. "I liked him too. He was sweet."

"He finished the painting of his mother, but she likes the drawing he did of you."

Valerie pauses. Had she told Nan about the painting of his mother? He must have, of course.

"Can I see it the drawing?" Nan's happy as she turns her gaze to Valerie. "She said it's in your bag."

Valerie glances at the wall and back to Nan. "I don't think I have it." The only bag she has is the one she'd packed the Saturday night of the party. She'd been in a rage, grabbing things; she doesn't remember picking it up. But, at Nan's request, she searches her bag. There it is, at the bottom, looking a little worse for wear. She returns to Nan, flattening it out before handing it to her.

Nan studies it. "He really did capture your spirit. He sees you." She lies back, drawing held to her chest as she nods off. Valerie can't help but beam at Nan's beautiful smile.

Before Alexander had her phone turned off, she'd left one last message for Jack. She hadn't heard anything, no text messages, no calls, so she'd left a vague and positive message. "Miss you. Hope you're doing well."

She loosens the drawing from Nan's hands and holds it to her own chest. Anything could have happened, she thinks. "Jack, wherever you are, I wish you well." She adjusts Nan's pillow and kisses her cheek. She doesn't know what will happen next, but she has to be grateful for the time she had with him, the time she now with Nan.

Valerie wakes early, the guest room faces north. It's not the rays of daylight that call to her, but Nan's murmuring. She seems to have slept soundly. Nan's eyes are closed, but under the lids they dart back and forth, "Papa, Papa, I missed you," Nan whispers.

Papa is what they called her grandfather, Nan's husband. Valerie smiles to herself. She makes tea and carries two cups to the bedroom. She shimmies open the curtains so she and Nan can welcome the morning. When she turns back toward Nan, her eyes have stopped moving, her lips stilled. The light on Nan's face makes her skin appear pale to the point of translucent. Valerie knows her time is near.

"Nan, I'm here."

Nan's breathing is shallow, almost undetectable.

"Nan, I know I'll be alright. I love you."

A single tear drop forms at the outer corner of Nan's eye. Then, Nan is gone.

Valerie leans over her grandmother and cries.

*

"You should come down," the nurse says to Valerie.

When they reach the front desk, her grandmother's friends wait outside between the door and the ambulance. As the gurney comes through, the crowd parts. Char says, "You were a good daughter to her. You're always welcome here." Walter adds, "she was a good woman," and Nan's other friends, "We will miss her."

"Valerie, if there's anything you need," as she walks back up toward the door. When the door opens, they become quiet. As the glass door closes behind her, the crowd of friends begin to dissipate, shuffle off in their own directions.

The nurse concierge at the desk stands. "It's a tradition." He nods toward the crowd dispersing outside. He hands her a paper. "Everything is taken care of for the family. This is a list of what will happen next."

She takes the paper upstairs and lays it on the table to be read later. She's alone, for the first time, in Nan's place, in the world. She sits and stares at the ocean for a long time.

*

The association handles almost everything. Her grandmother's possessions will be stored or donated. The Neptune Society will deliver her grandmother's remains. Valerie works her way through the condo tagging the things S for those to be stored and D for those things to be donated. Although she's allowed to take whatever she wants, Valerie packs a small box with photos, her grandmother's favorite shell, the antique jewelry box from her grandmother's grandmother. She takes the photo of her family from the coffee table and finds the printed picture Nan asked a passing stranger to take of Valerie, Nan, and Jack on the beach. A tear forms in her eyes as she holds the photograph to her chest before putting it in the box. She gathers her duffle bag, the box, and takes a last look around.

The concierge is a nice young man she's come to know as Keith. "Ready to sign out?"

Valerie nods. "I don't have an address yet, can I call when I settle?"

"Please do."

Char, Walter, and a few other of Nan's friends come through the door as she finishes the paperwork.

"You can always stay with me," Char says. "Or me," another offers.

"Thank you, but I'll be okay." Valerie hugs them.

"You'll call?"

"Or write?"

"Yes. I'll let you all know where I am. Thank you for making me feel like I still have family."

Valerie pops the trunk and tucks the bag and box in. One last look behind her, and she starts the car. "Busted flat in Baton Rouge..." Janis Joplin's voice fills the stale air. Valerie reverses, pulls forward to the exit and waits at the light; she wonders, north or south? "...rode us all the way to New Orleans."

East.

30

"Addiction is all about chasing that first high that we can never really have again. It's all an illusion. Running around in circles, lying to ourselves, and hurting the people around us all in order to get what we can never really have.

Our body and our brain cells get used to that chase, that longing and desire to be right on the edge there, believing that the very next thing we take or do is going to get us to that point - but it doesn't happen.

When I was young and first introduced to recovery, I said, nah, man, that's bullshit. You have to keep doing the same thing over and over and that's recovery? But, what I didn't get is that is exactly what addicts do - the same thing over and over. So recovery is about doing the opposite thing, but over and over, so you stay straight. People talk about recovery like it's a noun. It's a person, place, or thing. But recovery is a verb. It's an action. It's a consistent action of staying on the right path so we don't fuck our lives again.

That's not what I've been doing. Street racing is chasing that high. I realized and I quit. Just like that. My recovery means everything to me. Without it, I have nothing.

But then, there's this woman. Guys, I am in love. I have never in my life wanted something so bad as I want her. And I tell myself, I'm not pressuring her. I'm not rushing her. I'm not chasing her. But I'm wondering guys. See, she's married.

I'm programming this app into her phone so I can reach her without her husband knowing and the realization kicks me in the stomach like a bronco bucking. I go back into my house, and I think, oh, shit, am I just chasing something else I can never have? I wonder if I'm fucking myself, then I start to panic because I'm messing with other people's lives here. This woman... oh my god... she's the sweetest, kindest, the kind of beauty that starts in the soul and grows outward.

From the moment I first saw her, she's dancing with kids all around her. Then I meet her. I touch her. Sparks blow up in my face. Damn.

I keep telling myself that we can be friends. Every time I see her. Every time I inhale her scent. I lie to myself and say, friends. It's a lie because you can't feel the way that I feel and not reach for the magic. And it was magic, guys. When we finally got together. Blew my mind. Let me tell you, it's been a long, loooonnngggg time, but it felt like the first time I was really there, present, part of something special and beautiful.

But I feel, too, that this might be part of that chase. It might be the game of the illusion we addicts all take part in. Would I feel this way if she were attainable? If she didn't have a husband holding her back, if I could tell Clair and Danny and little Toms? I feel like it would, I feel like it is real. But how many times have we all picked up that hit and said, it's only once or I can quit any time or this is the last time. We're lying to ourselves. I love her more than I've loved anyone in my whole life. Am I lying to myself?

I was this close to losing it all. This freaking close. I called my sponsor. My hand shaking the whole time. All those numbers for my dealers leaking out of my head. He made me stay on the phone with him until he drove over. Had he not, I would have lost it.

I knew I was messin' up. I tried to reign it in. Thought I had a handle on it. But I forgot the number one rule. I have no control!

I stopped street racing but needed to deal with the consequences.

I didn't deal with the V situation. I could not let her go.

Then my dad appears. Pissed off as usual. He heard about the street racing, heard about V, and shows up at my door, raging and screamin', you're screwing up, you're screwing up… and I was so down, I was shakin'. Had my sponsor not answered the phone…. Thank you, brother, thank you.

My sponsor put me in lock down. 30 days. No contact for the first week. That's the way it works, you know.

My first call, I have to admit, was to V, but nothing. Straight to vm. I call Claire and she's so happy to hear my voice, she begins bawling. She can't even talk. Danny gets on the phone. I tell him where I am, what's happening. Tell him - I got in too deep, dude, needed to take care of myself.

He understands. They ain't mad. I beg Claire to tell V what happened. She doesn't tell me then that V left the school. Quit, fired, whatever. She was right to do that. I would've bolted. I think I would have bolted. Gone to look for her. Make sure she was okay.

When I get out, I go see my Dad. I gotta have it out with him. He doesn't want a relationship, that's fine, but then he's gotta give me space. He's gotta not come over to my place and get in my face.

I'm tryin' I tell him. I'm tryin' and you don't have to be part of my life, but you can't be a problem in my life.

And we have a heart to heart. Straight out, all through the night talk. By morning, we chug a gallon of coffee and we begin a new relationship. We both know it won't be easy, there's gonna be hard times, times I mess up and times he messes up, but now, at least, we know we're tryin' and that feels damn good.

Gotta a lotta catch up work at Saffarri's, so I spend my time working late and working weekends. But I gotta be honest - I drive by V's house more than once. If she doesn't want to see me, I can handle that, but I gotta hear her say it, I gotta see her, make sure she's okay. But I don't see her car, I don't see her. Then one night, I see some other woman there and I know she must have left him.

One Sunday, I got my kids workin at the garage with me. They offer to help me catch up and as long as they're staying out of trouble, I let 'em. It's good for me to have them around and not spend too much time by myself.

So I'm under a Pontiac GTO, droppin' the tranny, when Brian says, don't you know where her Grandma lives? And his girl says, get your ass down there. So, I hop in my car right then and there and pedal to the metal, I'm at her Nan's. I go in and I pour it all out to some poor sap who's pullin' a double shift and he's looking at me like I'm a stalker or some love sick pup, he's not sure. But he holds steady on, 'not allowed to give out any private information on our residents.'

He don't know me from any street urchin, I gotta give him a break. I show up in my jeans and my oil stained t-shirt. I turn to leave, then I think about that picture I snapped when Nan and I sat at the pic-nic table.

I show him the photo and his face twists all up and I get a bad, bad feeling. He looks at me again and says, 'sorry, I'm not allowed to give out any information.'

'She pass?' I ask. A glob forms in my throat when I think of V dealing with that all by herself. The not knowing is just killing me.

The guy looks around and then gives me a slight nod.

I figure it's worth a try, so I ask, 'Her granddaughter, Valerie. You know where she is?'

He purses his lips like he's not sure he should give me any info, but then he just shakes his head side to side.

I blast the music and take a slow drive back, hop on the 1 when I can. Roll down the window, feel the ocean breeze on my face; it's damn near sunset when I get back. The kids are all sitting on the curb, shop's all closed up.

The kids hang with me for a while longer before I head home. I spend the night in my studio, painting. Grab a couple of hours before heading back to work the next day.

After a month of hangin' low, down in the mouth, ruining every weekend, so my family says; we're sitting out back enjoying the pool and eatin' up some grill, when my dad says, 'Why don't you just go to her house and ask her?!'

'I did,' I say.

'You try internet stalking her?' Danny chimes in.

'I tried.'

'What happened when you went to her house?'

'She was gone, hubby got another woman in there already.'

'What an ass!' Claire says.

'Well, damn it, she's gotta be somewhere,' my father says. I'm kinda surprised he's offering to help. I think I must look like a pathetic fool if he's wanting to help me.

'Her husband must know.' Danny offers. 'If he has another woman, they must be getting a divorce. He must know where she is.'

I shrug. 'Want me to go up to his door and say, hey, I'm in love with your wife and I'm looking for her, can I have her phone number?'

Danny chuckles, 'Maybe not quite that.'

My dad jumps up. 'Let's go. I'm tired of this whining.'

Danny jumps up to go with us and Claire pops up too. 'Now, wait a minute,' Claire grabs my arm. 'What are you guys going to do?'

My dad answers, 'What the hell do you think we're going to do? I'm retired LAPD. We're going to ask the man some questions.'

Claire calms down. Danny kisses her cheek and we're out of there. It feels good, I gotta tell ya. We're riding over there in my dad's Lincoln MKZ. It's a Saturday afternoon and at first looks like no one's home, but then we see him and his new girl pull up and go in. We give them a minute or two then my dad takes the lead, gives his cop knock on the door. Three hard fists to the door. I see his mouth start to move and think he's ready to say, LAPD, but he doesn't. Old habits die hard, even for him.

In a minute, we hear footsteps and the door opens. The husband eyes us all. My dad does the talking; he's got a presence that doesn't fade. Straight spine, broad shoulders, chest puffed out, 'We're looking for Valerie Graham,' he says without explanation.

I see the girl behind him, trying to see who's at the door, 'who?' she says softly.

'Your wife,' my father barks. 'Where's your wife, Mr. Graham?'

His eyes focus on me. He knows me, no doubt. If he was trackin' her phone, he probably followed her once or twice; he steps out and raises his fist to punch me in the mouth. I weave, but my Dad catches his arm, pins him to the door and Danny takes up the other side, twisting his other arm. Danny's all round and seemingly soft in the middle, but I've seen him moving engines, pick up a motorcycle and shit like that, so he's stronger than he looks and they got this guy flat to the door.

I kinda chuckle at the husband. He looks like a damn fool. He's mad too. He's embarrassed. 'He's a lawyer.' I tell my dad, want to remind him so we won't get into any legal trouble.

'We're looking for your wife who seems to have disappeared. Do you have any evidence she is alive and well or should I call the local PD to search your house?'

The woman looks scared and I kinda feel bad for her. She's standing on the other side of the living room with her hands to her mouth.

My dad and Danny let the lawyer go and he straightens his shirt, walks back into the house. I hear the woman say, 'Did he say wife? You married?'

'Go into the kitchen for a minute.'

I feel bad for her. Hope this is a warning for her and she steers clear of this guy.

He grabs a large envelope from the pages of a book sitting on the coffee table and brings it over to us. 'This came from her attorney.'

It's empty, but we walk away with it. The attorney's return

address is in New Orleans.

I sat in the back of the Lincoln on the way back to Claire and Danny's laughing my ass off and my dad and Danny are looking at each other all worried. My days in New Orleans are mostly a fog. I lived there for like six months, I can remember maybe three whole days and a lot of little scenes here and there.

I know what they're thinking and it occurs to me too, but I'm not worried about a trigger and I'm not worried about backsliding. I feel stronger than ever. I feel more focused, with more purpose and I don't think of the consequences. I don't think what if I get there and she doesn't want to see me, but I do think - what if I get there and I can't find her?

31

The summer heat in New Orleans is thick. The streets are largely absent of locals who opt for air-conditioned homes or shaded yards with iced drinks. Even in the hottest parts of the day, the streets thin of tourists who hide in the casino, local restaurants, or their hotels waiting for the late afternoon and hope for a cool breeze.

The psychics still line the square telling fortunes and the shops along Bourbon Street still blast their air conditioning, trying to lure guests in for the cold air, which works on a day like today. They buy baubles and beads and trinkets that say, Bourbon Street, or New Orleans, that show masks or other landmarks that will remind them of NoLa

His sponsor warned him against going, but he promised to call at the first inkling of weakness. His dad wanted to come with, but he couldn't find Valerie with his father in tow. But the last thing Jack is feeling is the desire to use. The smell of the streets and the summer heat makes him feel nauseous.

Too much information is on the internet, and with a little searching of public records, birth, death, marriage, and divorce, he believes Valerie is using her maiden name and staying just outside of the quarter. He hesitates at the corner, glances at all the two-story houses, plants hanging from balconies, and neighbor sitting on patios. Glancing at the residents, he offers a smile, but they take him for a tourist, someone lost or looking for trouble.

Jeans are a mistake; the backpack hanging from his shoulder creates a patch of sweat that drips down to his hip as he steps up to a big green quartered house. Many years ago, the house belonged to one family. The family may have been upper middle class. They had great gardens in the back, horses, a servants' entrance to the side. But it's been passed down and sold, resold, and now quartered into four apartments with four separate patios. The units are separated by the stairwells, one that goes to the second floor from the front porch, one that runs from the back yard to the basement which probably smells of mold and wet concrete in the hottest parts of the year. If it rains too hard, there will be an inch or two of water swirling in the lowest parts of the concrete basement.

When he lived here in New Orleans, it was at one of the little places built specifically for short term rentals. No yard, no side, no basement. Just a building plopped onto the concrete with modern conveniences. No class. No beauty. But, of course, Valerie would live in something like this, ornate, tender, gentle, and off the main drag of noise and parties.

Jack walks up to the front door and checks the names on the mailboxes; only one lacks a name. Second floor. This is it. He wonders if the lack of a name is to throw off a stalking husband, or just a single woman in a new city being safe. It is the safest thing she could do. She's smart. His heart beats harder, and for a moment he forgets the heat as he excites at the thought of her.

The bell rings a tinny old fashion sound that he can hear as it echoes down the stairs. No sound of movement; the heat closes in the silence of the neighborhood.

A woman watches him from the balcony next door. "Whatcha doin there?" she calls out.

He smiles and holds his hand up, but it is not a welcomed

gesture and not returned. She backs up far enough that she can't see him. He glances around at other houses, other patios, there's a few more people watching. Saturday, plenty of people are home and the neighbors are keeping an eye on the sweet young woman who came into their fold. He likes it. He retrieves an envelope from his backpack and sticks it in the mailbox.

Jack walks toward the riverfront in search of a cool beverage and something to eat. Cafe DuMonde is humming with business, people line up out of the shop as well as a line waiting to order, another waiting for tables. He turns left and heads for the open marketplace. He doesn't want to be closed in or stuck in a line. He buys the first bottled water he sees and drinks it down, walks further and buys another with a burger.

Wandering under the covered part of the open marketplace, it's a few degrees cooler, but Jack's reminded the humidity doesn't cut you a break from the heat, even in the shade, like it does in California. Six or seven so years ago was a lifetime. An alternate timeline he never wants to cross paths with again. He heads back to Valerie's. If she's not home, he's booked a hotel on the other side of the French Quarter, far away from anything he's familiar with.

All the tourists seem familiar, the faces are the same, the laughs, even at noon, people walk around with footlong margaritas, and there's some sort of celebration. Both men and women are wearing red, some wear tutus and march down the street. Jack emits a chuckle as he tries to avoid the parade and nearly finds himself turning down the wrong street toward his old hunting grounds.

The city is haunted, full of people's demons. They will leave here with regrets, with fogged memories, with little trinkets that they'll throw in a drawer or give to a niece, and they'll tell tales of Cafe DuMonde and Bourbon street, not as it really is, but as a stereotype of a good time. He turns tail and jogs back in the opposite direction, cutting across the crowd.

If Valerie's not home, Jack intends to call his sponsor.

*

The humidity makes Valerie feel like she's slogging through mud, but she likes the first taste of freedom, of making decisions that are completely her own. She wakes slow in the morning, the fan moving at a snail's pace over her head, tossing the reflections of the morning light all around the room. She rolls toward the open windows and kicks off the sheet she laid over herself the night before. Her hair is up in a circle, a loose bun that strings apart even as she lifts her head off the pillow. She searches her hair for the little plastic clip she placed in it last night. Her hips have filled out from the beignets and her legs have definition from walking. She walks everywhere these days, her car garaged since she arrived. Everything is in the Square or the shopping center blocks to the south. Her lawyer is here, the cafes she frequents, her yoga studio, and the center where she works. If you can call it work, she smiles to herself. Until they get the grant and are able to set up the learning and rec center for the local kids, it's volunteer. Even then, the majority of the money will go for furniture, programs, upkeep of the building. Hurricane Katrina, fifteen years ago, wiped out everything, leaving some areas still without schools or recreation centers.

Thankfully, Nan left her enough to live on. And she feels, for the first time in a long time, she is home. She has found a purpose, place, friends.

The sheer curtains lick the windowpanes. There's no breeze today to push them off. She lifts herself up and pauses at her dresser to drop the clip next to a glass sculpture with an oval base that splits into winding spindles twisting around themselves. It's blue and white, traces of green, like the ocean; the urn which holds Nan's remains. Next to it is the photo of her family; her mother, father, Nan and she in front of her family's home. The mousy paint is peeling and chipped, the patio is concrete with matching steps, painted an odd off white. She thinks of it with a smile. The mismatched dishes stacked in a kitchen filled with appliances and extras, a bread machine used twice, a food processor rarely needed, two toasters - one for bagels and the other still good and not worth throwing away. Chaos, she beams. But home. The other photo is taped to the mirror behind the sculpture, Nan, Jack, and herself on the beach near Nan's. Another home. More Nan's than hers, but that didn't mean she didn't feel welcome or didn't feel at home when she was there.

And now here. She glances around her little space, the bed with flowered sheets, the green curtains and carpets that came with the place, heavy patterned wallpaper - the crowd of color and pattern sires feelings of warmth and safety.

She combs her fingers through her hair and pulls the mass of waves into a ponytail, grabs her yoga mat, and walks the three blocks to her yoga studio. An hour and a half later, after a little chit chat with the regulars, she slows her pace home. The heat has risen and she stops by a local shop for a bottled tea.

"Nothing else for you?" The clerk holds up a scone in one hand, a muffin in the other.

Her sweet tooth has left a lasting impression, she thinks as she declines. She has promised herself a salad today, fresh vegetables bouncing on a bed of greens. She drops the emptied Snapple Peach Iced Tea in a trash can as she crosses to her little apartment. The deep, dark green stands out among the brown, red, and lighter green houses. NoLa is full of color and sound and activity. It's alive, she thinks. The whole city sings. She watches the rest of the celebration, men and women in red tutus, pass the end of her block.

She waves to her neighbors and takes the concrete steps slowly. She wiggles the key into the door and turns the knob, setting her mat down when she sees an envelope sticking from her box. On the front of the long white business envelope, V is written in script. She opens it and pulls out a single, long, light-pink feather. Her face twists in confusion, maybe there's a tinge of uncertainty. She twirls the feather between her thumb and forefinger and turns.

The scene waves in front of her and she doesn't believe what she sees: Jack, on the stairs leading up to her. How many times had she thought she'd seen him among the tourists in the streets? Excitement flushes through her, reddening her cheeks as she steps forward with open arms.

He moves into them, wraps his arms around her and squeezes, breathes in her lavender sweat, coconut shampoo.

"I can't believe it's really you!" She loosens her hold. Each stare at the other, words lost, until she forces out, "Can you stay for lunch? I'm starving."

"Yes."

"Come on up, I have to change and you can drop your bag."

He waits, shuffling his feet, glancing around the small room. How long had it been and what else had changed?

When she emerges from her bedroom, her hair is freed, she's wearing a light skirt and tank top. She looks lovely, free, and happy.

"I can't believe you're in New Orleans," Jack says as they walk down the street.

"I can't believe you are in New Orleans!" She exhales a waterfall of giggle.

"How did you end up here?" They walk further away from the French Quarter; a neighborhood he's never been, but someplace she's quite familiar with.

"Me and Bobby McGee played on the radio as I left Nan's and I remember both you and Nan had been here. I know it sounds silly, but that's the best explanation I have"

"I owe you an apology. A huge apology. And an explanation."

"You don't owe me anything, Jack." They stop at the light, wait to cross the main street. She touches his face.

"I feel like I abandoned you. I feel like you needed me and I wasn't there."

"I needed me." She drops her hand, steadies her gaze. "I was worried about you though."

The light changes and others surround them as they cross the street. He's unfamiliar with the area; it's where the locals go, he thinks. She's a local now, comfortable in a city and in a life far away from him. "I was having a hard time. I didn't want to back slide.

My sponsor got me in a program." He doesn't think she understands how close he was and how important it was. If he's going to be good for anyone, he must save himself.

"Jack, it's okay. It's really okay. You don't owe me an explanation. But I am glad you're well."

He gives up the explanation for the moment as she opens the door to a little cafe and waves him in. Once they have their salads and twice refilled ice waters, he slips his hands on to hers, thinking of the first time he sat across the table from her. "I want you to understand I was in trouble. I was close to using again and I can't ever, ever go back to that."

She grabs his hand and squeezes tight. "I am so happy you took the time to take care of yourself." She stares at him, wants him to hear her, wants him to know she means it.

A relieved breath hisses out of him. "Thank you."

They update, their heads bobbing slowly together, moving even slower a part, each glossing over the ugly parts, luxuriating in the good things. And by the time they run out of breath and things to tell one another, they are at Valerie's door.

"I'm staying right up the street. Can I see you again before I leave?" His flight is tomorrow afternoon. The latest he could get and still make it home in time for a sleep before work on Monday. She looks up the street and then back to Jack. "Do you want to come up?"

For a single moment the thought of a refusal floats through his mind, a gentlemanly behavior, or some stray idea of when you want something too much, you should back off, but no, he nearly leaps up the stairs and takes her open hand in his. There are many things he should refuse, he will refuse, but not her, not this - he seizes the moment for however long it may last.

He watches her in the kitchen, water from the faucet and ice from the fridge, and she carries two tall glasses, setting them on the table before she plops down next to him.

"Do you miss it?"

"What's that?" she asks.

"California, the coast, the big house?" He's sorry he said it the minute it leaves his mouth. He's already shaking his head, starting to apologize. "I mean…"

Valerie chuckles, "I have everything I need." She waves her arm around the small apartment. Everything can be seen from where they sit, her bed, unmade, to the right, the kitchen in front of them. "There's something nice about a small space," she adds. Her eyes linger on her books in a basket next to the couch, no room for a bookshelf, the one wall is closet, the other is all windows. She's learned more about need and want in the last few months than she'd even learned from the tiny, shared dorm room in college.

"It's nearly as small as my place, maybe smaller."

"It's so good to see you." She curls her legs up on the couch, turns her body, her full attention to him.

Jack sips, sets the glass down. He's nervous. They'd parted as friends, a little more than friends. Where are they now? He lifts his arm, "Can I put my arm around you?" On her nod, he wraps his arm around her. She curls into him.

"I don't think I've ever missed anyone so much in my life."

"Hmm mmm." She hums in agreement and lifts her head, puckers her lips and moves closer, but stops short. He always asks, she should as well. "Kiss?"

"You have carte blanche." He leans into their kiss, pulls her closer. Kisses her again, wrapping both arms around her. "You do understand, I came here for you."

Valerie nods and kisses him again.

His breath is heavy, moist, but he still feels like he can't take in enough air as he buries his face in her neck and inhales her, kisses her soft skin, gently sips in the soft divots above her collarbone. When her breath turns into a moan, he feels he might lose his mind. He moves to stand without releasing her. Ask, always ask, he thinks. "Can I, we, make…?"

Her breath sighs out, "yessss."

He gathers her into his arms as she giggles and carries her to her bedroom.

*

Covered in sweat, she stirs. The sheets bunch around her, around them. She turns to look at him in the darkness, a hint of light from the streetlamp illuminates the side of his face, his closed eyes, the scruff of a beard she longs to touch even now. She moves slowly and quietly, disentangles herself from Jack's arm, breathing him in as if forming a memory. She pushes open the curtains. The sky is a rich blue, and there's a cool breeze slipping in through the slit opening. She lifts the window and listens to the New Orleans summer night. Far off voices, the trill of a screech owl, soft music drifting up.

She's come to love the city, the simplicity of a life on her own. Grabbing her summer robe from the back of the door. She wanders into the kitchen and pours herself a glass of water. She drinks it down, then wanders onto the back patio. It's a small wooden rectangle, barely large enough for her little breakfast set. The heat peels off in streams of sweat. She pulls her hair from her neck, fans it with her hand. Then the wished for soft but elusive cool breeze passes by. A smattering of clouds cover and reveal stars, the arc of the milky way opposes the new moon, a light flickers on and off in a nearby house, the sound of a car in someone's driveway, and somewhere far away, laughter rises above the night.

After a time, she meanders back to the bedroom.

Jack sprawls flat on his back, arms and legs outstretched, sweat dripping from his forehead.

She notches the ceiling fan to high before working her way back to bed. Half asleep, Jack rolls toward her. "Everything okay?"

"Perfect," she whispers.

He rubs his hand up and down her arm, she takes his hand in hers and holds it tight.

*

It's late morning when the streaks of sun poke at them through the window. Jack stretches, yawns silently, allows his eyes to roam her room. They land on her dresser, sculpture, photos, feather. When he squints, he can see himself both in the photo and the unkempt reflection in the mirror. Something inside him dances as he drops his head to the pillow. She hadn't forgotten him.

Jack will fly back this afternoon, but neither of them talk about it. They go to the marketplace for fresh fruit, walk along the river front and then turn around to head back to Valerie's through the local neighborhoods.

They walk arm in arm, kiss, laugh together.

When they get back to her place, her phone rings. Jack sees a man's name pop up and Valerie checks before answering but does answer in front of him. He can't hear what's being said, just the mumblings from a man's deep voice, slow and thick with a Louisiana accent.

"In the kitchen closet," she responds. "Upstairs. See you tomorrow."

When she sees Jack's face, she says, "work colleague," and drops the last of the fruit in the refrigerator. Whatever Jack imagined her work was, grant writing, fixing up an old building for the local youth, he didn't imagine a man in her life in any form. He should have, he thinks. She's free to date, see, work with whom she wants. He has to trust that this thing they had this weekend wasn't just for old times, that it means as much to her as it does to him.

"You need a ride to the airport?"

"No. I have a shuttle, but it's meeting me at the Square." He must ask her. He must say something to find out what she's thinking. He grabs his backpack and they walk to the square together, hand in hand, Jack thinking the whole time about what to say, how to say it.

When the shuttle is in sight, he only has moments. He puts his hands on her arms, "Come with me," he says.

Valerie chuckles. "I can't come with you." she pauses and sees he's serious. "I have an apartment and a job, well sort of job. This is my…" she stops short of saying "home," but she means it all the same.

The shuttle stops, the door opens. Jack steps backward toward it, "Can I see you again then? Can I come back and see you?"

"Yes." Valerie steps toward him as he climbs aboard the shuttle.

"You mean a lot to me." How much can he say in the moment, how much can he say without scaring her off?

"Come anytime. Carte blanche."

*

He gives it a few days and then calls, catches her at work.

"Hello!" she squeals.

The background is filled with noises, music, voices, and under it all he again hears that deep thick voice with the southern accent.

"Did I catch you at a bad time?"

"No. No. It's perfect. We just found out we got the funding. We're celebrating" she gushes. "We are building a school, Jack. We are changing lives!"

"That's great." He means it. But he also knows that will keep her there, in her new home, with her new friends, and whoever it is she's working with.

"I have a few days off," he says.

"Wonderful. Are you able to visit? You can see the school."

"Ain't a school yet."

Jack hears that voice, so close to Valerie.

"It will be," she responds; her voice is warm and casual. It's a tone that tells Jack she trusts the man, feels close to him. She turns her attention back to Jack. "When?"

"I can be there Thursday." He told Danny Friday through Monday, but he feels the need to get there, to check out this guy, to discover the scope of her project. Is it weeks, months, forever?

*

The shuttle drops him in the square at noon. Valerie jogs toward him. "Jack," she calls out. When he turns, she runs into his arms, kisses him hard.

"I need to get back to the center, want to come?"

"Lead on, lady."

248

The center is a two-story red brick building, a windowless frame on the second floor, a concrete walkway, overgrown bushes surround a dirt lot. Inside - teenagers sweep the floor, an electrician breaks through a wall, and music drips from the second floor.

"We have such plans," she says. "Classrooms on the second floor, but not just any classrooms, we want them full of color and activity. Here, on this wall, the kids want a mural. Over there - we're going to add windows, this place needs way more natural light, and a garden, Jack, come and see our agricultural center." She pulls Jack through the kitchen into a yard, overgrown with weeds.

When they return, the music has died down and he hears that deep rich voice talking to the kids.

"He's here," she gushes, "you finally get to meet the brain behind this whole operation." Jack follows her through the kitchen and back into the large, echoing main room. The man is big, thick with dark skin and darker hair. He leans on a table, simultaneously looking at plans and pointing the teenagers to a task. He turns slowly, and somehow, seems familiar.

"Jack, meet Marlon."

"You must be the young man that has put the sparkle in her eyes." He offers an open hand, which Jack takes.

Valerie giggles.

The man has at least twenty years on both of them, gray highlighting his temples. He's slow to move, slow to speak, and Jack guiltily feels relief.

"You look familiar," Jack says. "Ever been to California?"

"Can't say that I have. Been 'round these parts for long as I can remember."

The turn of his head, the shrug of the shoulder. Jack knows him. "You're... you used to play at the Blues clubs up in Treme."

"That was a long time ago, young man."

"I spent some time here in my youth, I used to come and see ya."

The older man shakes his head. "Can't say I remember much about those days, I was fightin' some demons back then."

"Weren't we all." Jack says reflectively, which causes Marlon to give him a long look. "You were great. You still play?"

"Once in a while," he says noncommittally and glances back to the plans.

The kids make giant sweeping motions, argue over the mural they want on the wall. One kid wants musicians, another says artists, and the last one says "us."

"You guys can do all of them, you should." Jack walks over to the kids, "Do the greats of New Orleans history with crowds in the background, or down here. Put yourselves in the crowd"

"How, man? How we going to do that all?"

"Paint it. You guys can do it. I can help."

"You're going to let that guy paint? He's still using crayons," the one kid throws a cleaning rag at the other.

Jack spins to Valerie and Marlon. "I do this with my kids at the shop. I draw it, they paint the basics, then I can come back and help. What do you think?"

Valerie looks to Marlon. Marlon dips his head and says, "looks like we got us another volunteer."

Jack spends every weekend he can in New Orleans. By the end of summer, the place is nearly finished. In a few weeks, they will begin hiring people to teach classes. Another week or two and his official reasons for coming will be gone. He wanted more out of this time, some sort of understanding, but he was too afraid to ask, too afraid to interrupt the smooth flow of their new routine. Asking could change everything, it could end everything.

It's mid-August swampy hot. A window air conditioner blows cool air from the living room, but with dinner cooking and them moving around the small kitchen, they can't feel it. Valerie stirs the sauce, turns off the heat, and reaches for the strainer to rinse the pasta through.

Jack gathers papers from the table, catching a glance at the paperwork. He turns it sideways, sees they are more grant applications for the center. Valerie is listed as co-director. Maybe he'd hoped she'd come home to California with him. He glances up at her, he'd not asked her though. New Orleans has become a home. She's become her own woman, not held down by anyone or anything, not defined by her past. All of it has only made him fall more deeply in love with her.

"You can put those anywhere." She catches his eye. Something's on his mind. She forks pasta on each plate.

Jack lays the paperwork aside, spoons the sauce onto the plates, picks up a meatball with the serving spoon. "How many?"

"Five!" she giggles. "Mm… two."

She brings the plates to the table as he follows with garlic bread in a basket. They've reached a good rhythm. At the center and here for two or three nights a week. They are roommates, friends, and lovers.

He pushes the bread toward her. "This is my special recipe, try." Every part of his body vibrates with the question. He notices Valerie watching him. He smiles, sips his sweet tea, and says, "What is it?"

They've come to know each other well.

"You've got something to say."

He nods, sets his fork on the plate, and meets her eyes. He loves the work, loves the kids, but on the way home, deep in conversation and in each other's eyes, they meandered too far north and by the time they'd reached The Blacksmith's Bar, he could smell Bourbon Street, the alcohol, the ragweed, and urine mixing. The scent brought back memories, not good ones, and made him momentarily pause and lean over as if he was going to retch. Valerie paused too. "Are you okay?" He was then uncertain if he could ever live here again on a permanent basis.

"Are you ever coming home… ah.. I mean… to California?"

Valerie nods thoughtfully, considering her answer. She's thought about it in the in between times, when Jack's not there for those long days, those long weeks. She's thought about how they can or can't continue this way forever. "I've wanted to come, spend a weekend there with you, but you had to go and volunteer." She smiles, then continues a little more seriously. "I've been focused completely on this project, so…" She mines her thoughts, chooses her words carefully. If truth be told, she's a little afraid to go back. She's found so much of herself here. New Orleans feels like home. Lasch, the kids, her neighbors and friends, feel like family. What is it, she wonders, she'd be going back too? "I've thought about us, but I haven't come up with any answers."

They eat slowly, the last rays of the long summer days, reaching for them through the living room windows.

"I love you," Jack says. This isn't a fling. It's not a spring-time romance bound to burn out in the summer heat.

Valerie touches her hand to his. She's been careful with words, afraid to commit again, but her feelings for Jack have always been clear. It's the rest of it which gives her pause. "I love you." The warmth of the tone wends around the words.

"I'd like us to have a future together."

Her fingers trace his hands, pause on the paint on his knuckle. She gazes at his face, tries to picture Jack as an old man. He'll be thin, she thinks, too thin. He'll tinker in the driveway with cars, even then neighborhood kids will be drawn to him. "I'd like that too," she finally says.

He exhales a deep breath.

"I've just been so focused on this project. It feels good to help to change lives." She thinks about their video chat last week when she sang Itsy Bitsy Spider with Tommy so he could remember the words. Claire took the phone into the kitchen to show Valerie the cake she made. Jack snatched the phone back so his dad could say hello while Danny made faces at Jack in the background. "Wish you were here," they'd said, and she did too. "I don't know what comes next, but I'm willing to figure it out with you."

Jack suspects she's afraid to leave her new home. She's afraid to go back, just like he's afraid to come back here permanently.

"That dinner, movie studio stuff, is in two weeks. You can come, yes?"

"Already got my plane ticket," she says

"You do?" He picks himself up from the chair and leans far

over to kiss her.

"Yes, Claire will pick me up from the airport on Friday morning. We plan to go shoe shopping since I'm assuming I'll need something more than these." She flashes her broken-in sandals, waving her foot from under the table.

"Lady, you wear whatever you want. Yoga pants and sneakers are fine with me. As long as you're there, I'm a happy camper."

"I'm looking forward to seeing what you've been working on. You said you've made some changes."

"Lotsa changes," he digs his fork into his meatball, happy once again.

32

The following weekend, Jack stays home in Santa Clarita. He had to prepare, work, he said. Besides a stray text or two, she doesn't talk to him that weekend, and the hours add up. She rolls out of bed in the morning heat, the humidity so high she feels like she can't breathe.

She changes into her yoga clothes and glances at Nan's urn. "I'd like to order a New Orleans, minus the humidity." She wonders what Nan's response would be, can almost hear her. "Gotta take the good with the bad."

At yoga, the ladies ask, "Where's Jack today?" Many of the women are taken with his dedication, his kind words after classes. "Wish I could get my partner to take an interest." Some of their husbands or boyfriends, inspired by the few male regulars, do show, but not on a regular basis. She walks back home alone, the cafe owners ask, "Where's your handsome fella?"

Short answer, "working." Jack has already become so much a part of her life.

He texts her later, "hope you're having a great day, Sweetie. Miss you." She curls up on the couch, can't get comfortable. She cleans the apartment. Finds his t-shirt and holds it to her face, breathes deeply, then tosses it on to her bed instead of putting it in the laundry.

She trudges half-way down the steps with the laundry basket, then turns back, not willing to carry the load to the hot basement and steam up the city even more. From her patio, she can see her neighbors fanning themselves on their balconies, they give her a wave. She throws together a salad, chomps through half of it before deciding she's not that hungry. She knows this is partly due to the heat. She downs glass after glass of water and takes a cool shower. It's barely sunset when she finds herself climbing into bed with a book. She's bored, lonely, and she doesn't like it. She pulls Jack's shirt from the sheets and lays it on her pillow.

She wakes to splashes of an early morning rain on the windowsill. The rain feels good, but it's done little to alleviate the heat. She decides she will spend the day at the center. If the rain clears up, the kids might show up to finish the painting, Marlon might pop by for want of something to do. She's been there nonstop for a few months, and thought she'd take the weekend to herself, but finds it's not as satisfying as she hoped.

When she puts the key in the lock, bagels and coffee in hand, she's surprised to find three of the kids and Marlon already at work.

"Look who's rolling in at this hour."

The rain has turned to a drizzle. She chuckles. "I didn't think you guys would be here with the rain."

"Jack said not to do too much because of the heat and rain," one of the kids says.

"You talked to Jack?"

Marlon catches the look in her eyes. "Ut oh, someone's missing her honey."

"Oh, stop. Anyone hungry?"

"She got it bad," says one of the kids.

"What happened to taking a few days…"

"Okay, guys, I'm here. We all know why. Let's just get some

work done."

The kids snicker as they take the bagels from the box.

Her phone lays on the table. She glances at it every so often.

It's late afternoon when it finally rings. She clicks on the video call from Jack. He's in half frame, holding the phone so she can see Danny and Claire, hears the laughter of Tommy with one of his friends in the background.

"Honey, I was hoping to catch you. Wanted you to say hello to everyone!" He turns the phone around and scans it around the yard, Claire - "Hi, Valerie, nice to see you!" Danny waves. His father comes into view, he gives her a wink and a smile. "Hello, Mr..." Don't you dare. The name's John." Tommy comes running and screams into frame. "Ms. V! Ms. V. I'm six."

"Six? Is it your birthday?" she says in her old teacher voice and suddenly realizes how much she misses the kindergarteners, and even Lucy. She shakes off the nostalgia.

"No, it was tomorrow." His friend squirts him with a machine-squirt-gun and he runs away.

Valerie chuckles, "Jack, I would have come had I known."

He waves his hand. "His birthday is next week." Jack laughs. "We just stopped for eats, we gotta head back."

Claire takes the phone and goes in the house, closing the patio door to the noise outside. "What time are you coming in? Tommy will be at summer camp until afternoon so we can go shopping, get some dresses for dinner. I don't know about you, but I haven't got a thing to wear," she chuckles. "It'll be fun!"

"It will be fun."

"There's a new coffee place at the shopping center. I'm so excited. I rarely get out of the house without Tommy during the summer."

The noise rises and then softens again as the door opens and closes, "stop hogging my girlfriend." Jack wrangles the phone back from his sister.

"My honey," Jack says, "I miss you so much."

"I miss you.... so much."

"Gotta run. I'll try to call you before bed. Love you."

"Love you."

He kisses at the phone and she does too. Then she turns to see all of them staring at her. Her face shines five shades of red before they all burst out in laughter.

"Okay, okay, get back to work."

She sits down next to Marlon, her elbows on the table as she sighs heavily at the nearly finished mural.

"Sounds like we might be losing you soon."

Valerie straightens up. "Nothing's been decided."

"That's your head talkin', girl."

She searches his dark eyes. "How can I leave when this feels so much like home?"

"Seems to me home is where family is. And that looked like family to me." He tilts his head to the phone, sits back on his stool.

A tear gathers in the corner of her eye.

"Looks like the ceiling has a leak."

Valerie turns her gaze up, searches the ceiling. When she looks at Marlon again, he's smiling.

"It's raining on the inside." Marlon points his thick finger toward her.

She leans in and hugs him. He pats her back, "It's okay, lady. When you find that love, you gotta go for it. No one's gonna hold it against you."

Valerie starts for home. The rain has passed, yet the heat still rises. In California, Santa Clarita smells clean after the rain passes; the sky is soft blue, and the city smells fresh. Here, the rain has just begun the cleanup; the scent of animals and sweat and humans float above the sidewalk. Her shoes stick and click on the tacky concrete. Once in her apartment, she opens the freezer and waves the cool air at her face, then opts for a cool shower before bed.

33

Burbank's Bob Hope Airport is small and friendly. A short walk from the runway to the luggage turnstile on the lip of the exit. It's easy to navigate, to leave and rush into the sunshine and dry warmth of Southern California. Given all of this, Valerie's stomach is still fluttering.

She left school one Monday with a husband, a grandmother, and some sort of certainty in her life. But it all changed within hours. It's a Friday, nearly three months since she left, and her life has changed and changed again. She's not the same young woman who left, and that makes her happy as she walks into the dry August heat with her overnight bag hanging from her shoulder.

Claire's gray Subaru Outback slows and pauses at the curb. Valerie waves and tosses her bag in the back, belts herself in the front. Traffic is Friday light as they swing onto the main street and find the freeway that will take them back home to Santa Clarita.

"How was your flight? Wow, you look great," Claire offers after giving her a once over. "Your hair is so long and your skin..."

"It's all the humidity there." Valerie chuckles. "It's like being in a sauna all the time."

"Maybe I should go for a weekend." Claire squints her eyes as she releases a giggle. Her hair is longer, blonder; she is tanner.

"How did your classes go?"

"Oh," Claire has momentarily forgotten she told Ms. V, Tommy's teacher, she was finishing school. The Ms. V she chit-chatted with for five minutes a day and this Valerie, Jack's V, seem so different. Ms. V was reserved, hair straightened or pulled back, wearing teacher dresses, boxy shirts, straight leg slacks; Valerie, next to her, wears yoga pants, a loose top, and her hair is untamed, blonded around her face, which brightens her light eyes. "One more year. It might kill me, but I'm going to do it."

As they pull into the shopping center, Claire offers, "Jack told me to buy you the dress, so anything you want."

"No." Valerie declines nicely but firmly.

"Well, he thinks since it's his event, his and Danny's…"

"No, thank you." Valerie believes she can't start a new life by making old choices.

"Uhm, okay." Claire shrugs. "The guys say we should wear whatever we want. At the studios, some people will wear Oscar De La Renta, others in jeans," Claire titters.

"Anything but those three-inch heels!" Valerie muses, thankful, she'll never place those toe traps on her feet again.

"Right? If these people want to look at my feet, they can see my unpainted toes in my DSW specials."

The ladies' laugh as they pass the Krispy Kreme, the movie theater. The fluttering is gone, and Valerie feels oddly comfortable in her old haunts, even energized as she and Claire make their way to the shops.

They spend the afternoon preparing. Claire chose a short black dress with black kitten heels. The A-line, loose fit complements her slim build. Her shoulder length blonde hair and bright blue eyes stand out against the contrast. She looks beautiful. Valerie decided on a tea length white flowered dress with a form fitting top and flowing skirt with pink sandals. Claire helps her curl the ends of her long hair and she straightens Claire's.

"I never had a sister to do this with." Claire smiles as she lines her lips. "Is this a good color?"

"Me neither, this is kinda fun." Valerie tries the same lip color, puckering before pressing her lips together.

"Danny was so nervous, he lost ten pounds."

"I thought this was just a regular dinner thing. Don't they go every year?"

"Not every year. Once or twice. I think he's worried about losing Jack, too."

"Where would Jack go? He loves working..." Valerie turns suddenly to Claire, the implication weakening her smile.

Claire turns away, grimaces. "Ready?" She heads for the door.

Valerie follows, but they both pause at the mirror's reflection, side by side, Claire giggles and squeezes Valerie's hand before they open the door. Valerie's flutters return.

Danny sits next to a napping Tommy and jumps up when he sees his wife. He kisses her on the cheek. "I do not take you out enough, honey. You look so beautiful."

Then Jack sees Valerie, the style he's come to know, beautiful and free. He stands still, admiring.

Danny and Jack wear black suits, light blue shirts, and before Jack can move, John hands his phone to him, moves to the ladies. "Me first, take a picture of me with these beautiful women." He hugs them, kisses each on their cheeks. "My beautiful daughters." He squeezes between them, puts his arms around them proudly as Jack snaps photos. John moves away, pushes Danny and Jack over to the women. Valerie glances up at Jack. He has shaved recently; the summer thickness of his stubble is gone. A day or two of growth is fresh, his face is more mature, a line around his eyes she hasn't noticed before. Jack gazes down at Valerie. The soft summer dress, the locks curling under, her eyes bright. He feels lucky. John snaps the picture. Jack and Valerie, Danny and Claire turn forward, arms around one another for another photo, and Danny says, "one for the road." They strike funny poses, make funny faces, all laughing before John snaps the last photo.

Under the stars, in the Universal Studios backlot, tables are circular in the street of a movie-set neighborhood. A stage sits in front of one house, the buffet in another's front yard, the corner houses a cardboard three sided Starbucks and a barista ready to brew. The dessert bar is at the far end, under the streetlights where flags strung between them spell out, "We Thank You." Music pours from a front porch, where a DJ dances with headphones. "Congratulations" placards strewn in various places along the small street.

Tonight, the studios honor those behind the scenes. The companies who provide sets, props, extras, and even catering. Danny and Jack talk to a few people, introduce Valerie and Claire around before moving to their table somewhere in the center.

Once seated, Jack runs his hand over the fresh five-o-clock shadow.

"You miss it?" Valerie leans in, the voices and music overtaking her voice.

"Nah, it was getting itchy. But I didn't want these guys to think I did it for them." He winks. "You miss it?"

Valerie rubs her hand over the fresh stubble, "Oooo, pokey," and giggles.

"The more to rash you with, my girl." He brushes his cheek to hers.

"Nooo," she titters and tilts her head away.

"Claire told me you wouldn't let me pay for the dress. I know, it's important to you to be your own person. I respect that. And I did this for me," he winks. "But I'm so happy you're here tonight for the only reason that you are here. I don't care what these people think."

A mic hisses and squeaks to life and a speaker takes the stage in front of them. Those still meandering move in toward their tables and ready themselves to listen. At first, it seems, Caitlyn Jenner has taken the microphone, but it quickly becomes clear as Elton John, Bette Midler, and Madonna line up next to the stage that Celebrity Impersonators will be their MCs.

"Don't worry, we'll have a break so you can have more dessert and more drinks. Trust me, you'll need it by the end of this."

There's laughter and applause.

"Tonight, we honor you."

"And us," says Midler's double.

"Yes, all of us who make the studios look good! When we announce the winners, no ten-minute speeches thanking your first-grade teacher to your therapist." Jenner's impersonator puts her hand on her hip and pauses, "Just thank your therapist and get off the stage." She snaps her fingers.

There's more laughter from the crowd.

"Every year thousands of people help us make good movies but, tonight, we recognize those who have made the greatest contributions to the most successful movies. You will receive this award."

With some effort, Elton's double picks up a triangular clear crystal award with a gold plaque on it.

"And a check for .01% of the movie's net."

Another impersonator waves an envelope in the air.

Oooos and aaahhhs rise as he pauses.

"Now that may not sound like much, but it does depend on the movie!"

The impersonators take turns making jokes and introducing the award winners.

It's nearly thirty minutes in, when the speaker announces, "Supplying the studios cars' with some of the most innovative, outrageous, and beautiful art, is Saffarri's Automotive of Santa Clarita. Danny Saffarri and Jack Rose, owner operators."

Claire applauds while Valerie's mouth falls open. Jack kisses her and jumps out of his seat, follows Danny up to the stage. Valerie raises her hands to clap, and leans over to Claire, "Did you know this?"

She nods vigorously, "Jack told me not to tell you."

Danny holds the award while Jack waves the envelope in the

air.

"I just have to thank my lovely wife, Claire, for believing in me."

Claire tears up, presses her lips together and smiles.

Jack pushes in next to him, nearly bouncing in place. "Must always acknowledge the women who inspire us. V, you are my muse."

They return to their seats, kissing the women's cheeks. Claire is tearing up, fingering the award. Valerie is shocked, staring at Jack's face. He waves the check and hands it over to Danny.

After the awards, there is dancing and champagne in the cul de sac of the movie-set neighborhood. But their little group begs off, says goodnight to friends and meanders through the sets to the valet.

Jetlag and excitement catching up with her, Valerie rests her head on Jack's shoulder.

"Danny, can you drop us off at my place?"

"You sure?"

"Yeah, I think V's done for the evening." He kisses the top of her head.

Jack leads the yawning Valerie to the door. "Someone is tired." He offers her a t-shirt to sleep in. She washes up, shuffles to the bed, and is nearly asleep by the time he climbs in.

In the middle of the night, she stretches and turns toward the window, realizing quickly this is not her little apartment, the window not in the same place. She takes a deep breath, a cool breeze whispers over her. It feels so good. She's not sweating, she can breathe; she's not dying of thirst, but out of habit she gets out of bed and feels her way along the walls to the kitchen, where she opens one cabinet door and then another until she finds a cup and pours herself a glass of water. Her eyes adjust to the dark. The window over his kitchen table is gone; it's now a patio door and the small table with two chairs sit outside. Nearly like her patio in New Orleans, he's used an ornate iron railing. He's turned the once painting studio into a living room, and a board separates the kitchen from new construction.

She feels her way back to the bedroom. Jack hasn't stirred; he is starred with arms out, legs sprawling across the bed. She moves back into the cool sheets. She has missed the cool California nights. She sits, curls her legs in front of her.

She thinks of Claire's slip earlier, Danny losing Jack. She's noticed how Jack avoids Washington Square, walks completely around Bourbon Street, how the scent twists him. She pokes Jack lightly, he moves over, offering more room. "Jack," she whispers and pokes him again.

"Everything okay?" His head pops off the pillow.

"Yeah, I have to ask you something."

"Okay." He's sleepily breathless as his head falls back to the pillow. "Shoot."

"Why do you love me?"

"Huh? Uhm." He takes a deep breath and shakes off sleep. He glances over at her sitting up in his bed. "Okay. Serious talk." He inhales deeply, blows out a breath and shakes his head. "Okay. What now?"

Valerie restrains herself from giggling at his sleepiness. "I'm sorry."

"No. No. It's okay." He pushes his body upright, leans on an elbow.

"Why do you love me?"

He runs a hand over his face, brushing away the last remnants of sleep. "Why do I love you? Okay." He takes a deep breath and gazes at her in the shadows, reaches for her hand. "You're kind. You're gentle."

He pauses, but just when Valerie thinks he's faltered, he begins again. "I saw you a few times before I ever met you. Claire wanted me to know where to pick up Tommy. Once you and Miss Jenny were trying to teach the kids dance steps for the Christmas show. And the kids kept getting it wrong, and you would just smile and start again. One kid would go running off, and you would just turn him around and bring him back. The whole time you had this giant genuine smile on your face as if you loved each and every one of those little souls. And then that first day I met you, Tommy smashed your hand and you still had that smile. Then you turned it to me." Jack's rubbing his fingers over her hand, like he did on that very first day. "And I thought this is someone who sees people, who cares about others and gives part of herself to everyone she meets. That's special. That's really special, V."

Valerie is speechless.

"Did you fall asleep?" Jack chuckles and rubs his hand on her arm.

"Ah, no." She leans in and hugs Jack.

"Okay, so why do you love me?" he jokes.

She drops herself to the bed. "Sleep time."

Jack laughs. "Oh, I see how you are." He reaches over to tickle her.

She giggles and squirms away from the tickle, pushes his hands from her sensitive spots and moves her body onto his. "I love your stubble. I love that you don't care what other people think. I love that you are so kind, and funny. You are so funny, Jack. I love the way you are with Tommy and your family. Is that enough?"

"Enough? No. You're just getting started, go on, go on. Say how humble I am." He reaches to her waist, finding those ticklish spots again. She kisses him.

*

In the morning, Jack shows her all the changes he's made around the place, the plans to add the living room north of the kitchen as she suggested, art studio in the back, and another room, left unidentified on the plans.

"And this? she asks.

He smiles shyly. "I don't know, kids' room, baby's room. If I sell it, it'll be whatever…"

"Sell?"

"Well, I don't know, maybe. I don't know what's going to happen."

*

Tommy's birthday party is at Claire and Danny's house. She remembers the first time she sat here under the jasmine. Tommy is bigger; he runs around with the kids. She recognizes some of the kids from kindergarten and hugs them hard. When they sing Happy Birthday, Danny lights the candles; Claire leans in to tell him to make a wish. Tommy's nose crinkles up like Claire's, and John seems to stand guard at the end of the table. Jack catches her eyes before leaning in to help Tommy blow out the candles.

She's quiet as she hugs them all good-bye.

"Wait, Ms. V." Tommy runs out of his room, as Valerie stands in the door. When he returns, he has her feather jar from the kindergarten classroom cradled in his arms.

Her eyes moisten as she leans down to hug Tommy.

"We asked the substitute if we could take it and hold it for you," Claire offers. "Tommy put more feathers in it."

Valerie spins the jar filled with so many more feathers than she remembers. She wants to cry. She hands the jar back to Tommy. "Do you think you could keep it for me a little while longer?"

Tommy jumps up and down. "Yes!"

"He really didn't want to give it back to you," Jack offers as he drives her to the airport. "That was nice of you."

When she doesn't respond, he takes her hand. "You okay? You've been quiet today."

She presses her lips together to stop herself from saying more. "Yeah."

She can't let him change his whole life for her. Jack will finish the painting the following weekend. She'll tell him then, at the end of the weekend.

34

August's end throws the French Quarter into a momentary lull. It's a single breath before the fall season begins. People will come to watch the leaves change, to see the array of Blue's Shows, the parties will continue, the parades and mock funerals, the tours of graveyards. It's still hot, summer steam rises off the Mississippi, offering not quite the last of the city's humidity. In fact, this weekend seems like someone set the city on high.

Valerie fans herself, sitting under the three-hundred-year-old live oak behind the center. Ferns grow around the base. The yard has turned green and thick with little encouragement. Tomato and Pepper plants bloom with fruit, Squash and pumpkin offer flowers, fattening in the center.

"Almost done, Ms. V." One of the teenagers calls to her. They will unveil the last of the painting today.

Jack stands back, covered in brown, white, blue paint. Marlon waits at the door. They've gathered more teenagers who have been in and out, offering to help, wanting to be a part of the center, their parents, neighbors, and friends stand outside.

A few of the teenagers hold a canvas over the last part of the painting, "Ready? Now?"

"Yes, yes, go ahead!" Jack calls.

Marlon opens the door and the neighbors and friends enter; the kids drop the canvas. Between Jack at the front of the room, nearest the painting and Valerie at the back of the room, they are lost to one another as the crowd moves in. Somewhere in the middle they find one another as the people look and point, call out names of faces they recognize, "Louis Armstrong," "Buddy Bolden," "Is that Jelly Roll?"

Pitchers of drinks and cookies are set out along tables in the back as people meander the school, the rec center and the gardens, and someone calls out, "There he is," and "Who is that?" Jack guides Valerie and Marlon over to the corner. In the crowd of faces, the teenagers added the everyday people of New Orleans, including themselves, Marlon, Valerie, and Jack among them.

Marlon hmmfs approvingly before he shuffles away. Valerie thanks the kids, hugs Jack, and slips into the crowd. Jack leans down, small paint brush in hand. "This is the most important part kids, watch." He makes a J symbol to sign his name. "Now, you guys sign your artwork."

Excitedly, they line up, sign next to Jack's symbol.

At the back of the center, Valerie talks to two women, hands them a list and a set of keys. Jack watches from a distance, approaching as the women work themselves closer to Marlon.

Someone brings a cake from the kitchen, people take turns congratulating Marlon and Valerie, saying thank you, and we'll miss you.

When Jack works his way in close to Valerie, he says, "What's up, what else are we celebrating?"

"We're on a short list, Jack, for the funding. That funding will keep the school going throughout the year! Isn't that great?!"

"It is." Although he smiles, his words don't carry the same excitement. It'll keep her in New Orleans for another year. "I.. a.. don't…"

A trombone sounds at the front of the room and Jack spins.

He works his way through the crowd to watch Marlon Lasch play. The center goes quiet as Valerie finds him, slips his hand in hers. He'll make it work, he thinks. Somehow, he'll make it work.

It's dark by the time they lock up the center, their stomachs filled from Po Boys and cake. They make their way to her place, climbing the steps slowly, and she mixes some iced tea that they take to small back patio. The plant once adorning her railing is gone, the knick-knacks along the shelf in the window are missing.

He starts to say something, but she interrupts, "yoga tomorrow? We'll walk to the waterfront, have some beignets and coffee after yoga, yes?"

"Yeah."

In the morning, they take their yoga mats and collect beignets and coffee from Cafe Du'Monde. They move slow and quiet, barely talking, holding hands in the oppressive end of the summer heat.

They take the long way, pass the center. Once, it was a plain brick building, nearly gutted and empty, now it sings with life. Valerie did that, he thinks. "You're pretty amazing," he says.

She smiles, leans into him. "So are you."

"Another year," he says quietly.

"And hopefully, the center will go on and on. Become a place that the next generation will have."

Jack nods. He's trying to work things out in his head. How will this work? Can he live here?

They walk up the steps to Valerie's place. In the bright light of day, it seems too empty and sparse. Her books are gone from the basket, a closet door waggles open and inside it's empty.

"Where is all your stuff, woman?"

She walks into the bedroom. "Jack, can you help me with this?"

He follows her. The drawers of the dresser are slightly open, as if she just opened and closed each of them, and there's a box on the bed. She's lifting Nan's glass urn into the box; he rushes over and places his hands on hers, helps her guide it into the box. She grabs at the photos and then the feather.

"What are you doing?"

"I need this in the backseat of my car. I saved it for last because I didn't want to take a chance of it being broken."

"In your car? Why?" He glances around the sparse room.

"Road trip!" she says. She makes a few last checks of the kitchen, the closets as he follows, box in hand.

"Where are you going?"

"I don't know," she says half joking. "I guess it depends on the song that plays on the radio."

"Oh, damn. Let me in that car first." He tries to hurry past her.

"Uh ut, you be careful with my Nan."

He sets the box down on the chair. "Road trip, for real?" He pulls her close.

"That was part going away party yesterday. I handed off the paperwork, the job. Although I'll come back if they need some help, I thought I might head West."

"Mmm... West. I do like that idea. Right into the sunset. Keep driving til you can't drive anymore, then turn right, go north." He kisses her lips.

"North?" She runs her hands up his arms.

"Just a little North. There's this little house I know about; it's small but loving. It needs you."

"It does?"

"I do."

"Me, too." She snuggles into his hug, wraps her arms around him.

"Okay, okay." He grabs the box with Nan's ashes. "I'll cancel my ticket, call Danny. I promised you and Nan a road trip, didn't I?"

"Already taken care of." She grabs his backpack, locks the door behind them, slides the keys into a locked mailbox downstairs.

"Yeah?"

"Claire helped. We are so far ahead of you."

"You two are gonna keep me on my toes."

She nods, reaches over the box and gives him a kiss. "I'm driving."

He sets the box carefully in the back seat, slips into the front, and holds her hand as the car purrs to life. "Marry me girl, be my fairy to the world…" The Red Hot Chili Peppers fill the car, Jack laughs loudly.

"What?"

"Listen, listen!" He points to the radio.

"…. buy me a star on the boulevard, it's Californication…"

As they wait for the parade of people waving white linens to pass, they lean in for a kiss.

ABOUT THE AUTHOR

Noreen Lace earned her MFA from California State University where she now teaches. She has authored over 60 publications of short fiction, memoir, and poetry in journals such as *The Chicago Tribune's Printers Row Journal*, *The Maine Review*, and *The Oleander Review*, among others. *Our Gentle Sins* is her first novel (June 2022). www.NoreenLace.com

More from Noreen Lace:

How to Throw a Psychic a Surprise Party

Eddy

The Crier

Grandma's Last Secret

Coming Soon from Noreen Lace:

If you loved these characters, join them in the next installment:

She Laughs Like You

Jack is jailed for a crime. Their daughter is missing. And Alexander rides in to win (or force) Valerie back.

Also available from ReadLips Press:

Halfway to Impossible   M.R. Koch

The Red Wing Chronicles   Ron Terranova

Tourists in the Country of Love   Jo Rousseau